WHAT BOOKS PRESS

AN IMPRINT OF

THE GLASS TABLE

COLLECTIVE

LOS ANGELES

Imagine if you will, a Bosch painting rendered in Froot Loops, projected onto the ceiling of a cathedral, and then sprinkled with glitter. In other words, imagine reading *The Eight Mile Suspended Carnival*, a vault of riches and innovation, whose very sentences squirm with life, strangeness, and weirdly cheerful foreboding. In other words, this is a book that must be read in order to be believed.

—Jim Krusoe, author of *The Sleep Garden*

THE
EIGHT MILE
SUSPENDED
CARNIVAL

THE
EIGHT MILE
SUSPENDED
CARNIVAL

REBECCA
KUDER

WHAT
BOOKS
PRESS

LOS ANGELES

Published in the United States by What Books Press,
the imprint of the Glass Table Collective, Los Angeles.

Library of Congress Cataloging-in-Publication Data
Names: Kuder, Rebecca, 1966- author.
Title: The eight mile suspended carnival / Rebecca Kuder.
Description: Los Angeles : What Books Press, [2021] | Summary: "A tornado drops
a young woman, Mim, near a carnival. There, without her own memories but able
to see other people's memories, she becomes entangled with the carnival boss and his
intricate vendetta, and propels vengeance into motion"-- Provided by publisher.
Identifiers: LCCN 2021022943 (print) | LCCN 2021022944 (ebook)
| ISBN 9780984578245 (paperback) | ISBN 9780988924888 (epub)
Subjects: LCSH: Carnivals--Fiction. | GSAFD: Fantasy fiction. | LCGFT:
Fantasy fiction. | Novels.
Classification: LCC PS3611.U325 E38 2021 (print) | LCC PS3611.U325 (ebook)
| DDC 813/.6--dc23
LC record available at https://lccn.loc.gov/2021022943
LC ebook record available at https://lccn.loc.gov/2021022944

ISBN: 978-0-9845782-4-5

Cover art: Gronk, *untitled*, mixed media on paper, Copyright © 2020.

Book design by Ash Good, ashgood.com

Excerpt from "Reeperbahn" by Tom Waits, Kathleen Brennan.
Copyright © 2002, Jalma Music (ASCAP). Used by permission. All rights reserved.

Exerpt from "May Day" by Jack Hardy. Copyright © 1978, 1998, 2006
Jack Hardy Music (BMI). Used by permission. All rights reserved.

Exerpt from "Grandmothers" by Luisa Bieri. Copyright © 2015 Luisa Bieri.
Recorded with Sol Rising healing arts troupe. Used by permission. All rights reserved.

Rebecca Kuder was awarded the Ohio Arts Council's
Individual Excellence Award for 2018.

What Books Press
363 South Topanga Canyon Boulevard
Topanga, CA 90290

WHATBOOKSPRESS.COM

For Robert and Merida

Behind every window, behind every door
The apple is gone but there's always the core
The seeds will sprout up right through the floor
Down there in the Reeperbahn

—Tom Waits and Kathleen Brennan

PART ONE

ONE

SCRATCH-LAND

I

During a year not unlike 1917. In a place like most places.

Scratch-land spread across the horizon. Occasional shrubs and rusted weeds interrupted the otherwise blank canvas. A world faded from lack of notice, rot of time. Things weren't alive and green here. This stillness, this dry, dusty shadow, offered only memory and its silent repercussions.

Years before, opportunity had stolen all mature trees. Bend, snap, cut went the rhythm of thieves. Sure, trees fall naturally sometimes, and storms leave carnage, but these logs were felled, too many, too fast, and rafted down the river. Money to be made. Trees would grow back, some said, then forgot to plant seedlings, no thought beyond the next greed-meal. Along the river, a few bushes spangled the banks, a fringe of sorry lush. No matter the abuse, no matter what, usually some form of life will survive.

And so after the trees were taken, the dry season came and stayed. The river was now only deep enough for flatboats, their poles callousing shoulders of men, men without time to look up and consider the missing trees, the meager flora, and what it meant.

Empty. Except in one direction: machines, buildings, spines of steel sprung from the ground, seeded by metal bits. Come closer, observe the metal monster machines that loom round the Tower of Misfortune. A huddle of canvas tents trembling, light peeking from openings like eyes and silent mouths, afraid to waken the sleeping machines.

From the main road, a path of dust leads the curious to a gate in a tall iron fence. Strung above the gate, behold, a painted banner, wide proclaiming letters:

THE EIGHT MILE SUSPENDED CARNIVAL

Should you look closer, you might notice layers, the banner, repainted, year upon year, canvas clutching paint. The place itself might otherwise be mute, might disappear. *Look,* the scabs on the steadfast banner say, *I exist!*

Nearby, civilization eroded. Stagnant holes languished, hollowed out long ago. The holes were never filled in. The work was left mid-sentence.

The Eight Mile Suspended Carnival meanwhile sighed, but stood, what else could it do? Undeparted, beliefs, notions, curated imagery: *The Eight Mile Suspended Carnival,* faded remembrance and forgetting, existence and extinction, faded paint on the carnival sign, unclinging surfaces, pink and blue and rusty red, and the dust of the paint mixed with the dust of the ground, and the raindogs barked (what else would raindogs do?) and with gusto, gobbled from their dog dishes the forgotten layers of wonderment: death, reincarnation, and how-much-longer-before-its-next-death-and-rebirth carnival.

Maybe you can imagine such a place.

In sunlight, the ground shimmied like uneven scales from here to there, and back again to here, to a young woman who didn't move. Couldn't move. Body slick with mysterious wet.

II

The young woman remembered only the wall of wind, how wind had burnished and bruised. She was a tossed stone. The soil, magnetic, seized her arms and legs, held her body on the cracked ground. Light seared her eyes. Misery, a grinding symphony. Drums, cymbals, shouts, and trumpets, a cacophony of sting, rip, ache. Outside her surrounding thickness, she heard water, its constant call, and not far away. And other sounds. Not watery. The sounds came closer. Words moving toward her.

She had lain on that scratch-land forever. Viscosity enveloped her when she was born onto this ground. Like oil? But tightened into crust, a shell, and inside the shell were pulses of pain and heat. She strained to move, discover which parts worked. Her anguished muscles and bones collided, screamed, but only echoes filled the air where there might have been motion.

Her throat throbbed. She needed water.

III

A voice said, "Who's this naked creature?"

The young woman opened her eyes. A blur, face of the divine feminine. Something leathery touched the young woman's forehead, and she cried out.

"No, Beatrice!" the divine feminine said.

The young woman strained to clarify the shapes in front of her.

The divine feminine was a human person. The leather was a tongue: narrow snout-head, long neck, grey and brown feather-fur, all perched on two tall legs. This tongue tickled the young woman's forehead, distracted her from the shell of pain.

"Beatrice!" The divine feminine held the animal back and leaned toward the young woman. Warm human, metal jangle. Jangle draped from every visible part of the woman's body, except her hands. "Wait, I know your name." The woman closed her eyes. Her lids were powdered bright green, which collided with the dark purple underneath. "It's Mim," the woman said, "and you can call me Cleopatra. What's that swill you're covered in?"

"I don't know." Mim's throat burned.

"We'll take care of you."

Cleopatra offered Mim her thin, velvet hands. Hands velvet, not what they seem. Mim cringed and let herself be pulled up to sitting. *Cleopatra has someone else's hands.* Cleopatra wrapped her shawl around Mim, pungent, like sweet soil. Cleopatra plucked a pin from her hair and secured the shawl under Mim's neck and held her. So much pain. Good to be held.

"I'm thirsty," Mim said.

Sharpness coursed through her hip. The shaggy animal pushed and dug into the ground beneath her.

"Beatrice, *vámonos.*"

Agony charred Mim's shell as Cleopatra helped her stand. "Where are your people?"

"The wind was a wall," Mim said.

"Yes, a twister. Not much damage by us, amazingly. Still. Never know what you might find. That's why I came hunting."

"I can't remember anything."

"Well, you'll stay with us till someone comes for you."

Beatrice inspected the ground where Mim's body had been. "Beatrice, leave that be!" Cleopatra nudged the animal, turned to Mim, pointed down. "The moon has visited."

Burgundy seeped from between Mim's legs. "Must be," she said.

Beatrice snuffled the ground, and clamped her jaws to a vole. Gnawed a bit, dropped a chunk of something unnamable, and trotted onward.

"Can you walk?" Cleopatra asked.

With each step, pain slunk from the dirt into Mim's legs and frayed her bones. Finally they approached a gate in a tall iron fence. Within the fence, a cluster of spidery structures stood, fancy like giant metal flowers. A banner, paint clutching canvas.

"Welcome to the Eight Mile Suspended Carnival," Cleopatra said.

Inside the gate was a freestanding doorway, but instead of a door, there was a metal slab with a list of words and numbers.

"What's that?" Mim asked.

"The Rules." Cleopatra pushed the metal slab open and they went through.

They passed tents and pens and booths, metal wrapped with cloth. A greasy smell invaded Mim's nostrils. Ahead was a grand building, with a porch as wide as its front. Curl-topped columns stood like stalky teeth, fangs to hold up the porch roof. The words above the porch said OASIS HOTEL. A bald man was sitting there on a low stool. He looked up from a piece of wood he was scraping.

"Went out to see what the storm brought, and look who I found," Cleopatra said. "Says she was dropped by the twister. Doesn't know from whence she came. Give her your water, would you?"

The man handed Mim a wineskin. She drank. Her bones recalled their weight.

"Where was she? We already salvaged everything," he said.

Cleopatra pointed to where Mim had been. He turned the wood in his hand several times, rubbed the surface, stared at Mim. "Survived the twister. How unlikely you are." His smile was a glint, a live thing. "Can you do anything, foundling? Some sort of work? We can't collect strays."

"Meet the boss. Mr. Suspender," Cleopatra said.

"Hello," Mim said.

"Charmed," he said.

"Let her rest in my room first. She's all torn up. Look at her," Cleopatra said.

"There's plenty of rooms," Mr. Suspender said. "She might want privacy."

"She shouldn't be alone. She needs care."

"Where are your clothes?" Suspender asked Mim.

"I don't know."

"Wind must have torn them off, poor cowdling," Cleopatra said. "She'll stay here till her people find her."

He studied Mim. "Where did you come from?"

"I don't know," Mim said. "I can't remember." She started to cry. Had wind sucked her from something important, maybe people, a family? Beyond the grit and violence of the wind, all she remembered was waking on the ground, bruised, cut, and naked.

Suspender held his knife as if to resume carving, but did not. His hands formed a beauteous sculpture. Somehow he gazed into her body. His scrutiny made her warm. "Did you show her the rules?" he asked.

"That can wait," Cleopatra said.

"Yes, I suppose so," he said. "Fine, she stays with you. Go on and patch her up."

Cleopatra bowed and led Mim in. Inside the Oasis Hotel lobby, lamps glowed like moonbeams. "He built this whole world, and gathered us," Cleopatra said. Up a staircase to the first landing, then down a hall. Cleopatra opened a door. Mim coughed. The room smelled like burned rice. Cleopatra lit a multitude of candles, fireflies of light. From every surface, the room's intricacy accumulated into something heroic.

"I'll find a dress for you to wear. Then rest and a sponge bath." Cleopatra pulled aside an iridescent curtain, revealing a rack of garments. She chose a worn, dark blue dress. "This is mine. You'll swim in it. You're too small. But it won't trouble your skin, and I don't mind if it gets that mess on it, it's just an old rag." She helped Mim remove the shawl and put on the dress, then produced a pair of bloomers and a thick flannel pad with eight short ribbons attached, and handed it to Mim. "Wear it between your legs," she said. "It'll catch the moon."

"I've bled like this before," Mim said. "I think. Feels familiar."

"Well, I'm sure you've never had something this clever. Nelda's own design."

"Who's Nelda?"

"Nelda, she's at Wistmount now—you'll meet her when she's home. Wash the pad when it's full. The little corner is next door. If you can't make it that far, use the bedpan."

A short movable screen of black carved wood and red silk divided the room. Silver stitches sailed across the silk, silver birds and butterflies trembled upon an imagined wind.

Mim studied the screen. "Five butterflies."

"Oh? I never counted."

After Mim was dressed, she rested on the bed.

Cleopatra took something from her pocket. Cards. She placed them on a silk-draped table beside the bed. "Now, let us figure you out. You must remember something, a face, a dream, some echo? I can't purchase this idea of nothing. Cards might help. Or not. No. Let's try the other way." She put away the cards. "How old are you? You're slim, but the breasts. And full of moon, of course. It wasn't your first time? Seventeen? Eighteen? Anyway you can't be twenty."

"The wind has talons," Mim said. She surveyed the collection of glass and feathers, but all this beauty pained her eyes. Along with the grease of the Eight Mile Suspended Carnival, Mim smelled something else, something powdery and bad. The twister had stirred up whatever had been sleeping; the odor took shape and seeped into her pores. She touched textures: rough floor, smooth dress, and worn blanket that covered her.

The symphony of pain toured her body. She tried to muffle it, but breathing didn't help. The band made sounds like steps, but then they weren't inside her, they were real steps, voices, and the door opened.

Suspender came in with Cleopatra. Mim hadn't heard her leave. He rolled a metal box into the room, unlocked it, rearranged parts, and in a few maneuvers, clattered together a second bed. "Behold your cot," he said.

Cleopatra helped Mim sit, and offered a glass jar full of something. "Drink it fast," she said. The stuff was green, with sediment that tasted like metal and dirt.

12

"What was that?" Mim asked.

"A helpful substance," Cleopatra said.

"Yes, our fortune-teller is very helpful," Suspender said. "Alright. You can stay, but you'll need to abide by the rules."

Of Suspender, Mim saw two parts: the outer crust, and something inside, barely visible, something tender.

"That can wait," Cleopatra said. She lifted another vessel from the tray and offered it to Mim, who drank—warm, sugary.

"I'll take care of your skin later. For now, rest," Cleopatra said.

Warmth dribbled down Mim's throat, and soon she was gently falling, slowly curling her shell into the shape of a claw, which offered some relief.

IV

In the blur of paper, metal, and shadow, a thin layer of obscurity clung to the windows of the hotel; this obscurity like loss and detachment covered every surface of the Eight Mile Suspended Carnival. If you polish something, if you bathe it in water that isn't full of sulfur, the sensation is only a momentary clarity. Nothing stays tidy long. Vision and perception shift and keep shifting like dry clots of earth, dust, clang. The only thing that shines is oil, or maybe blood. *Those* substances can't be dulled by grime or tired toil, not by cynicism, Time, nor distance. Blood and oil are the substances that endure. Blood and oil, and some other stuff in a bucket, you'll see, those three are the unassuming charmed matter, those are what cling, and throb, and inspire. They are breath, when there's no water and no air, these thick things are all you can see, all you can taste, they overflow the sorry container of any edifice, fill cracks and ooze and if anything, in error, gapes (a mouth, say, or a heart) they fill what's become vacant. If there were a way to frame their chemistry, their essence, those three—blood, oil, and the stuff in the bucket—would change from words into things, would flap and take wing, and using the fissure between thought and word, spring into story, use that air and rise and cover the whole of life, the act of living; those three would cover the sky, blot the sun, birds, everything else in the space they would command and eat and shit out. A big life machine of sticky dark.

But let's keep things where they belong: in bodies, in built machines, in buckets, covered, though sometimes, if we're not watchful, leaking onto the ground, spilling over; pugilism and carelessness invite them from their bindings into the open, to lead the world one step closer to oblivion.

These three cavorters have always existed. They have patience. They know who's in charge. They can wait. They will.

V

Sick-sleep troubled Mim for hours, days, textures combined: the swirling wind, and grit, and other things she couldn't see or pronounce . . . sweat and thirst and torrents and boxes of clocks and gears that needed oil . . . oily substances that further obscured her ability to see, to taste, to breathe. This greasy film of nothing and everything gyrated, its center unbalanced, undulating, undying and unforgiving and unlashing unleashing . . . the least sound was an echo-room inhabiting her warm head.

What connects us to the world? What spits us out, lets us flounder, lets us splash, alone, through the stench? Being tossed away. Being left behind, forgotten. Forgotten and forgetting. You might think you have a place but how secure is it? How deep is the hidey-hole, how soon will the wind fly it all away, leave you exposed and covered in grime.

There was nothing green in Mim's memory. The silky oil of her soul mixed into the gossamer of Cleopatra's room, where everything crouched and waited. Where Cleopatra's musk stole into the shadows. Mim was aware the door opened and closed because the air shifted, shifted, so surely time was passing, yes? It must be. It must be. Time, too, spun into the tunnel, the wall of wind from which she was born, but no, that couldn't be, or *could* wind create a life? Was that howl and heave, was the wind her mother? *Are you?* she asked the wind. Something knocked around inside that swirl, folded her psyche, already frail as worn silk, already translucent, already near failing, but then somehow the beat persisted.

As hearts tend to do.

And there was Cleopatra, strong arm with velvet hand pressing a cool rag to her forehead.

Suspender brought a bowl of food and handed it to Cleopatra. "Eat-up time," she said. She fed Mim a spoonful. Warm and soft and somewhat bitter.

Again, Suspender's gaze invaded and thawed Mim. "You up to some work?" he said.

"Don't be simple. Look at her," Cleopatra said. "She needs time. We'll show her the boulevard when she's better. Now, let her rest."

"She could help the chef."

Mim sat up. "Everything still hurts," she said.

"Leave her," Cleopatra said.

"Sure, sure, rest, but shortly we need the miraculous survivor to do more than lay about. Chosen or not, we can't feed a slack mouth indefinitely." His voice sounded like two people speaking in unison.

"Don't worry about him, he's got imperfections," Cleopatra said.

He laughed. "That depends on who you talk to."

Mim took the spoon and ate three more bites.

Another time, someone new entered Mim's room. Another of the divine feminine, who wore dungarees belted with a rope. "I'm Nelda." She handed Mim her dose. "Oh, look at you. Poor thing."

"Thank you," Mim said, and drank the stuff.

"And I found gingerroot in town—made a batch of tea. I didn't strain it, better if it's thick. It'll sustain the bones. Have some." Her kindness warmed Mim more thoroughly than the spicy sludge.

"It burns!" Mim said.

"I know. That's perfect," Nelda said. "And I'm glad you're here."

Mim smiled. Glad, such a simple word. Yes, glad. An exhalation. Sometimes things can be simple, like *glad*.

"Me, too," Mim said.

VI

Some nights, while she recuperated, Mim was back inside the roar, the wall of wind. Wind flung her from one place to another, where all people resembled all other people. For Mim, looking at faces was a waste of effort, faces from what Suspender called the death pill factory across the tired bridge, faces from the town . . . he said they were spent guests. Wind makes things happen, wind is all there is sometimes, wind keeps pushing, and quiets the inessential, and forces everything to stop and celebrate its feats of terror.

Some nights, Mim's skin betrayed her . . . tugged as if to uncover her and float away, or crinkle to the ground, leave her with crumbs, whatever was underneath. This pang woke her at night. Ever since that wall of wind had birthed her, had named her *Mim*.

Some nights, Mim dreamed that Suspender crossed the tired bridge and merged with the other men, and entered the factory, and like Beatrice, Mim herself was draped with feathers or fur. And some nights, all faces were insignificant because Mim could see their insides. Could see their memories.

Some especially horrid nights, she dreamed of finding herself in a ditch, skin torn off, body all red and warbling, eyes screaming back at her, hungry, no shell, hungry for skin, desperate for a container. The one without skin, the Mim in the ditch, she needed her skin back.

If she woke and stayed extra still, and tried not to breathe, sometimes she could make these agonies stop.

TWO

THE RULES

I

The smell of edibles invaded the hollow in Mim's gut and woke her. Midday light crept across the fortune-teller's horde of round objects. Through a thick porridge of soreness, she went to use the little corner, then downstairs, where she found a hallway leading from the lobby deeper into the building. Aroma and clang beckoned her through a doorway, then into a large room with many tables and benches, a kitchen.

At the stove, a man sang and stirred a pot of something. Black ribbons were woven into his long braids.

Mim bumped into a sideboard, and a stack of tin bowls tumbled, clattered on the floor. The man yelped and turned toward the noise.

"Mangry Mittens! Don't sneak up like that. You'll scare a guy."

"I didn't mean to."

"You invaded my kitchen! Put those things back."

"Sorry." She gathered and replaced the bowls.

"Sit down, windling. You're late, but there's plenty. Not everyone gets room service, windy. Breakfast at eleven, lunch at four, dinner at midnight after we close."

Mim sat on a bench. The man handed her a bowl full of reddish soupy stuff, and a spoon.

"No one should eat alone." He filled a bowl for himself, and sat across from her. "So you're our new wastrel? Arrived by twister. Messy. I've seen worse. I hear they're rebuilding what they can of Grayville, north of Wistmount. We were lucky. Dry as a skeleton here, though the sky wasn't pretty. That wind! And cramming all those guests in the basement was a hell of a tale. The which I'll spare you. You're welcome. They call me Lo-Lo."

On the table a metal cylinder surrounded a lamp. He spun the cylinder. Through slits on the side of the cylinder, the sun rose and set, then the moon, likewise.

"You are paler than sad milk. Tornado must have snatched off your color. Tell me about yourself, scrawny," he said.

"Cleopatra found me."

Lo-Lo laughed. "You mean the fortune-teller? Her name ain't Cleopatra, dolly. Far from it."

"What's her name?" Mim asked.

"Ask herself! Anyway, what about you? I tried to meet you, but the fortune-teller wouldn't let me. Nelda, yes, but not me."

"I can't remember anything. Only wind." When she conjured the wind, her skin woke and quivered.

Lo-Lo took a bite of food. "More honey." From a jar, he drizzled amber into his bowl. "You'll want some too," he said. He drizzled hers.

She tasted the reddish stuff, which made her tongue tingle, but it was sweet and she was hungry. Lo-lo talked on about the hotel's history.

Suspender came into the room. "You got up?" he asked Mim.

"Good morning yourself," Lo-Lo said.

"I ate before dawn," Suspender said. "Electric Trampoline needed realignment. Someone fell last night."

"Oops," Lo-Lo said.

Suspender lit a burner on the stove to boil water. Into a graceful bowl with pink flowers on each side, he spooned brown powder. When the kettle screamed, he filled the bowl and stirred. He put the flowered bowl on the table, then filled a larger bowl with food. Sat and ate. Lo-Lo passed him the honey but he said, "No, thanks."

No words while they ate. Mim wondered if Suspender was named after the Eight Mile Suspended Carnival or vice versa. He had precisely three outfits: each a pair of canvas coveralls. Mim would only realize there were three because of the faded color beneath the dinge, one blue, one grey, and one brown. Today was blue.

After a while, Mim asked Suspender, "Do you have another name?"

He looked up at her. "Pelle. What they called me as a child," he said.

"Pelle."

"Yes, Pelle." He squinted at her like a puzzle to solve. "But no one calls me that." To Lo-Lo, he said, "You show her the rules. She can't stay unless she's proper oriented."

"Me? Why me?" Lo-Lo asked. "I still need to visit the livestock."

Suspender sipped from his tea bowl and looked at Mim. *Was that a leaf in the air, above his head? Translucent?* But if so, the leaf faded. "The foundling can go with you. Show her around," he said.

"But . . . I hate to be rude . . . you don't smell very good, dear," Lo-Lo said.

"Did you bathe? Hygiene?" Suspender asked her.

"No," she said.

"Second floor, end of the hall," Suspender said. "Clean up, then you'll get the tour."

Mim didn't want to bathe or tour, but didn't have the strength to object. Being told what to do was a comfort.

She walked up to the second floor, turned left, and went to the end of the hall but was met by a locked door. Must be the other end. She found a wide, copper-wrapped door, and opened and went through.

Lo-Lo had explained that the hotel used to be full of bathers when it was a health resort. Now, the large, open room was a stately shell, walls lined with greenish copper tiles, impressions of flowers and vines coiled around each square. Some tiles were more turquoise than green, depending on how the light encroached. She found a pile of thin linen towels and at the last tub on the left, turned the faucet. Air sputtered, then water spilled into the tub. Impossible to balance hot and cold. She undressed, stepped into the water, and flinched when the water lapped her wounds. She was bruised and scraped badly along her right hip and thigh. She submerged and rested her eyes a moment.

She looked around, confused until she remembered. The water was cloudy and cool. She stepped out and patted her skin with the towel, odd, like an echo, like her body was hollow. She couldn't separate this strange sensation from the strangeness of this new place. It felt good to be clean. She dressed and returned to the kitchen.

At the table, Lo-Lo rearranged many paper scraps, wrote on a couple of them. "Shh," he said, "don't speak." After a little while he gathered the scraps, stuffed them in his bib pocket, then said, "Much better. Come along, tidbit. Meet the menagerie. The goats are teasing the foul again, so Beatrice and I shall go happify them." He led Mim out the back kitchen door. The kitchen was one-story, sewn to the back of the hotel, with a metal roof that sloped toward the door. The seam between the kitchen and the rest of the hotel had been patched with pieces of metal sheet and wire. The menagerie was kept between the kitchen and the river.

"I didn't realize how close the river was," Mim said.

"Don't step on that dock. It's rotten."

Beatrice lounged outside atop a wooden box, eyes closed. Lo-Lo shooed her to get up. "Damn thing, how many times must I express it: you are not a chicken." He picked up the box. "You lead her."

"Why me?" Mim asked.

"Scared?" he asked.

"What *is* Beatrice?" she asked.

"Some say her mother was a Russian wolfhound and her father an emu. Think upon that. No one knows, really. The fortune-teller brought her."

Beatrice, the beast, the attraction. Perpetually vexed. Mim wanted to run fingers through Beatrice's feathery fur, but those bloodshot eyes stopped her conveying affection. Lo-Lo said Beatrice provided security, roaming, nudging, and alarming anyone suspected of cheating the carnival or otherwise causing disarray.

Goats were another kind of odd. Nine goats. Goat eyes were globes; goat ears stuck out, like unflying, useless wings, trying to lift their tight gourd bodies as the beasts trotted around the pen. Most had brown coats of varied shades. The white goat, Zlateh, had pink eyes. Some had horns, at least one or two, some did not. Beatrice leaned across the slatted fence and made a low booming sound. One of the taller goats licked her plumage.

"Good thing goats can live on clutchweed. Not much else for them to scrounge," Lo-Lo said.

Goat. A simple word for something unfathomable. Lo-Lo said he made cheese from goat milk.

"Fresh, grassy-smelling. They adore Beatrice, but she gives back eternal disdain. Nevertheless, she keeps them in order, even the littles," Lo-Lo said.

The littles were sweet in their ugliness, but the grown goats had no manners. He said they only obeyed Beatrice, so you had to enlist her if you needed action from goats. It was tricky. But her power over them was like sunshine on flowers. In her presence, they bloomed into responsible citizens. Suppliants, they offered themselves wholly. Beatrice looked down upon them, yawned, and scratched her back with her snout.

Next they went to gather chicken eggs. *Something wicked about the chickens,* Mim thought. *Too unpredictable.* Lo-Lo said Beatrice tended them, too. Said her scent scared off foxes and other poachers.

He catalogued the animals they had kept from the start of time, when the carnival was elsewhere. "Even sweet martens. Years ago."

"What's that?"

"Pine martens, or in Spanish, *martas.* 'Finer than foxes, charming as a child's cuddle toy,' Suspender used to yell. Until someone snuck in and stole them for pelt."

"That's horrible," she said.

"Yes." He handed her an egg. Such tiny weight in her hand. "Plenty this morning. Let's have one. Nothing like a fresh egg." He cracked a shell and slurped the contents into his mouth. He cracked another. Inside was a red bit. "Red means good luck. Open up!"

She did, and he fed it to her; she gagged, spit it out. "How can you eat that?"

"Oh, so little courage," he said. "Just put them away, then."

She opened the box and placed eggs in their felt beds.

"Livestock is trouble. A week after we arrived, the munitions factory had an explosion. In the morning, a dozen chickens were dead. Twitchy, too fragile. Chickens come and go."

Lo-Lo had to woo one hen to steal her egg. "Come on, poor darling, cough it up. Think about your youth, all you would give up! She's fallen in love with the possibility of motherhood." Finally, after cooing and kissing her beak, Lo-Lo scooped the egg from the sad-looking hen. "Plenty eggies even for tomorrow's lunch. Today, I think fritters with ground corn, or eggs in lard. Beauty! Bitty sunshines in the pan. Tomorrow, terrines, or maybe fluff eggs."

He said he would bake the empty eggshells until they were clean, and grind them to powder, so Cleopatra could make her good coffee in the morning. She alone had the gift, he said.

"You don't remember anything?" he asked. "Not where you came from?"

"No."

"Cheer up. Maybe someone will come hunting you." Lo-Lo set the egg box inside the back door. He took Mim's hand. "Now, we tour. Beatrice, come on. Behold the morning!" They walked away from the river, past the hotel, out toward the carnival.

II

The Eight Mile Suspended Carnival stood trembling but determined, surrounded by scrubby bush and dry nothing, across the river from the Spurlock Munitions Company. Black powder works, the death pill factory. Suspender said, "That place exists and profits by wrecking whatever's noble and pure about humanity." Small fall-down buildings lined the bank over there, tracks with carts connected it all. Suspender said the death pill factory was built diffuse so when a man did something stupid, like smoke a cigar, and blew something up, the damage wouldn't be complete. Everyone knew about the explosion at Eddystone. Those poor girls in F Building killed, mangled beyond recognition, *95 Girls' Bodies at the Morgue.*

The array of structures at Spurlock Munitions reminded Mim of the carnival's family of tents, but the carnival's intentions were not likely so sinister, not likely.

The morning of Mim's tour was juicy, sunshine liquid and fresh, as if trying to replace rain. Had it been months, years? Mim didn't know, but it certainly was dry. After lack of exercise, turned out her limbs were grateful for the walk. *Relief, being somewhere—being here. Not lost.* They trolled counterclockwise around the perimeter: booths, tents, rides in a rangy circle surrounded the Tower of Misfortune.

"Less straightforward, but more like Paris, circles inside of circles," Lo-Lo said. He kicked a ball of something nasty toward Beatrice. "Eat-up time!" Beatrice grunted and ate.

"The hotel has been here for ages, since it was a health resort. Aside from that, the boss will claim he built everything, and that's part true. True he is an artist. He'll raise a metal monster by himself, but on most, he had help. I helped, we all did, all of us who've been here awhile. Tiger broke his back on that one." Lo-Lo pointed at a round spidery edifice, about half as tall as the hotel. "That's why we call it The Rack. It was just an emotional backache. But Tiger truly could not stand up. Cleopatra worked on him.

She's the strongest one here. He was okay after awhile, after The Rack was finished. Must've brought to mind what he didn't want to remember."

The rides on the outer ring were simple—wood strung together and waxed, bits of glass for fancy. Some had full staircases, to carry guests closer to the firmament.

While they walked, Lo-Lo pointed at attractions. "Boat ride, costume shop—you'll find more robement there. Take what you like and Nelda will make it fit. She's the relevant artist to consult. There's the wine tent. You can read, right?"

"Yes," she said.

"Read that sign to me."

"'Notice: No staff admitted during business hours except in pursuit of official business,'" Mim read.

"A proper and stern warning. Extra carny feet make things too hard for us to manage. No staff during open hours, except me and Anton the Younger. I serve wine, and Anton provides security," Lo-Lo said.

He pointed at things, and named some other things. "All these signs need to be repainted. Alas, who has time?"

Mim smelled something repulsive. "What's that?" She covered her nose and mouth, but the stench was eternal.

"That stink? Snake pit. Eyelash viper." They quickly moved on. "Rides, rides, rides, mostly for infants. The Ringer. The Slanting World. The Electric Trampoline, adults only. Perilous!" He pointed to a gap. "The wine tent used to stand there, but the ground got saturated—you don't want to know—so we moved it."

III

Atop the pole by the entrance was the Carnival Moon—an electric masterpiece. Inside the gate, the doorway holding a slab of metal covered with words.

"I saw that when I got here," Mim said.

"The boss rigged it so a person has to read the rules and agree before they can come in," Lo-Lo said. "Guests and carnies all need to read it out loud and audibly agree. Carnies only have to do it once. Unless they break a rule. Read it," he said.

A stenciled list, white on black. Freshly painted.

THE RULES

1. NEVER UNDERESTIMATE ANOTHER FELLOW.
2. KEEP YOUR HANDS STRONG.
3. DON'T KEEP WHAT YOU CAN'T CARRY.
4. THOSE WHO SEEK GIRLY PLEASURES SHOULD GO HOME TO THE WIFE.
5. CLOSE YOUR EYES ONLY WHEN NECESSARY.
6. NO SPITTING.
7. NO PUGILISM.
8. A THING ISN'T YOURS UNTIL SOMEONE GIVES IT YOU.
9. MACHINES SHALL REMAIN PRISTINE.
10. DON'T BE TOO SUPERSTITIOUS.
11. BE A LITTLE SUPERSTITIOUS.
12. TRUST US.

Lo-Lo said, "Congratulations, carny. *Allons-y!*" They spiraled inward, passed the fortune-teller's tent, the tall man stilts, the Hi-Striker, the Camera of Illusion, more rides, rides embroidered by air, and finally, Lo-Lo said, "Behold the Tower of Misfortune. There are stories, words in my brain, let's see . . . Tower of Misfortune, no one has fallen off and died, not yet. But if you're near the tower when he calls for a move, walk away. You'll want to be elsewhere."

"Why?" Mim asked, but Lo-Lo had moved on.

"Cabinet of the Fallen, that's mostly spirit stuff. Knife man, he's long gone. Calhoun's Corner, he's gone too, but who wants to repaint a sign for something so irrelevant?"

Mim hurried to keep up.

He catalogued the tired colors of the Eight Mile Suspended Carnival, as if the things themselves were small creatures, voles, from underground, now exposed in the aching bright.

"We need to do some painting, sure. Wind harmed our signage. Cheap materials will peel off. Suspender ain't interested, claims the two-dimensional is beneath his art. Yet he's never happy with anyone else's work.

Maybe you can pass. I'll mix some paint later and we'll see. Been experimenting with binding agents."

(He did. She did. But that was later.)

"Oh, I forgot the Room of Doom. I'll show you another time. Suspender's construction shop, invitation only, never uninvited."

Poles, moons, fashioned for your amusement, not unlike the dumb machinery that generates bodies, ours, the breathing mess that rises from mineral, roars loud or breaks quiet, gasps that move us toward the last. *A man with ragged virtue runs this discoverable world.* Do you know the name of your father, the pole that roughed you to life? Do you know the moon, She Who Knows, the one inside, from which you emerged?

What do you see?

Where is the light coming from?

How is the man holding his head, and from the angle, can you determine a damn thing? Can you read him, his intentions?

What if you discern, assemble letters, the wrong letters? Spell the wrong words?

What will you make of your mistakes?

Room of Doom saved for later, Lo-Lo and Mim continued onward. Beatrice trotted toward a tall grey mountain, almost as tall as the Tower of Misfortune. Shifting sounds grumbled from the heap. The sign said *Mount Detritus.*

Lo-Lo said, "Make something of the remnants, make it tall. Consider things usually unconsidered. For instance: when bits of melted metal washed up on our side, Suspender saw opportunity. Especially after the explosion. No one knows what caused it to go boom. Bits of bridge, bits of war. He tossed out a net and dredged it up, took a long while. It was a mess until he considered the magnet. Now behold its unflawed elegance. Clean up isn't too hard with the magnet. Reshape it every so often, let the people climb."

What you did, Lo-Lo explained, was climb the mountain, then slide down.

"What's the point?" Mim asked.

"It's amusing and diverting! Take off your boots," he said.

Beatrice sighed and lay down beside the mountain. Under Mim's feet, cool droplets of metal shifted, like halted tears.

"Once you get up here, you have to yell your father's name," Lo-Lo said.

"I don't know my father's name," Mim said.

"Just yell anything." Lo-Lo yelled, "Jeremiah!" and slid down.

Mim yelled, "Jeremiah!" Beneath her bum, the cold, hard tears stirred her skin all the way down to the dry ground.

Near the carnival gate, where she lurked to glimpse the night's crowd, Mim saw Suspender hop onto a drum-shaped platform, veined with silver and painted the color of dried blood. Above his head, the Carnival Moon shone brighter than its celestial inspiration. A constellation of people lined up for admittance. Some thin, some thick, some drab, some fine, the people spoke in buzzing voices, like flies unwittingly waiting for their spider. At a ticket booth, a younger carny, unknown to Mim, waited.

Suspender whistled. The people quieted. With a spinning copper coin he held their gaze, then lifted a dented shout-horn and spoke through it, his voice a tinny invocation:

"Friends, if you seek the mundane, I apologize. If you seek the mundane, please leave now. Here, you'll not find the mundane. Common magic you'll find at any carnival, in any town. Not here, not here. This is the Eight Mile Suspended Carnival. No tigers to pluck feathers from fowl. Here, friends, here you will find the unnamed and impossible. Curiosities that lurk in unlit corners of your dreams, dreams too obscure to remember—what, upon waking, you can't recall but can't quite shake. Those dreams that cling might be found within this place. You'll find things you didn't know you had lost! The key to your crate full of treasures." He pointed at a young woman who wore an olive green hat. "You know the one, don't you? Yes! That key. Access, that's the gift we provide, friends. Access to everything holy and unholy, all of it. Textures and sounds of the sun, the moon, the warbling of the smallest creature, magnified by ten thousand. I'm talking about *stories*, friends, imaginings and creations, enchantments you will not soon forget." He laughed, as if just then remembering something. "I am speaking, simply, of the stuff of life.

"It's sacred work we do here, sacred what we perform. And it's all for you. Step right up." He gestured to the ticket booth carny, spun his copper coin again, and ushered people through the gate.

He looked at Mim, and she felt an odd desire to touch his bald head, so shiny beneath the electric moon.

IV

Master of Foods, Lo-Lo orchestrated concessions and cooked for the carnies. Breakfast at eleven, lunch at four, dinner at midnight. His victuals elevated food beyond what human tongue-buds had ever met. Lo-Lo was grime-covered most of the time. Everyone was. But his dirt smelled like an open window. He kept his face clean and hair bright. Braided or not, he had so much hair, especially compared with Suspender. Lo-Lo was a beauty, but from his insides, or what Mim could see of his insides: his insides shone, unlike the sad hole inside Suspender. *Pelle.*

Some of the carnies, Mim would never know their names. Suspender spoke of others, some had taken off, some had been exiled. There was a whole category of carnies called Tobeys. They did various load-bearing jobs, set up, take down, rearrange, whatever was needed. They were called Tobeys because, apparently, the first one who joined the carnival in the early days was named Tobey, as was the second one. The two were called the Tobeys, but after they left, the name persisted.

Suspender and Lo-Lo and the others resembled the carnival machines. Everywhere, metal clanged. Carnies ate their cakes from dented metal plates, which, emptied, resounded in the zinc basin for washing. Even boots in the hallway sounded sharp—tin talons scraped the floorboards. One night, Mim dreamt of carny-cakes made from paste: equal parts wine, water, and dry ground, the mineral upon which this carnival had been planted.

And how did the carnival wonders move? Whence the motion? Most were self-perpetuating, employing truths and principles of weights, pulleys, fulcrum . . . winding and unwinding bands. Wires. Wind helped, when they had wind—if effort wasn't overly ambitious. Wheels did their share. But whatever needed light and power were fed by the HydroWheel. This was a shockingly small but dense wheel that robbed current from the river and transmogrified it into electricity. An invention of Suspender. He claimed he would make another to sell, someday, someday.

V

Uncurl the shell. Go outside. Watch the craggy faces of these carnies who didn't even know for sure, but accepted she was, in fact, Mim. Who else should she be? She was grateful for their food and shelter.

Mim wore her name like the fortune-teller's worn blue dress. She had nothing else, really, to prove her being. Mim would have to be enough.

This body did—and also didn't—feel new: every month, she would bleed.

Your body cannot contain all that you are, else how to traverse the day? Fool yourself into trying; the fool may provide comfort. Fit it all in, let the bones build a cage and let the skin hide the deepest grim, that glub glub, that wanting. Skin is all that's hiding the glub glub for the unfortunate human whose story unfolds before you, on the lines of black, on searing white— these tattooed shapes stretching across digested trees, trying to make sense, the parade of line grinding to make meaning. A story.

Stop, stranger. Stop and rest as you pick pebbles from your boots. Hear this story, the one that depicts someone young and full of whisper and hope. Sometimes we're good—we can be good. We'll quiet down. We won't spoil it for her.

The first time Mim saw someone's memory, she mistook it for a leaf.

THREE

MACHINERY AND MEMORIES

I

The four elements. Make of each a fancy glass bead; string them into a necklace. Is there a natural order? Air, earth, water, fire? Does not a baby breathe, when first born? Or sooner, does not the womb cushion with water? Does not the fire of conception bring spirit into that watery womb? Does not one earth-laden body collide with its mate to turn fire into spirit, to swim little spirit through the water inside each muddy body, and does not spirit, eventually, breathe?

How to separate these substances, and why? Absent one, the others smile and take over. No rain, you get cracks in the earth. No fire, you cannot see, cannot perform alchemy. No air, and soon you turn the most stunning shade of blue.

Why, in our thoughts, must we separate them? Why not instead seek equilibrium, and help us all keep cheating death?

A rainbow of velvet, Cleopatra so splendidly adorned her body that when she moved, music arose. But she never wore rings. Round and strong, this one of the carnival's two deities proclaimed herself Mim's protector. Now that Mim was up and recovered, Cleopatra disclosed to her the fortune tent and its workings. When they arrived, they found, already, a line of customers.

Cleopatra said to the people, "Kindly wait until the preparations are complete."

Inside the tent, Cleopatra told Mim, "First, we ready the space." She clapped her hands in each corner. "Join me, more power in two of us."

Mim clapped, too.

"Now candles." Cleopatra lit the candles, which they placed in every corner of the tent. Across the tablecloth, from the center and spiraling outward, Cleopatra ran her hands, covered it with her essence, she said, and spoke words about air, earth, water, and fire.

Beatrice nosed into the tent, shook her feathers and spit something onto the plank floor. Cleopatra petted her. "Beatrice, you know I need privacy when I work. Please don't distract the guests. Take Mim round to see the other wonders. And Mim, thank you for your service."

Cleopatra steered her toward Mim. Beatrice balked.

"I don't think she likes me," Mim said.

"Pet her, like this. Don't be scared." Cleopatra showed Mim, starting with the shoulder blades. Mim touched the plumage, which was much more fragile than it looked. Beatrice frowned.

"Never touch her head. She only lets me. But beneath her reticence, she craves company."

"Like this?" Mim rested her hand gently between the creature's shoulders. Beatrice exhaled and blinked slowly.

"Yes, good. Now Beatrice, dearling, go find Nelda."

Beatrice led Mim past the line of people, past the Chess Game, where guests could straddle a stool that abutted a backdrop painting: a human-sized pawn pondered a chess board, his painted chin resting on hand, elbow resting on painted table, waiting for the living opponent's move. On the north side of Mount Detritus, Beatrice stopped, bit at the ground, and disgorged a dark lump, about the size of a small apple. Her digestive processes were ornate and incessant. Nearby, Suspender tidied the mountain with his magnet. The shape of his back as he worked forged a human contraption.

A fancy man in a long brown coat approached Suspender. "Doorman said I might find you here. I do admire your machinery," the man said.

"Thank you, Mr. Spurlock."

Spurlock? Factory Spurlock, boss of the death pill factory?

Spurlock said to Suspender, "I need something to put out fires. You recall that explosion. The river's right there. We need to move water to the buildings. Nothing my men think up operates worth a damn. Ever use your sweat on endeavors beyond amusement? Can you do it?"

Suspender twirled the magnet. "Depends. My own work is rather tall. Besides, I'm not fond of the war business."

"This is security. Safety. Say a fire gets lit. Make it easier to put out. Save a few souls from being burned or killed. Supports your fellow man."

Suspender laughed. Was that funny? Beatrice bit the lump into chunks, snorted, and masticated the pulp.

Spurlock said, "I'll pay you plenty, don't worry."

Suspender rubbed his head and exhaled. His bald head was the cleanest thing at the carnival, lustrous. Its shape captivated her.

"I might consider an offer," Suspender said.

Spurlock laughed. "Course you might. And you'll like it."

"I'll come take a look. Meanwhile enjoy your liberty, a game of chance, a libation."

Beatrice took another bite of her stuff and coughed.

"I suppose I might. Kind to invite me," Spurlock said.

"Goodnight," Suspender said, and resumed rebuilding Mount Detritus.

Work to be done. You lift your foot, and I'll lift mine. The toil is righteous, the sweat clean, cleans grit from our eyes, flushes out what's nasty and unnecessary, uses water, the water missing from the world, all the missing rain, water from our bodies to provide new vistas, bodies that need the work, the food, the fuel, the cash, will do what is presented just to keep beating heart beating, will keep moving onward, toward. Beat, breath, its own reward.

Suspender came around the Mount to Mim and Beatrice, shoved Beatrice with his foot. "Don't eat up my metal!"

She stepped back, growled, and kept chewing.

To Mim, he said, "You! Don't let her do that."

"Sorry. She coughed it up."

"What are you doing over here?"

She hadn't meant to spy on him. Maybe he didn't want eavesdroppers, so she didn't mention what she heard. "Beatrice was leading me to Nelda, but she stopped."

"Wishing Well is that way." He pointed to the left. "Beatrice knows how to find it."

"Okay," Mim said.

They walked past guests at play, past the snake pit, the Electric Trampoline. People veered away from Beatrice. Shortly they reached a rusty outgrowth, maybe twice the diameter of a trundling hoop, erupting from the ground. Above it, a filigree spiderweb sign said, *Nelda's Wishing Well.* Nelda, in green satin, sat on a green-painted throne, and called out, "Wishing Well, Wishing Well, make your wish but never tell." Opalescence on her cheeks, and orange-red rouge on her lips. Guests talked to Nelda and chucked coins into the well. Beatrice careened toward Nelda, and Mim followed.

"Hello, dearlings," Nelda said.

"Cleopatra sent us to visit while she works," Mim said.

Nelda petted Beatrice, who leaned lovingly toward her. "Glad for friendly company. How's business tonight?" Nelda asked.

"People were lined up for her already!"

"Over here is decent, too. So many tossers, aspiration everywhere. Can't blame them, right? We all need something to clutch."

"I'm not sure what I need to clutch," Mim said.

"Maybe Beatrice will do." Nelda petted the beast. "We were two, and now we're three. I love having another deity around, even if someday you remember yourself and find your way out of here. For now, it's my delight to know you." She gave Mim a coin. "Make a wish."

"Wouldn't know what to wish."

"Save it for when you know." Nelda hugged Beatrice, turned to a couple new guests, and called, "Wishing Well, Wishing Well, make your wish but never tell."

Mim watched Nelda talk to guests for a while. *A memory, anything,* Mim thought, and tossed the coin into the water.

Later that night, after the carnival closed and they had finished midnight dinner, Mim curled on the cot in Cleopatra's room. On her way to bed, Nelda stopped in and gave Mim a handful of coins. "We've accomplished tonight."

"Sure did," Cleopatra said.

"Thank you," Mim said.

"You're welcome." Nelda yawned.

"Want to stay over?" Cleopatra asked. "You can share with me."

"I'll wake up freezing, with you."

"I can share!" Cleopatra patted her bed.

"Not actually. No, tonight I need sleep. Goodnight, my dearlings—until the morn." Nelda kissed them each and left.

"Keep that money safe," Cleopatra said. She handed Mim a small bowl. "For now. But sew a pocket inside your dress. Can you sew? Nelda can help. Pockets are ever-helpful."

Mim put her coins in the bowl and held it carefully. Cleopatra unwound accouterments, removed from her neck a length of gold chain that held a gold ring. She kissed the ring, then showed it to Mim: a murky brown square hemmed in by tiny pearls. The miniature square looked like a drop of pond water, a tear from the Wishing Well. In the dim light, the decadent burnt red of Cleopatra's fingernail polish shone.

"Why don't you wear that ring on your finger?" Mim asked.

"What's this?" Cleopatra lifted a slipper and swatted a vole from its warm bed. The vole scurried under the door and off somewhere. "These damn rashy feet. I need salts," Cleopatra said. "Do the getting, will you, Mim?"

Mim poured salt into a metal basin, then pitcher water.

"Thanks everso." Gaps stretched between Cleopatra's fading words . . . "had to fight my way out of that unjust family. . . ."

Mim's injured wrist throbbed as it still did sometimes. A square-ish leaf materialized above Cleopatra's left ear, then the leaf spread into motion: a girl, shining coils of hair, runs through a field, away from a house, and Mim sees broken skin on the girl's cheek, and behind her eyes, desperation lifts and propels the girl's feet, bright quick steps on scratchy grass; the girl's feet are unshod but Mim can feel they're tough, like Cleopatra's feet in the basin. Mim feels the girl's stout soles as if her own feet have grown pads so she, too, can run however far she needs to go. So she, too, can escape.

Then Mim looked at Cleopatra, simply the woman in the room, soaking her feet, which no longer belonged to Mim. Cleopatra's eyes were closed.

What was that? What had Mim *seen*? She tried to see more, but there was only the room and its baubles, quivering.

33

Sleep was impossible, until a couple hours before dawn, when her body simply let go.

II

If you closed your eyes for a week at the Eight Mile Suspended Carnival, your body would absorb seven days of plunk and plod, the sounds necessary to create so much wonder.

After lunch the next day, Suspender declared Mim should learn some jobs. He told her to follow Tiger, who ran Just Knock 'Em Down, meaning a wall of milk bottles, stacked five, four, three, two, one. Mim was to help re-stack the bottles.

"Two for three, two for three!" Tiger yelled. He was a scabby old man who hated to wear a shirt, so he had torn off all the buttons.

He explained to Mim that if the top bottles weren't properly balanced, guests with any aim could knock them down. "I hate to give away even one of those ugly babies." He pointed at a shelf of rubber cherubim. "Chafes my backside!"

Tiger nagged Mim through several clumsy starts. Finally she figured out how to align the bottles so they held sturdy as the pyramids. No one could knock them down. Night's end, Tiger gave her two scoops of pennies and three fat silvers and said she was welcome to work again tomorrow.

Hands like spiders, creeping round hips or through pages, or pulling ropes, hands do what we ask of them, hands do what we don't even know they are doing. Without thought, we plunk metal in the box, eager for the show to begin, to lift us above the bestial. Noble, isn't it, in a way? How the hands reach toward story, toward song?

Mim paid attention, everywhere, to the ropes that tethered the canvas and raised the roof, the lines that defined the architecture of the Eight Mile Suspended Carnival.

Nights were for adults: wicked, rough, full of games and wine. After dusk, the rides closed.

A gramophone Suspender had rigged to work on a timer supplied the carnival's music. Between five o'clock in the evening when the carnival opened, and midnight, when it closed, songs warbled from the machine, crackled through speakers. Each day, Nelda switched gramophone records. If, for instance, you hear harp music, you know 'tis Tuesday. One record for each carnival day. After awhile, the sound melted into the background of the carnival, became texture, a rhythm for the week. From morning till five was quiet, aside from the clatter and gab of the carnies. Sunday morning and all day Monday were quiet, too, when the carnival rested.

When you need to build, throw disparate and warring elements together to make one. Use whatever motions you can imagine. Sometimes it's necessary to string through holes, like beads, and make a line of things unified by their gaps, unified by what's missing. In this case, use string, or use rope. Unified by the negative space, by the omissions, scars, wounds. Unified by the ghosts, whatever was torn from one's spirit. There may be discarded parts somewhere, but no matter how the water or tears have washed your eye-pans, you won't be able to make them appear. They appear only in your grief. Their loss allows us to string our parts together, to make something useful and new.

To practice.

And sometimes, to untie.

III

When the carnival had wine to sell, Lo-Lo raised the tent and poured the wine. The Eight Mile Suspended Carnival had no official dispensation to vend intoxicants, but the risk was worth it. The burden of inhibition faded when people drank, and the inebriated were generous with their money. Wine fattened a night: the selling of drinks, and the increasingly foolhardy acts of the novice. Those who just wanted to drink would come back, never sure the tent would be open—but ever searching, ever hopeful.

Mim stood in a shadow outside the wine tent entrance. She wanted to see inside, but that sign reminded her carnies were not welcome during open hours unless you had a job to do, and she didn't want the *malocchio* from Lo-Lo or Anton the Younger.

Two women emerged, one propping the other up. A group of death pill factory boys followed them out.

"Beautiful ladies," said a hatless man with white hair.

A man in a gray hat said to White Hair, "You drank it all!"

"Fuck off," White Hair said, and shoved Gray Hat.

Gray Hat hit White Hair, who hit back, ignoring Rule Number Seven.

Usually when this happened, Suspender would douse the combatants with water, but tonight he was elsewhere, and so was Anton. A crowd of yellers coagulated.

Lo-Lo rushed from the tent and saw Mim. "Come on now. No place for a waif like you," he said, but they didn't leave. "Where the hell did Anton go?" Lo-Lo yelled.

Beatrice galloped toward the fighters and knocked Gray Hat over. White Hair jumped on top of him and punched him in the face. A third factory man pulled White Hair off. Beatrice thundered into the third man, too. He stumbled and lost his grip on White Hair, who fell down. But, like a dancer, the third man caught himself. White Hair screamed at Beatrice. Gray Hat jumped onto White Hair and punched him, but the third man pulled him off, and with catlike tread, unraveled the fight. Persuasive, slinking low.

Finally Lo-Lo yelled, "Get out of here, all of you!"

"Exactly what I was about to say," the third man said. To his colleagues, he said, "Come on. Go sleep it off, and get back to work."

People grumbled and began to disperse.

"We'll clean up tomorrow." Lo-Lo fastened the tent door, took Mim by the arm, and they went toward the hotel.

IV

The untying of things began when Mim saw that first leaf, the girl running, Cleopatra's memory. Spin, untie, loosen, loop, connect slivers of time, what ties marrow to marrow, the river of marrow that runs through the bones of a world, the paths, the ways, the center. *Was she running from someone, like that girl, like Cleopatra?* There must be something, some past. What came before the wind? *She's here so she came from somewhere; a person doesn't just fall from the sky, knowing things, how to walk.* Are there ways of being connected besides marrow? Even the narrowest path is still a path, leads somewhere, follows itself backward; even a thin hair has a direction, here to there, or there to here. It can't just fold into itself like layers of crust. *Everything has a moment, a place on the path; where is hers? She saw the girl, running. Was it a memory? Was it true, or was it a story she told inside her head? Can people see inside her? They don't act like it. But Suspender—Pelle—sometimes looks at her as if he's studying. Does everyone hide secret stories inside?*

What ties her to the world, what's her tether to mother, to mineral?

Is there no start, no end to a person? No border? No skin?

V

Mim loved night, after the carnival closed, after midnight dinner. Loved to lounge in Cleopatra's room, body exhausted, the edges of the day softened.

Maybe Mim had powers that she didn't comprehend. The carnival housed invisible vaults of stories and imaginings, and maybe someone had opened a vault, and maybe while it was open, Mim had breathed in something. Maybe she had inhaled a substance that changed her. Inhaled something of the fantastic.

One such night, Mim and Cleopatra reclined.

Mim said, "Tell me about Pelle."

"Who?"

"Suspender."

"What's to tell?"

"How old is he?"

Cleopatra sipped from her blue jar of wine. "Younger than you think. He's not old with years. Only seems so. The miles have left him shabby."

Between sips of wine, Cleopatra told of strangers' fortunes, stories prolonged by grape. Her rounded words wrapped the room with thick, warm humanity; her whole impressive mountain of person expanded.

"Those silver candlesticks are from my wedding table." She pointed at the light.

"Once upon a time, a blind woman click click clicked her wooden cane to my booth. Soon as she appeared, I knew she would gain wild riches within eight days. So that's how I spun the cards, of course. Several months later, she returned, in a resplendent velvet coat, trimmed in lace violets. Hat like the Queen's wedding cake. She looked cozy. But she cried dry tears."

"If the tears were dry, how could you see them?" Mim asked.

"That's how blind people cry. And the blind woman said that six days after I read her fortune, she was listening to the wireless when a knock came at the door. The dreaded blue-uniformed man stood there—well, I've got to embellish, for she couldn't see his uniform, nor stature, but all good stories need leeway—this man told the blind woman of her lost parents' luckless death in a mining explosion. But you see, Mim, the blind woman's parents had never shown her any love, in life. She had run from them, up and left, yes, despite the trials of being blind and alone! I had seen all this in her reading. Turns out, these parents left the blind woman a copious fortune, which the man (embellished in his speculative blue uniform) said was all for her. He read her a letter, and said a key to a treasure box would be delivered the next day. And since you asked, her dry tears were shed not for sorrow over their shroud—as you might expect—but for the love she had lacked. No amount of velvet and silk trappings can replace love. An orphan like you should know that."

"I'm not an orphan," Mim said.

"Really? I haven't noticed hordes of people hunting you."

Mim considered being an orphan, that word, so exposed. She stared at the sputtering twin candle flames, their low waxy cores, watched embellished uniforms shimmer and disappear, uniforms grainy, like the candlelight, but that story was enough to warm Mim into the lull that approaches before sleep, almost as delicious as she imagined love must feel.

VI

If a person could climb a ladder to the sky and look down at the Eight Mile Suspended Carnival, the looker would see a living beast, its spine the Tower of Misfortune, its arms the tents, its legs the rides, wheels, gears; its blood the wine and food and excrement that flowed through the bodies of carnies and guests; the air in the beast's lungs breathed by the humans who worked and wandered inside the cave of the beast's body. Its head the hotel, its mouth and ass the doorway into and out of a corrugated skin of wonder.

Mim learned the body of the beast by walking its perimeter, marking things in her mind. If you walked with Mim, you would see boat rides, jewelry tents, the Wishing Well, the Room of Doom, snake pit, wine tent, and so on and so on. And you would see Suspender's construction shop, but you would never see his treehouse. Camouflaged so fully that no one saw the treehouse until much, much later.

For, sometimes, a place can hide. Even a beast like the Eight Mile Suspended Carnival is more complicated than it, at first, appears. For isn't *The Imagined Unseen* a tantalizer, a true and legitimate aspect of wonder?

VII

Lo-Lo, cook and chemist, paint maker. He suggested that it was time for Mim to repaint the carnival signs. Suspender agreed. She painted, and showed Suspender her work. He approved. Painting became Mim's second occupation at the Eight Mile Suspended Carnival.

Each day, after breakfast, Anton the Younger would bring a sign for her to repaint, those that could be taken down. First, the banner above the entrance. Anton un-rigged and lay it on the ground. Layer upon layer, how many times had they painted this banner? First, she jabbed and scraped at the dry chips, then, with brushes, followed faded lines, shapes, letters. Mean work. But there was something about the offish smell of paint. Something good.

After she had worked through all the removables, she turned to those that couldn't be detached.

Above the Electric Trampoline, for instance, a red and yellow caution sign, a disclaimer, had been nailed to a board. The carnies weren't overly concerned with legalities, but if something went rotten, they didn't want the blame. What was really true was that Suspender cultivated a variety of risk. And the perception of risk. And the disclaimer's location, so far from the ground, added mystery, heightened the necessary commitment before jumping: climb a tall ladder to a platform, read what it says, raise your hand and swear you're taking responsibility for your own hide. (Then jump.) This procedure weeded out the less hearty. Many chose instead to climb down.

It was Lo-Lo who made the paint. "Electric Trampoline, you need black, yellow, and red. Adhesive, water, powder." He gathered empty bin-cans outside the kitchen door. "Munitions ain't the only powder in town," he said.

Mim helped him mix until everything was smooth. The paint smelled of metal and also something sweet, sticky.

"Here, you." He shoved buckets at her.

"I can't carry them all!" Mim said.

"The smart one will figure it out." He smiled and fled to the kitchen.

Mim lugged two and came back for the third, and brushes.

Mim ascended to the platform, carrying one can at a time, brushes strapped to her side. The air was cooler today, the breeze cold, up so high. The top of the sign was barely within reach. She began on tiptoes with the top, a thick black border. The paint syrup dripped down her arm. When she stooped to dip her brush again, pain swiped her shoulder and neck.

Next yellow, then red, increasingly smaller borders of warning. The words in black, on yellow. So as not to erase the words, she painted carefully, sometimes with fingers when the crevasses were narrow between letters. So as not to obscure the message. Gnash, the only carny allowed to operate the Trampoline, had also poeted the piece.

> One shall take care when approaching this contraption!
> For it requires skill beyond the normal humdrum.
> You've never experienced terror and outrage such as this.
> To sustain yourself requires endurance beyond endurance.
> Be Your Whole Self sober! and think fully before you sign your doom!
> Hazard is a thrill, yes.
> We warned you.

She painted until the carnival opened, then, to avoid more work, she hid in the hotel lobby. By midnight dinner she was still sore everywhere, but she admired how the dripped paint clung to her skin. She hoped the beautification would never wear off. Her skin was still sad milk. All the browns and beiges of the carnies' skin seemed to stay where it belonged, on bodies.

Cleopatra's wrapper was ruddy, Nelda's was dark wet wood, all magnificent, and permanent, unlike Mim's pallid skin. Mim adored this new paint-skin, how it tethered her to the world.

Lo-Lo scoured the main table, clanked dinner dishes in time with the music of the carnival, then poured tea into Mim's metal carny-cup. She liked the tea, liked to chew the twiggy dregs.

Cleopatra spun the cylinder that held the sun and the moon, then removed a brown stick-like item from her pocket. "I recently acquired this lovely cigar from the pocket of a guest."

"Share?" Nelda asked.

Cleopatra cut the cigar and handed the larger half to Nelda.

Suspender drank from his special tea bowl; the pretty one with pink flowers painted on each side, the one he never let Lo-Lo or anyone else wash, lest it be broken. He banged his fist thrice on the table.

"Now we'll discuss the Crossing," he said.

Cleopatra lit her cigar and waved it in the air at Suspender. "A thoroughly worn tune, that one," she said. She continued talking to Nelda. "Anyway, the guest bragged he got this specimen from some simpler Spurlock cousin, said he's rebuilding a roof for a dunce they keep hidden. Apparently the dunce smokes well."

"Apparently," Nelda said.

Suspender banged on the table again. "Respect, please! The Crossing."

Cleopatra removed her cigar and pointed it at him. "Your plan was simply to winter here. Remember the good fat spots? Dunberry, Tallulah? Springdale? How long has it been now? I'll tell you. It's been seven months this week. Seven months!"

"So what? It's solid here," Suspender said. "We were spared much blow-down in the twister. Where else would we have done so well? Luxury! Our own hotel! Despite the lack of rain. We were even able to drag those guests down to the hotel basement. Where else have we had a basement? We wouldn't want their heads lopped off, not in the best interest of the carnival. Unpleasant stories grow legs." He looked at Mim. "Or maybe we were waiting for this human gift to tumble from the sky. Still don't know how you survived all that wind," he said.

"Neither do I." Mim touched her painted arm.

"If we had left here before the twister. Right. We would have no Mim," Cleopatra said.

Anton the Elder, father of the Younger, pointed at Mim and said, "Painted girl, you would be alone and dead!"

If she could find it, she would run back to the wall of wind, the twister. To discover how it worked, see if it smelled like a mother. *But you survived that twister,* Suspender had said last week, not to Mim, but to Beatrice's back, picking burrs from the beast's matted foliage. He had said so. Mim had survived. Had stayed.

Now, Suspender said, "Enough sap. Back to the Crossing."

Nelda groaned.

The Crossing was a grand, vague pilgrimage, across the plain, across everything, to wherever people were naïve and lonely, and wanted a good time.

Lo-Lo sang, "The Crossing! Where coins pour from pockets like water down a chute." He looked at Suspender. "Carnivals aren't meant to stay put this long. All this stagnation is tainted. Unnatural."

Suspender stared at Lo-Lo and deliberately sprinkled bread bits on the table.

Cleopatra held up her blue jar. "Just pour it, Lo-Lo."

Lo-Lo filled her jar.

"Mmmm, helps my food settle," Cleopatra said.

That was a big job: Cleopatra ate twice, three times what Mim ate, and Mim herself ate at least two platefuls that night. Cleopatra drank from her blue jar and licked the corner of her mouth like a cat.

"What's your true name?" Mim asked Cleopatra.

Lo-Lo laughed. Everyone looked at Mim.

Cleopatra sat up, and plunked the blue jar on the table. "You're not clever, are you?" she said. "Give the name, give away the power! No, it's eternally unwise to give the name." Cleopatra's smile was built of glass.

Faces don't matter, Mim thought, *only insides.*

"What a load of shite," Suspender said.

"Not a load of anything," Cleopatra said.

"Her name's Mildred!" Lo-Lo said.

"Hortense!" Tiger said.

"Pauline!" Lo-Lo said.

Nelda laughed. Others donated names, and even Cleopatra eventually laughed. Only Suspender didn't guess. He picked up his knitting, which danced into shape in his hands. He was quiet as a tree without leaves. Maybe he knew the answer. "The Crossing," he finally said, not looking up.

Then Mim saw a leaf above his head. Silvery, elongated . . . different from Cleopatra's.

Bang clang, bang clang, metal hits metal and metal hits heat, everything is wrapped, twined with silvery thread, woven and corded and magnificent. A towering edifice, planned and unplanned. Suspender consults his sketches and models but also improvises. Mim feels locomotion in the brain, finds solutions. When one metal gear needs to be balanced, she, like Suspender, knows the precise *how*, feels the road inside her bones. And from under Suspender's ingenious hands, and somehow also from under Mim's hands, what emerges through the scent of grease and metal is massive and ferocious and beautiful. An unignorable form, a shadow, hangs and sways at the left of his vision, apparently suspended from a beam, is it a barn? Another dusty man approaches, walks the perimeter of the tent-sized machine, pulls levers and tests strength. "Nothing breaks. Everything works in unison," Suspender says to the man. "I leave you my final creation, for I am headed west, to make a thing of my own." As he speaks, Mim feels the words escape *her* mouth. As if she had spoken them herself.

In the hotel kitchen, Suspender stared at her. Did he know what she had seen? His gaze returned to his knitting.

Whose insides? Whose shell, whose skin? Mim needed her own, but others kept appearing, blurring where she began and ended. They named her; was Permission Granted to subject her to *their* insides? Mirrors collapsed and refracted, and now it was not only bloody wine behind the Room of Doom; now tricks lived inside everything she knew, or could know.

VIII

Curl, uncurl: the shell moves into different positions, but it's still a shell. What's inside? *Mim* doesn't fill the shell. The shell is empty, though sometimes it feels pain. Less pain now. Maybe it's not entirely empty. *If Mim isn't the name, what is?* And does it matter? *Everyone says Mim.* A name can't be all, nor is it everything. *If Mim isn't the name, maybe there's unnamed potential. Maybe there's something more, coiled inside.*

But potential won't fill the shell. Cleopatra is so complete, full of shine, and wine, all tumbled together, meat-cakes and mist, and thick letters stuffed into flimsy envelopes, frayed at the corners, the pages peeking through, full of words, and Cleopatra is full of running children, a child, a girl, that girl (with bruised cheek) who runs through that field; that girl alone could fill a person, even without thick letters and mist and meat-cakes. Memories fill a person. Even without sea foam and things that smell of dead flowers (but are probably something else, because even smells can deceive) and spices and metal machines . . . *that girl, who runs through that field, would be enough to fill my shell.*

At bedtime, Cleopatra arranged her bulk amiably and told Mim the story of the death pill factory. "You can spot factory men from their dungarees. In the morning, while most of us sleep, and Nipsy clears the rubbish, the factory men move from the dormitory toward the smaller buildings, and all day and into the night in those shabby shacks they pulverize, melt, and reshape their death stuff until the sun falls behind the world."

Nipsy, younger than Lo-Lo but not as slight, had many jobs. He cleared whatever debris Beatrice wouldn't eat. He sold entry tickets and kept chiselers from sneaking through the gate and sometimes played xylophone there. After Lo-Lo cooked, Nipsy had to clean the kitchen.

"Every day, at three intervals—work early, work late—men clomp out, slower than when they entered. Bodies spent from work. They remove hats and wipe eyes, too tired to smile. Then they disappear around the corner, past another shack and they're gone. At any hour, there is always some group at work. Except Sundays. Sometimes they go to Wistmount to raise the devil. And many times, they come here. But only the ones who have energy, or need wine, which is not allowed at the factory; I hear they are strict about the law.

"There are new men coming, I hear, to make enterprise run *plus vite*, pump out more of the stuff, for the war.

"Never question, only perform foulness. Make death pills, smelt and sweat, full of stale hopes, toil for the whims of the underworld, toil for naught."

"Why do they do it, then?" Mim's skin quivered, so she wrapped her blanket tighter.

Cleopatra stretched and examined her velvet hands. "I have no answer. There are larger considerations. Most characters are motored by food and shelter. And sometimes incorporeals like recognition, or love. There's a thing called hubris, where people undertake the role to make worlds, or break them."

Cleopatra grumbled something else about death, and rolled toward the wall, where shadows from the silver candle-snakes continued to dance.

But Mim didn't sleep. Not yet. A broad, rounded leaf flattened above Cleopatra, then quivered open.

A younger Cleopatra, wearing a dress gathered below her breasts. The silk of the gown glows, as if a candle flickers behind the fabric, inside Cleopatra's torso. The palest yellow. Beneath a grape arbor, she stands with a tall man, his face strangely still, and a couple who, from appearance, must be his parents. The older man and woman share his nose and jaw, features built by a stonemason, with weights and measures to make sure the overall effect is tedious balance. But the stonemason forgot to leave gaps where humanity might escape, or be revealed, that is: the older man and woman appear to be asleep with eyes open, having wrapped in tight twine any sentiments they may have about the proceedings. (They won't give over to Mim or to anyone.) A minister stands with the older couple, looks up every few moments, *will this soft rain affect the day?* Mim feels a twinge, a flutter inside Cleopatra, and Mim looks down and notices that beneath Cleopatra's breasts, the palest yellow of the gown drapes over a swell of flesh: inside, blood, bones, and a diminutive person who isn't quite a person yet.

A rustle comes from the woods behind the arbor. Another young man, hair paler but other architecture resembling the groom and his parents, walks quickly toward the group. A woman with a parasol treads gracelessly through the sweet, damp grass, well behind him.

"So sorry we're late," he says, and grabs the tall man's hand, shakes it with vigor. "Father, Mother," he says, not touching them. The father's face is still a mountain; the mother's lip twitches, a flicker in the lower right corner. "Hilary's fault, of course," the dark-haired man says. Laughs. The woman with the parasol shakes her head, but doesn't contradict.

"Please proceed, Reverend," the father says.

Mim feels Cleopatra's warmth, the flush of carrying a child inside, but also a hand at the small of her back. The hand not of her intended, but the

second man, her soon-to-be-husband's brother. A hand that claims owner-
ship. Mim thinks Cleopatra might be falling asleep, because of the tingle in
her own limbs, until Mim wiggles her toes and a spark crawls up toward her
womb, and meets the glimmer within.

Then Cleopatra's leaf folded shut: brittle paper, half-dry, dry enough to
tear.

FOUR

THE HANGED MAN

I

When Mim was alone, she was haunted by a belief that her skin might slip away. With other people, even if they ignored her, she was fairly certain it wouldn't *vámonos*, as Cleopatra said to Beatrice. Sometimes, Mim would stare at the skin on her arm. Stare to see with her naked eye whether it moved. Suspender often invoked the naked eye to describe the radiance contained inside the Eight Mile Suspended Carnival. He invoked the naked eye to tantalize guests through his shout-horn, which Lo-Lo had found in the Wistmount dump and restored. "Of course you can't see it with the naked eye," he would say, and detail this or that astonishing aspect, for instance: the fifteenth toe, or the rainbow skin, *not a tattoo, folks! That's a drop of verifiable rainbow on her cheek.*

Things flickered beneath the surface, Mim knew. The naked eye was a lie.

One night, after the carnival closed but before midnight dinner, Mim's skin wouldn't let her sit still. She didn't want to help Lo-Lo prepare food, but she had to move, so she slipped out toward the menagerie.

Beatrice slept outside the goats' pen, standing on her right leg. She switched legs periodically, left, then right, all the while asleep. Only when she was ill would she lie down.

47

Voices came from the front of the hotel. Suspender and some of the death pill factory men . . . Spurlock in his brown coat, and a few others. Not wanting to see or be seen, Mim crouched behind the prickle-crack bush, between the chicken coop and the river. The factory men must have come to the carnival hunting wine. Suspender rarely imbibed, but now, he must have. He moved with less precision, all shiny and loose.

Spurlock walked alongside, talked to Suspender.

Spurlock said, " . . . pulley . . . if . . . works . . . believe . . . we'll no longer have to concern our humble establishment with fires in the powder house. Good. But that's simple. To fix a bridge is simple. I'm cogitating a new type of machine, one that'll smooth over the works. Sad fact is, those engineers aren't clever enough to build what I want. Despite their blab about augmenting output. There is a war coming."

Suspender fiddled with something small, must be the nail and hand-sized piece of metal, spun wire around the nail. Mim had seen this toy, seen him remake and test its movement. He shoved the toy in his pocket, and retrieved his tobacco pipe. "We've chewed upon this theme before." He struck a match and lit the pipe.

Spurlock said, "Come over next week, take a look. I'll show you what's brewing." They stopped near Beatrice. Spurlock said, "What *is* that thing?" The other men caught up with them.

"One of our many attractions," Suspender said.

"Not very attractive, if you asked me," Spurlock said. The other men laughed.

One of the men said, "Stick your pipe in its mouth. See if the critter can smoke."

"That would be amusing," Spurlock said.

Suspender said, "Likely not. I know you don't want to lose a hand."

"Oh, come on, everyone needs a little fun," another man said. He reached toward Beatrice but she flailed and bashed at him, chomped down on his hand and did not let go.

The man yelled.

Suspender said, "Shut your yap so I can calm her!" He knelt next to Beatrice. "Easy," he said. She growled without releasing the man's hand. Suspender stroked her side, put his arm around her. After a moment, she let go of the man's now bloody appendage, spit at the man, and strutted back toward the chicken coop.

The man warbled in pain.

Spurlock yanked the man up and chuckled. "That's a good one. That's got to smart."

"Warned you," Suspender said. "You lot better clear out now."

Mim had to pee and maybe also vomit. The death pill men went toward the carnival gate. Suspender went to Beatrice, comforted her, said quiet things. After some minutes, he patted her and went back inside. Beatrice wandered off toward the river.

Mim peed on the ground. When she stood, not only her legs but her entire body trembled. She crouched again. The idea that Suspender could love like that . . . it was cold and hot, and she waited some time until, finally, the shivering passed, mostly.

Mim was still shaken when she helped Lo-Lo serve midnight dinner. She spooned rice soup and hard cheese into bowls. Lo-Lo rang the bell to call people to table. He turned on the radio. Something scratched forth, girl children singing. He said, "I strain to find the familiar, but naught arrives."

After most of the carnies had finished and left, Mim began to clean dishes. Suspender entered the kitchen.

"Boss needs food," Suspender said.

Lo-Lo handed him supper. "Had some juice tonight?"

"Turn that sound down."

"No, he just wired it! Let's listen," Nelda said.

Suspender took a bite of cheese, then soup, and put a dry lemon rind between his teeth.

"Poor Suspender, full of the juicy," Lo-Lo said.

"I blame those new death pill engineers and chemists. Spurlock and Dead Louie brought them over. They soused me."

"You'll take their money, though, right?" Cleopatra said. "Payday, I want some things around here. Some improvements. And a *fête*, I think."

"Job should be start to finish in not so many days," Suspender said. "And we cavort on this ground at the whim of Spurlock. Can't forget that."

"It's nobody's land, you said so yourself," Lo-Lo said.

"Perhaps, but tranquil neighborhood relations should never be taken for granted," Suspender said.

"War. They hate us; we hate them, who cares? Butter, butter the doom-drum," Lo-Lo said.

Nelda laughed. "Fine, you slink up to those ick-baddies. Please cleanse your hands liberally when you're done."

Lo-Lo stood near Mim at the sink, his hip touching hers. Close, connected, like Suspender had been with Beatrice.

"I gotta bring some stuff up for tomorrow," Lo-Lo said. "Nipsy!" He yelled. "Get in here! Wash up! Mim, help me carry." He went toward the basement door.

Mim looked at Suspender, who was still chewing rind, then she followed Lo-Lo. *Suspender. Also known as Pelle.* His care for Beatrice, his protection of the creature, of his tribe. Maybe that was a type of love.

II

String things together, string them up. On one strand, observe love, parts that fit, or don't fit, parts that rub each other into dust. Collision becomes a song of death and beauty. On the other strand, smell that stench; breathe it into your body. Walk through the day—don't slip in the sentiment that pools at your feet—don't look down or you'll never look up. Don't look at the color of bruise in the sky; don't see it as a bruise. Ignore the brutality of each next breath. Ignore what your captive yells from her cage inside your bones.

You have nothing else to collect, nothing else to hold your parts together. The stench is irrelevant. You need to carry something.

After a bruised-sky day, Cleopatra pulled Mim toward the fortune-teller tent. The outer canvas was painted to resemble early night sky, the color of chicory. Inside the tent, even before Cleopatra lit the candles, all was amber; the inner canvas gleamed. Cleopatra shook out drapery and arranged things to hide where the fabric was patched. "Perch over here and keep quiet," she told Mim, moving an upturned crate into the corner.

Mim sat. "How do you do it?"

"Don't speak," Cleopatra said.

Her first guest was a young woman, older than Mim but with a reasonable

50

portion of child undrained from her face. The young woman dropped coins into Cleopatra's bird-soft hand. Cleopatra invited her to sit.

"Cut the cards," Cleopatra said. The woman grasped the deck halfway (halfway, judicious, like it mattered) and cut. Cleopatra flipped cards over with a dull snap, and then said "hmm" and "ohh" and let what she saw saturate her thoughts. Then she looked up from the cards and told the young woman everything. *Take care before you dance with a drinker; Look behind if you see a rabbit with a split ear; etc.* The young woman blushed as Cleopatra unrolled her life for her. Cleopatra didn't need cards. She had told Mim this. But she used the cards so people wouldn't be scared when she knew so much truth.

At the end of the night, Cleopatra said, "The cards are tangible. People admire what they can see. Tangibles provide comfort." She put some coins aside for Suspender, and locked the rest in her box. She returned her blue jar of wine to the table, no longer needing to hide it from the public.

"Will you read my fortune?"

"Off duty."

"That's not fair."

"Fair is for customers who pay."

"I'll trade you something," Mim said.

"You've got nothing."

"I'll wash your linens tomorrow."

"Wash them all week."

"Three days."

"Four." Cleopatra pushed the cards toward Mim. "Cut."

Mim didn't split the deck like the young woman had; she did it unevenly on purpose, picked up all but a few cards. The cards were smooth and heavy, with soft edges like the flimsy envelopes that filled Cleopatra's shell. Cold, like slivers of stone.

Cleopatra flipped the top card. A figure hung upside down by the foot, mouth open, a silent yowl.

Wind pushed against Mim's face.

"This can't be right." Cleopatra took the card back, put it on top, face down with the others.

"Why don't you wear rings?" Mim asked.

Cleopatra hummed something, then cleared her throat. Drank from the blue jar. "Cut again." Cleopatra knocked on the table, knock knock. "Twice."

Mim did. Once, twice, both times uneven like the first time.

Cleopatra turned over the same card. "*Le Pendu.* The Hanged Man." She stared at Mim for a while, then said, "I can't see you."

Mim's left wrist throbbed. A succulent leaf shone above Cleopatra's head.

Cleopatra, younger and not as solid, peers at a young man who stands across a wooden counter etched with the initials of sweethearts. His jacket is pricked with metallic bits, warrior hardware spangling his chest. Mim loves this man, because Cleopatra loves him. But mixed with the love is also bitterness, tang in the sweet. Cleopatra pours the man a tumbler of wine. The man removes his square hat, picks up the glass, says, "Thank you." He walks away. Mim's chest burns as she watches him depart, and Cleopatra wipes the counter.

In the tent, Cleopatra said to Mim, "What's wrong with you? You look empty." Cleopatra's stare stung Mim's eyes, as if Mim stared inside herself. "Are you something, too? Some kind of reader."

"I don't know what you mean," Mim said.

"Just now, you saw what I saw, right?"

Mim nodded, afraid to drop her gaze.

Cleopatra pointed at Mim. "I don't need someone stepping into my memories. No. No. Don't intrude, *s'il vous plaît.*"

"I can't help it. Things sometimes come into my seement."

"Tell me."

Mim described the scene. Cleopatra stared at her. "Seeing memories, that's new. And can you hear things? Or just see?"

"I can hear."

"Did you hear my name?"

"No. No one said it."

"Good. We'll have to figure this out." Cleopatra drank some wine, then leaned closer and took hold of Mim's left wrist, the one that hadn't quite healed. Cleopatra's hand was small, but convincing.

"Ow," Mim said. "That hurts!"

"I know. Feel it. Now. Don't tell anyone else about this. Your fact you must keep safe. You never know who will exploit your fact." She released Mim's wrist. "Want a drink?"

"Yes, please."

52

Cleopatra handed Mim the jar. "You'll need my help. Be grateful I found you. I could turn you out! Allegiance. You better keep that word in your thoughts. Some people would say you need to find your home, but we know that's not important. Better off with the carnival than anywhere else. No. You need me. No one here has your protection in mind like I do."

"What about Nelda?"

"Of course, Nelda you can trust. But let me tell her. Now get out."

Mim waited outside. She considered walking somewhere, but where? If there were a safe place to go underground, if there were a safe place anywhere, she would go. Cleopatra knew. Nothing was safe now. Tiger stopped by and said things; words from his mouth whizzed, twirled, too fast to be properly arranged. How many words filled the air in this place, and what did any of it matter?

Canvas flapped and Cleopatra emerged from the shadowy tent. "Come with me. I know what to do. First, dinner."

III

After dinner, Cleopatra took Mim back to her room, and undressed behind the silk screen. "A body needs an amount of history, its own terrain," she said. "If not, then steal others? Maybe. A memory is a story, needs an opening." She stepped from behind the screen. "A person, like yourself, with your talent, can't uncrack another person if the object isn't comfortable. No. I can't just walk into a place and see the future of a person. For instance. A person must come to me, must be willing. Must want my assistance. People must be intimate, or tranquil, or desirous. Of course I can protect *myself* from you, now that I know." Cleopatra said more words. Began to brush Mim's hair. Said Mim would have to train herself.

"How do I train myself?" *And can't I just keep quiet, and steal what I can?*

"Listen," Cleopatra said. "The tidy deck of cards we each carry has been shuffled into the air and the world is thrown into chaos. It's chaos enough around here. One thing for certain: You won't crack me open, if I don't opt to be cracked. I'm sure of it. For instance."

"I don't want to crack anyone open. I want to sleep."

Mim went behind the screen, changed for bed, and bundled herself on the cot. She gave over to the comfort of the smooth sheets, the stale wrappings. She pretended to be safe from the words everywhere and the creeping rain falling in her head all the time, the timbre of those damn raindogs who trolled the roof of her being, those dogs that conspired with the wall of wind, and made a symphony of falling metal drops, drops like bullets.

In the morning, as usual, Mim woke first. She dressed quietly, tried not to wake Cleopatra, but after a few minutes, the fortune-teller turned and said, "Not sure if I want you far or near. Requires more brooding. If you stay at the carnival, you'll need borders. Borders can be cultivated. You and I have work to do."

"I'm still tired," Mim said.

"Tired is the mark of the amateur." Cleopatra claimed to know things that would help Mim survive. She claimed that, at age ten, a woman had taught her to ignore anything overheard unless someone specifically asked her to tell. There would be lessons, some of which Mim would have to do a hundred times each day. One was to try seeing memories on purpose. Together they drew a diagram and sewed small doors to cover important details. To be safe, they hid the diagram behind the screen in Cleopatra's room.

Mim agreed to these lessons. Otherwise, she had no home.

IV

Suspender didn't operate a ride. When the carnival was open, he ambled along the boulevard, cordial but reserved, and watched everything.

One evening, while Mim helped Smoot clean the snake pit, Suspender walked past. And above his head, a dry brown leaf.

A boy, hair wild like a lion's mane, stands in a field, while a man, maybe his father, aims a rifle. "I'm gonna fly up and dab down on you!" the man yells into the distance. The angry bullets bite meat, a beast larger than Beatrice but with four legs and no feathers. A burning stench. Antlers. Deer. And again, that dangling shadow, and along with the boy, Mim feels its slow-swaying weight. *What is that shadow?* The man runs toward the felled deer, grabs legs, and drags it to a cabin at the edge of the field. The boy sees the animal's huge brown eyes, open and bloodshot, and Mim shudders at what she finds in the boy's gut: anger, fear, and revulsion. The man has given all his love to his wife, the boy's mother, but she is gone, and the man has nothing left for his savage-haired son, only oatmeal dregs, thickened and cold, like this dying beast. Mim knows—as the boy knows—that despite the nausea, his father will make him eat the flesh. Knows this meat will feed his hunger. The boy will forever taste the bullet, that death moment, the flavor of the deer's final forgetting.

And though she knew everything along with the boy in Suspender's memory, why couldn't she see the face of the father who used the bullets? And why, again, always, that slack, swaying shadow?

The taste of bullets, how easy it is to kill. The boy in the memory must eat to stay alive . . . the taste of death . . . and now this man before Mim: Suspender dangling open with all his parts, a machine so intricate and fragile, the glory of the stunning fact of what it is to breathe, unseen—yet so near—another quivering life.

In Smoot's basin of cold water, Mim washed snake dirt from her hands.

There *was* a bullet aspect to the carnival machines. Those things, those rides, metal corners attached to planks, first flat, then bent, then angled with bits that dripped Suspender's memory of the bullet taste into Mim's mouth. On her way back to the hotel, she put her tongue against a metal plank on the Hi-Striker. It tasted like bullets. She would not go on the rides. She didn't want to depend on something that tasted so fierce. Most of all, she didn't want to go up in the air again . . . spun, tossed, lost by those machines, machines the flavor of bullets.

V

The lessons didn't change anything, except Cleopatra declared, repeatedly, that she herself was immune. It was easy. Mim taught her face to veil itself, to keep anyone—even Cleopatra—from realizing all that she could see.

FIVE

SUNDAY SPECIAL

I

Saturdays at the carnival, Wistmount brought their children. Shiny with grease and crazy with sweet cakes, they would slip from their parents, gloss dribbling from mouth corners, and sometimes, on rides, the children would vomit. One ran too fast toward the nethers of a machine, and when Mim scrambled to hold it back from getting hurt, it wailed and wailed and squealed away. Then father caught the child and gave it a sharp slap, which only fanned the tears.

One sunny day, a horde of unleashed children overwhelmed the sugar booths. Mim was helping Tiger when somehow a pair of sticky-handed children breached the back canvas and grabbed the Knock 'Em Down bottles. Tiger smacked the ringleader, and off they fled. He told Mim to rinse the bottles in the river.

"Sullied bottles sicken me, no matter how good you stack them," he said.

He closed the game. Mim piled the sticky bottles in a burlap sack.

At the Wishing Well, Mim rested the sack; work could wait. Nelda, on her throne, scraped her string-box and sang to guests, who tossed pennies into the water hoping for things unattainable. Days, Nelda wore men's clothes, a rope securing her dungarees, but nights, she wore her green satin gown.

"I love your gown," Mim said.

Nelda laughed. "Make a wish."

Mim rummaged in her new pocket but she had nothing.

"I can see you have a wish." Nelda dipped into the bosom of her gown, produced a penny, and dropped the warm coin into Mim's hand. "Close your eyes, think of your wish, but don't speak it aloud. Then give the coin a toss."

Does anyone miss me? Mim thought. The coin went down, down, down, disappeared into the murk, even though she knew a metal net covered the bottom, which later, Nelda would raise to capture all the penny wishes.

Mim needed to remember something. *All of what's new will be memories, someday.* But what about the first memories, those the wind blew away?

For Sunday Special afternoon breakfast Lo-Lo made corn porridge, potatoes, and meat-fry (when they had meat). Unless the chickens weren't laying, there were fluff eggs. In-aptly named, heavy and dense, with alarming, pungent bits. His food often hid surprises, but Mim trusted him, and of course, needed to eat.

The carnival was open all day on Saturday. But folks from town reserved Sunday mornings for spiritual pursuits. Even death pill production stopped on Sundays. Sundays, the carnival was closed until evening when they showed moving pictures.

Sunday Special was a favorite; no carnies dawdled on the way to table.

Suspender was carving an oblong piece of wood with holes on one end. Mim sat across from him and watched. "What is that?" she asked.

"A hatchet-stink for the snake pit."

Smoot clapped. "Finally!" he said. Smoot was the youngest generation of a family of snake-handlers. Sinewy and grey, he rarely spoke and, like his snakes, only ate on Tuesdays and Fridays. But he liked to sit with the carnies on fasting days. His imagination didn't fast.

"Yes, we'll make a happy Smoot," Suspender said.

Lo-Lo piled eggs and corn porridge onto platters. Yodeled while he stacked.

"Sing before breakfast and you'll cry before night," Suspender said.

"Leave that twig and have some grub while it's still young!" Lo-Lo said. He distributed platters. When all the tables were supplied, he sat beside

Mim. "Brownie of Cranshaws, bless the corn," he said, although no one had waited to eat.

Mim watched the moving pictures with the carnival guests. The pictures made her dream. Their flicker rattled metal plates through her head. Moving pictures changed time. The jolt of something simple: a man crosses a field toward a woman, a sputter—the man gives the woman a flower. This happens in fragments, not like the smoothness of life. A man crossing a field, in life, has weight uncapturable in pictures. Moving pictures jitter onward, forward, flickers magic but also dead. Suspender operated the moving pictures while Willie sang and performed poems. Sometimes he performed dance suites, unusual, angular maneuvers, with titles like, "The Delicacy of Bullets, Act I" and so on. Sometimes, Willie stood still for several minutes, hat upturned, brim balanced on two fingers. Tonight, the screen displayed a story of the tropics, birds with discombobulated anatomy, unfamiliar reptiles—some growing extraneous heads—and human-sized rodents, teeth gnashing. Slowly, slowly, Willie recited:

> "Audacity, you budge me, arose.
> Caribou, you featherbrain me, you mockernut.
> Gibbon, take your bronchitis, donate to Jacobus.
> Reminisce, you array me, crewmen. Cozy concertina.
> Azure, you soothsayer, you Adrian Bloodstone. Ineluctable admission
>   in our midst."

Finally he closed his eyes and whispered, "Go."

Behind him, the flicker continued, now a dance scene: ladies with lace beneath skirts flipped their hems like pendulums, spasmodically, embarrassed mute laughter silent on their metal-flashed faces.

Willie said, "Now, to cleanse your palate," and moved to the side, hat waiting.

It was Mim's favorite: The swimmers. A person went underwater with a camera and captured two humans who swam circles around each other, head to head, head to foot, foot to foot, foot to head. Lo-Lo told Mim that it was a fraud, for *do you not notice the lack of bubbles coming from their mouths? And noses?*

"Under water you still have to breathe," Lo-Lo said. He pointed at what he claimed were strings used for suspension, to make them appear to float.

"But I don't see strings," Mim said.

The couple danced underwater, moved together in a flicker, then darkness. When the lights came up, Willie stood by the exit, words gone, glad hat open, and waited for helpful coins from the crowd.

II

One day, before breakfast, Mim went walking. Clouds roiled the gun-grey sky, mingled like Cleopatra's paper merry-go-round that usually lulled Mim to sleep. She could swear the same clouds had passed already: the dark patch inside each one shifted in the wind but maintained its unity. At the outer ring of the carnival, she reached the Camera of Illusion, drew back the curtain, and peered into the eyepiece. (Suspender claimed that each time you looked, the camera revealed a different scene, but never what was actually in front of you.) Now a sea shone, green water danced, vastness only interrupted by a swollen island. On the island were three palm trees and a wooden barrel, knocked over, slats missing, like the rib cage of a monster. From the water, something glinted. A tail? And: metal, or flesh?

She left through the gate, toward the river. Past where Cleopatra found her. She ran, footsteps heavy on purpose to see if she could affect the crust beneath her. Her ankles and knees hurt before her lungs did. She slowed, passed over a low hump. The thin dark line, the river.

She considered the edge.

Ground met river in an ebony ribbon. Grey feathery plants fringed the water. The water, quick and quiet, the tongue of a snake. She crouched and trailed her fingers through the thin mud, then through water. Soft, just a whisper, and warmer than she expected. Dirt-swirls shimmied from her fingertips, echoes. *Things change but don't disappear;* mud from her hands mingled with the muck on the riverbed, then dissolved into the water. Everything, still there.

The river can have my dirt.

A passel of mud-painted frogs surfaced along the edge. Endearing! Sized like the tip of Mim's thumb. The frogs had other business, couldn't fathom

59

her. After they were gone, she looked toward the tired bridge. Downstream, the buildings of the death pill factory, open to the river, showed only bone-beams exposed to the air, though the building's other sides must be more solid.

From the factory, two men came toward the river, one carrying a bucket. The empty-handed man pointed upriver. The carrying man tipped the bucket into the water, rinsed the bucket and his hands in the river, and went back up the hill. The empty-handed man waved at Mim.

He got into a skiff and rowed toward her.

Blood, oil, and the other substance: they fill in where they can. Gravity and other principles, you may recall, allow their inheritance, allow the glub glub of their inhabitation, their confident squatting, never invited, never questioning whether they belong. Three friends ooze between gaps, between what we string or rope together, the stuff in the bucket, all that shine, all the drench of its weight . . . blood, oil, and the other one—third friend, He of the Bucket—laugh at each other, at intervals, not dependent on such a fragile branch as breath.

They don't need us at all. In fact, they only need us to look away, to *Look over there!* at all those dazzling, shiny distractions.

The man hauled the skiff up onto the bank. It was the man who had stopped that fight at the wine tent.

"Hello, you glorious wonder," he said. "Name's Lucien B. Dunavant, but my pals call me Beede."

Up close he had the squarest mouth, lips so red. A beautiful cat. He tried to stomp river muck from his boots.

"I've heard you shouldn't touch that water downriver," she said, "Isn't it poison?"

"Poison? Who says?"

"Carnival says."

"Clean enough for me!" He wiped his hands on a handkerchief and rinsed it in the river, wrung it out, and smiled at Mim.

"You're the one broke up that fight."

"I've broken up a thousand fights. What's your name, dear?"

Familiar with her, that pretty cat. "They call me Mim, but that's not my real name."

"What's your real name then?"

"Not telling."

"Why's that?"

"Not giving up my power."

"You got all the power you need in that smile." He stepped closer.

As he inhaled her, cold absence flooded his eyes, nothing but mirrors inside, reflecting and reflecting forever nothing. With his exhale, the absence became heat, became fire.

"Mim, your skin, it's alabaster."

She didn't know what that meant, but he noticed her skin, her skin! And said alabaster with a smile. Was it good?

"You work at the death pill factory?" she asked.

"The 'death pill' factory? Now why do you call it that?"

"That's what everybody calls it," she said.

He looked across the water. "Hmm, that's putting a twist on it. Cowardly collectives, too scared to fight. Who will protect their backsides when the baddies come? Depend on others for their veritable lives? Unbrave. Don't much like that made up death name. Independent thinkers over there, huh? I am curious about one thing. What's it like to work with coons? I've seen a lot of coons at your carnival. Mr. Spurlock won't hire them, not even to swab the latrine."

"What's a coon?"

"You know. A colored. Dark-skin."

"Oh."

"They don't work, do they?"

"Everyone works. Skin doesn't matter."

"Interesting. Independent thinkers at your carnival. 'Death pill' factory. Like they never used a bullet, shoot."

"They have names for everything."

"Even pretty girls like the new friend Mim? Mmm, Mim. Where did you come from, mmmMim? Mim feels good in my mouth."

She looked at his square mouth again, red like the velvet that covered Cleopatra's table, red like in Suspender's memory, gushing from the neck of the deer. Mim needed to watch Beede's red mouth.

"Tell me a story," she said.

"You want a story? Hmmm . . . " He took her hand. They sat together on a flat-top rock. "A pirate story then." He moved close, touched her hip. His scent brought to mind water, and bullets.

He told of a pirate who dove into the river. "This very river," he said. "Pirate found a boat and jumped aboard, straight onto a pile of bones. The bones spooked him, and he fainted and died! Lost at sea."

"I don't like that story. Tell me a good story. A sad one."

"Not a pirate girl, huh?"

"Tell me of when you were a boy."

"A real story? A history? Sure. A girl needs to know about her boy." He touched her hand, and the touch stirred her, scaled her arm, rounded her shoulders, her back, and tingled everywhere. His breath climbed right inside her skin, and helped itself.

"When I was a boy, my mother perished of the typhoid, then my father did, too. Then came inquirings, talk of shipping me to the waifs' home, but some folks down the line took me in. A good man and his son. The boy was smart, knew how to make things. With particles of scrap metal, ragged bits, he made the dangedest unnerving creations that would spin and swivel like they aimed to be useful but forgot how.

"That young rat hoarded his machines in the barn rafters, built a nest in the hayloft for the purpose. Machines were crammed and wire-wrapped into place so he could practice and improve their functions. Told me he didn't want prying father eyes. His mother was who-knows-where; she had run off and hadn't left a whiff behind. Maybe she drowned herself in the lake, like his father said, as he sat late one night, holding his face in craggy work hands, hand-shadows stretched long and cold across the table in the light of a candle nub.

"And the boy secreted away his papa's castoff parts: wire, string, anything needful, in his rafter-world, high, away from the ghostly maternal gap, the speculations of drowning.

"I watched the boy and tried to learn, but he wasn't fair, wouldn't show, wouldn't teach. His mind was a maze, its innards full up. Selfish, mean. I don't know why that rat never liked me."

Beede straightened his muddy boots, so his feet were parallel, and held his chin in his hands like his head was too heavy with remembering. Mim tried to see inside, but couldn't open him.

"After his father died—hung up in the barn—I waited to hear the train, grabbed that boy and we ran through the field. Tried to help him but he let go my hand. I jumped that train, and away I went. Never saw him again."

Mim watched Beede's face transmogrify from boy to man. Glimpsed fire in him. Then he kissed her, and that square-lip kiss burrowed into a corner of her body and found whatever had been wound up and waiting.

"I better get back," she said.

He hummed. "Mmm, Mim. I'll find you next time."

On her way back to the carnival, she turned to look. Beede was still there, arms outstretched, the letter Y. He waved at her. When she reached the iron gate, she looked again. Tiny, far away, he rowed back across the river.

At the hotel, Suspender sat on the porch, knitting. "Best if you stick by here, don't go wandering," he said. "I've seen a rabbit with a split ear down near the river more than once. Unlucky. Never know when pirates might row up and snatch. And whatever you do, don't put yourself in the water. Death pill's got some new kind of poison they donate to that unsuspecting river. Good thing we're upstream."

"I only took a walk."

"Well, stay by here."

Don't go swim, don't want to lose Mim . . . She watched his knitting . . . deep indigo yarn so pretty between his hands . . . *if only I could climb in . . . let the yarn in his hands swaddle me . . .*

SIX

THE EGG, AND OTHER POSSIBILITIES

I

And sometimes, the shiny beautiful colorful bits are enough. When they rise and, inside their song, we are renewed, uplifted to the stars. Complicates the story, sure, these gorgeous tendrils of green, these gasps at glory.

Did you expect something simple? A decorative object to hold sweetly in your hand?

On a busy night, the weather fine, Mim helped Tiger light the Carnival Moon, set up Just Knock 'Em Down, remove coin from tossers, and replace milk bottles. Around sunset, the line grew excessively long. Apparently Mim's pyramid building was too slow.

"Dang it girl, I'll do it myself," Tiger said.

The next man in line was Beede. He winked at Mim and handed Tiger three coins.

"Have a toss, try your luck, just knock 'em down! Take home the prize!" Tiger said, in his crackly show voice.

Beede pitched a ball at the tower of bottles. They wavered but didn't fall.

"Strike one!" Tiger said.

Beede hurled another ball, faster, and the high bottle toppled from the shoulders of the others.

"Strike two! Mmmmake this last one count, friend!"

Beede looked at Mim, then closed his eyes. His square mouth curled into a smile, kitty cat, and eyes still closed, he tossed.

Bottles clattered across the wood platform.

Tiger removed his hat. "And we have a winner," he said. "Pick your prize."

Mim stacked the bottles for the next guest.

"Lady's choice," Beede said.

"Me?" Mim asked.

"You." Beede said.

Mim chose a small stone egg spangled with hearts and diamonds and handed it to Beede.

"Next up, just knock 'em down!" Tiger called.

Mim left the booth and walked toward Beede. He held the egg, placed it in her hand, said, "Fancy," and pulled her toward the midway.

"Where you going, Mim?" Tiger said. "I still need you!"

"I'll be back!"

Mim laughed and let herself be stolen. Behind the snake pit, with its overgrown dirt creatures and alleged eyelash vipers thrashing through stench, Beede said lovely words, touched the stone egg in Mim's hand, and pressed his body against hers. All was heat. They kissed for a long time. Beede was not letting her go. Yearning danced in her bones . . . he touched her hair, her cheek, her hip.

"Alabaster," he said into her ear.

She pulled back. "I have to go back to work."

"I'll find you next time," he said.

She kissed him and ran back to Tiger's long line, where bottles awaited reconstruction, egg safely in her secret pocket.

II

During breakfast, Suspender pounded on the table until everyone was quiet. "Tomorrow, after we close, please attend the River Pulley Shindig! A carnival for yourselves, friends, given as a gift, a special, from me. Guests can't be the only ones to have fun, agreed?"

Carnies clapped and hooted.

"To Wistmount for provisions!" Lo-Lo said.

Suspender shook his hand. "I promise you money."

The carnies hurried work that day. And the next, and rushed guests along, impatient to start the party.

The real moon had almost vanished. Looking at that sneak-sliver moon was like a peek between canvas panels to see the dusty exhibits: small man in a bubble; or the Plasticine baby, a twenty-toed fraud plunked into a jar of yellowish water to Preserve and Promote. Mim hated to look at it but you couldn't look anywhere else. This was the premise upon which Suspender had built the whole carnival, actually. Curiosity and compulsion.

That night, Suspender locked the gate, grabbed his golden shout-horn and addressed the carnies with verbiage—though tonight's tone he calculated to entice the cynic.

He said, "Purveyors of mediocrity, most of your carnivals, yes. Not the Eight Mile Suspended Carnival, citizens. No mediocrity to be had here. If you seek the mundane, I apologize. If you seek the mundane, goodbye. Here, absolutely nothing mundane. Topographical marvels can henceforth be discovered.

"Stretch the truth, some say, but only, always, to tempt and benefit the public. I'll tell you a secret, friends. This is a holy place. A sacred place! We devote our lives and livelihoods to your temptation. We are your servants. Humankind needs pretendments. Needs imaginations to be manipulated, tugged like taffy, and by the way, the taffy booth is ready, friends, step right up!"

And all was jovial.

On that loud night, guests gone and gate closed, the Tobeys arranged a constellation of furniture outside. Cleopatra lit candles to warm the *fête*. Mim helped Lo-Lo lug platters of potato breads, cheeses, smoked belly, candied carrot with charred sweet-onions, juniper olives, and a slew of other glossy treats, and the earnest gorging began.

Suspender plunked bottles on tables, enough bottles for one apiece. "Welcome to the River Pulley Shindig. Violations of Rules number Nine, and Ten, Eleven, and Twelve, for that matter, shall be forgiven, *this night only*. A dot of madness stimulates the mind, a dot of chaos."

"Butter, butter the doom-drum!" Lo-Lo yelled, and uncorked his bottle.

Musical instruments and improvised assemblages were employed. "Everyone make some sound!" Suspender raised a mug and drank. He grabbed an empty platter and a spoon, and started beating. "Hands are good, but metal's better!"

In the din, Mim found a knife and used its dull edge to beat the rusted ribs of a tree barrel. Cleopatra took Nelda's hand, they got up on a table, and stomped and danced.

"Oh, Dear Beauties of the Tabletop!" Anton the Younger hollered.

Nelda helped Mim up, kissed her cheek, then whispered, "You've got a good secret."

"Cleopatra told you?"

Nelda smiled and fluttered her long green skirt. "Wishing Well, Wishing Well, make your wish but never tell."

What makes Beede think the color of skin affects work? Or anything? Nelda is my dearling, is my kin. Mim kissed her, and they danced.

The carnies sang, banged and slopped themselves toward intoxication until the arrival of daylight.

After the shindig, in Cleopatra's room, Mim fell to bed holding her stone egg, and slept . . .

Opaque with dust, Cleopatra's dressing table shelters a family of spherical bottles, grey, green, brown. The gossiping bottles whisper secrets to mirrored flowers and ephemera for the hair, face, body. Jewels. Piles shine and commune in the gloaming.

In that treasure chest of a room, Mim smells sweet powder, like dried roses at the Wishing Well, and hears voices, quiet laughter. Across the pink-tinged room, on a bed, is Cleopatra, much younger. A man stretches out next to her, still wears his uniform trousers. His jacket warms the back of a chair, like a short, attendant soldier. Loyal, waiting. Turned away from the couple, as if too modest. The man puts his hand against young Cleopatra's cheek. Mim feels that curious thing, a kiss, like Beede's kiss, that clash of hunger and admiration, pride at the man who tilts Cleopatra's face toward his, a petunia in sunshine. The couple is beyond speech, nothing to be said now; the thing is to *do*. The man unbuttons Cleopatra's dress, and undoes his belt. Mim knows, senses the man hasn't slept in days; she feels what Cleopatra feels, an echo of what keeps him awake, the burning sulfur of wherever he had been, across the world, inconceivably far away, but here now in this room she knows the torment of that smell, and how, in desperate dew-early hours, the soldier decided never to sleep again. Resignation seeps from his fingers and laps against Cleopatra, drains an imperceptible amount of bloom from her lips. Mim feels the shudder-chill Cleopatra feels, as, with his cold, sleep-defeated hands, the soldier takes a thin rope and ties her arms to the headboard. And Mim feels Cleopatra's whole body wish to warm him.

He touches Cleopatra's breast, and a new shudder ripples through Mim, more frantic, closer than his sleepy coldness. He puts his mouth on Cleopatra's nipple and heat lights Cleopatra, and Mim, and his head descends to the privacy between Cleopatra's legs, and he pulls off his trousers and tosses them to the floor. Mim feels the bedsprings sink, her own body pressed down. Then he slides between her legs, and moves up and down, and a bloom of fire billows through her.

Across her dank carnival room, Cleopatra sighed and moaned. Mim reached between her own legs with the stone egg and touched and touched until here came the happiness and fear. She fought her breath to keep quiet, counted until her heartbeat slowed its gallop, and eventually slept.

Good. Good. Every girl deserves, good. Good.

III

Mim woke to a scrape at the door, which then opened. Lo-Lo. "Lunch time, lazies," he said.

"Ooh, I'm hungry," Cleopatra said.

"Lift your arse and come downstairs," he said, then left.

Cleopatra began to dress, didn't bother with the screen. She rolled turquoise stockings up her legs. "I hope the laundry is done. Nipsy's been slow. Might need to do some of my own things."

"I want my own room," Mim said from her cot.

Cleopatra squinted at her. "You sure you feel well enough?"

"I feel fine," Mim said.

Cleopatra made an exaggerated frown. "But won't you miss me?"

"I'll see you every day."

"What about your training?"

"I can do the nightlies on my own. I know them well enough. We can work daytimes together."

"Well, keep track on the diagram, especially when you can see on purpose."

"I will."

"Fine. Time you had your own room anyway." Cleopatra tossed boots aside, hunting her red shoe's mate. "Every girl needs privacy. And there's room for all in this shabby hall. Go, find another compartment."

Mim found a companionable room down the hall, past the toilet, empty except for a small crate. She returned to Cleopatra's room, put the diagram on the cot, and dragged her things to the new room.

Cleopatra took one of her kerosene lamps and followed. "Slide the cot over that hole so you won't fall in." The hole was a rectangle of missing floor-plank. "Tell Lo-Lo to fix that. He's handier than he looks."

Cleopatra put the lamp on the crate. "Makes it nicer." She unwrapped a rosy scarf from her head and flung it over the cot.

"Thank you," Mim said. She put the diagram in the gap in the floor, and flopped on her cot, in this room, which was hers.

And when that part of you wakes, when you drag that part into the light, things may shift. May tumble.

Alone in the new room, Mim couldn't sleep, limbs itchy, thoughts clicking through the night. She was full of Beede, the stone egg, the kiss. Of Cleopatra and the soldier. Needing to move, she went to the door and out. Past the torn window-paper, past tin items that jingled in the wind outside, with Cleopatra's lamp, she went toward the back hall, through the back rooms, the former office, and through the basement door.

She had descended to the basement before, to fetch things, but always someone waited; she never had time to linger, always Lo-Lo needed root vegetables, or bent musical instruments were suddenly missed and wished for, or someone wanted jars of murk from cabinets described by painted numbers, *Get the amber whatsit from cabinet fifteen.*

69

Tonight she would explore. At the bottom of the stair, she perched the lamp on a shelf. Wooden shelves lined the walls: on the shelves, rows of boxes, cans, crates. She inhaled the smell of cold earth. Quieter than silence.

The Impossible ropes stared up at her from the wooden crate marked twenty-three. The Impossibles were ropes that had become too tangled, so bad that no one could untie them. Coiled in dense, snaky bundles, bent, broken, but still muscular, with a lick of venom waiting.

"Rope has memory," Lo-Lo had once said, while he trussed an elderly, butchered chicken. "Wants to stay kinked, knotted, tangled, hence: Impossible." He pointed at Suspender, who was carving a twig house. "But this one says keep them. Says toss them into that pile in crate twenty-three, to mingle with the rest of the mess."

"Never know when you'll need something," Suspender said.

Lo-Lo's falsetto made Mim laugh. "The ballad of the errant knot: Preparatory torture for the Crossing, *untie all ropes,* and curse and spit when refuseth any errant knot! The errant knot!"

How would the Impossibles feel if Mim cradled their weight, their gravity? She lifted the top rope. To untangle would be the great riddle solved. She studied loop and gnarl, noted where they were frayed, where fibers grappled like lonely children, arms interlocked, making a solid chain of orphan threads, remaking itself from the echo of solitude. She sat down with them and found the way.

Wove this into that, around that bend, loop through and through and eventually a tangle slackened and flopped to the dirt floor. She took another rope, thicker than the first. Following paths of fiber, the rope became a road, moved forward, faster than she could follow the solution's logic. She watched it race ahead, and finally, breath against her ribs, she caught up, until each supple rope spread simply on the floor. She looked down and smiled.

She wound liberated lengths as she had seen others do, loop around elbow and hand, and when she reached the end, wrapped the final vine around the bundle and tied a knot. One smallish rope was still kinked, still held memories. Diameter of about two pencils, but at one end, it widened, thick as her wrist. She imagined how it had been tied and retied, all previous abuses, how it had worked and helped and kept things from falling or falling apart. Now these Impossibles were possible.

Near the rope crate was a smaller crate that vibrated slightly. No number.

The deep red letters on the side were not a language she recognized. She slid open the lid and found a purple-red book. Ornate shapes danced along the gilt pages, glory itself. This book needed to be taken.

She crept back upstairs, carrying the uneven rope and the book. Back in bed, she coiled into herself, mimicked the ropes, and the snakes, and slept until she smelled buffalo bacon cooking downstairs. Light again.

She wrapped the blanket tighter and the book clunked to the floor. She rose and hid the new treasures in the hole in the floor with her training diagram and stone egg. *So none will be alone.*

String enough parts together and you start to see a shape emerge. A body, a building, a song. But a bodied song, a song pulsed full of the profound sticky stuff that must be present for life to persist. Thick, glistening, the stringing is crucial, how we link, for instance, a hat with a head, the rain with a cloud. We drool over the unknown, the hidden—false love, a turncoat, a traitor—a thing that is not what it is. If we focus on the thing that is not what it is long enough, occasionally we forget where we're headed, each of us, we fools who think we can fool Time, we gasping fools.

Forgetting becomes a comfort: watch the juggler, dingy pockets of pebbles, flung in the air, one after another, shape visible in the air, but only for one short breath, then disappeared. But watch, oh watch the juggler. Watch, let the tale the juggler spins with fabric and stones help you to forget.

IV

Everyone at the Eight Mile Suspended Carnival told stories. Time's textures in that place were a weave of the immediate and all that came before. There was life, daily life and business, mess making and clearing up for each new day, letting guests think they had power while quietly taking their money. There were the memories, other peoples' interiors that Mim could see. But the other texture was the stories. Some stories mustn't be true. *Just make some shite up,* Suspender would say. When a story had a reason, it might not be quite honest.

"When I was at the waifs' home," Cleopatra said, one night when Mim

71

visited before bed, "after my parents . . . You know, in those days, everyone was sickly, frail, maimed by some disease, inside or outside the corpus: compromised, I'm saying. With my parents gone, before I can remember much, really, I was hauled with my few scraps and pennies to the vilest worm pit imaginable. Only thing of value I had, I hid. Great grandmother's mourning ring, her woven hair inside. This." She indicated the pond-ish ring on the gold chain around her neck. "My mother must have sewn it into my coat hem. I didn't find it until much later. We poor children at the waif's home, orphans all. People pitied us. Well, some of those kids were true swindlers, would chisel what they could off a younger, and no bother about it. But most of us were only miserable and alone. Due to my gift, I was more alone than most. Tidy families formed there, children banded against the lash. To fatten the toy cupboards, as it were, to get a bit more to eat, plenty of trade goes on. An economy of stale bread and tea leaf dust, saved up until there's enough for a thimbleful of tea. And thimbles were a luxury! We girls had to sew *and* farm, and thimbles were only given to the bigger girls. You had to stick around, earn your thimble. Run away, escape the toil, but where, then, to go? A child alone in the woods, to beast on grubs and berries? (Like those fireflies toward Wistmount, poor embers.) At the waif's home, a few lucky or eye-catching ones might be scooped up by barren couples, or politically minded mothers who had lost men and babies, but even with this arrangement, it was not certain that you would romp, fat and well-fed in the sun. The accommodations at private homes were uneven affairs. The myth sang that it was better to get out, but some littles crawled back, bruised and swollen, silent about their new and newly discarded situations. Back to work they went.

"It was hard to sleep, too many in your bed, but with company, it was warmer. The thin blankets were never enough. I don't care who; childhood wasn't easy for anyone back then. It's not easy now, but it was worse then. My father, may he rest in peace, beat me at intervals. My body learned early to survive. But scars don't make it easier.

"I made shoes. Shoes for other children, to be sold at a smart shop in Livingston. The shoes we made were snowy, so clean, pearly buttons up the sides, three on a shoe. The buttons were hard to attach to the leather. Horrid work. The inevitable needle-pricks, dots of blood across white . . . if you didn't notice you had pricked your finger—and many of us had fingertips numb with cold and work—the blood sullied the shoe, and if you didn't clean it immediately, (and really, how do you clean blood off white?) the shoe wouldn't be right. Lashes would follow. My gift of knowing was no help in leaving shoes unbloody. You would think that our keepers, those hateful starched ladies, would do the buttons themselves. To yield more good shoes to sell! But sewing the buttons was hard, and they were lazy. They wanted reasons to beat us. It was ornately codified: for this infraction, ten lashes, for that, twenty. Infractions numbered in the hundreds, and the list grew like that famous beanstalk, so that new snarls became opportunities to bare a small behind, and air their own anger. Those starched ladies each had different names, Aunt This or Miss That, but they all wore the same sullen face. Strong jaws, fortresses for clenched teeth. Except for Aunt Sister Canary, sometimes she was kind.

"But you know what? Time passes. I've shed my anger. A snake peels off her old skin. It doesn't help to tyrannize anyone else. It was hard to halt that thrashing wheel. You have to wake up and stay awake to the souls around you. You don't learn to be better, once beaten. Only craftier. You learn to avoid more of the same. You try to escape what's impossible to escape."

"I can't remember a waifs' home," Mim said.

"Of course not," Cleopatra said.

"How did you get out?"

"I perceived extra even back then. All my life. When I was ten, a young woman with some money and an urge to rebel against her family took me. She had messed about with prognostication. Visiting with a church commission, she sensed my talent and taught me the arts. How to perambulate the world of words, and a few other things I would need. But alas, when I was about your age, my companion caught a brain fever. I was fortunate— soon after she died, a traveling community of similar souls, by name *Mr. Petersen's Whisking Shows*, passed through and I took up with them. Not bad, but Time revealed those people weren't the real gifted. They made money off the dreams and hardships of humanity. I discovered I had real talents for knowing what others couldn't.

"Petersen claimed he had stolen Beatrice from an Siberian jungle when she was just a pup. He forced her wildness into a side act, but she was unhappy with those ogres. She got my attention and during a late night *tête-à-tête* with myself, she decided to leave, and we left. I called us the *Illusory Bestiarum* and we set up tables at fairs when the weather was good, or private homes when it was not. My original benefactress had given me the ability to read literature and speak well, and a dab of finery, so I could impress the normals, the rich folks who were lonely, or bored. A girl should be able to take care of herself, that's my belief, and it's true. Some of us . . . some of the time . . . some . . . " Cleopatra paused, as if to search for what she meant. "Illusion and charnel, provided there's space . . . " She paused again, and chewed on indiscernible sounds, and the pause lengthened.

Was Cleopatra asleep? Her breath was shallow. Mim wondered if the story of waifs was true, or how much had been grown, like flowers, to bloom in others' imaginations, to donate a glimpse of what Cleopatra assumed (or hoped) people wanted. A yarn, a tale. A detail. A spark. The ignition Grandfather Spurlock so craved.

V

Mewling babies, mouths yowling to be fed, so needy and persistent, we wait to kill each other; we wait to kill each other. Rocks, bricks, guns, worse. Hurling fire, knives, sharpened metal or wood, all the ingenuity we can sweep into a pile, used for snubbing.

This is how it goes. Sprawl wet from the womb, wail, toddle, then walk, violence moving around on two feet, assaulting the air with our crusty, uncaring bodies. You see them everywhere—maybe you yourself have direct experience with the game.

Here you look at me dumbly, grapple for memory or stop trying, giving over to the comforting fog. Maybe any love that escapes into this world is pure, looping accident.

The carnies claimed that the munitions factory was born and died in Grandfather Spurlock's generation, and rose again, because of a spark. Maybe a story was like that. Stories spun and sputtered from carnies, and through the mist in her head, which never fully lifted, Mim watched and listened. Someday, she too would have stories to tell. Would regain her past, or collect and put on others' stories, hand-me-down clothes for hand-me-down children, like the children in the waifs' home, but Mim would make the stories her own, like Nelda would do with clothes. Nelda could nip the dress at the waist; decorate with a peony, a few French knots, a sash. The memories that fit her now: the sound of Nelda and Cleopatra, their laughter. Her friends. Lo-Lo as he whistled and sang at the stove or fixed the steam truck; the radiance emanating through the hotel's dingy windows, mornings; Suspender and the child that hid behind his face; the others at the Eight Mile Suspended Carnival, who juggled and scattered stories like pebbles, like sandy stars at her feet.

Mim clung to these stories, and the memories she could mine. She recorded details in the book from the basement. The pages of the book were full of symbols, curious ciphers like turned-around letters. Mim wrote in the margins and other empty spaces, captured what she could of the carnies' stories. When she ran her finger across the letters, symbols, shapes, a rustic tune entered her ears, swirled out from her mind, her would-be memory. Had she her own memories, this book would become part of their architecture, their pulse. She knew, however, that the book's sounds only echoed from a collective past, from the air of the basement where she had found the book, the space undisturbed since the hotel was built. A place below, so blind-mothish and alone, couldn't have seen the sun. Wasn't there only one book? Yet when Mim looked closer, it, too, echoed; the book in the crate had ghostly compatriots, other books, identical. Real enough, perhaps, to fill that large crate.

Next to stories, she wrote the letter "S" and whose initials had told it.

Next to memories, she wrote the letter "M" and whose initials had shown it.

One story, marked S/S (or P) in the margin of Mim's book: *Late night, Suspender (Pelle) takes a long drink of the grassy stuff he prefers to wine, and scowls into the candle nub. "Once we gather coin sufficient, we'll make the Crossing," he says.*

Fear lives in him. Necessity hides behind his eyes; he is hunted by an eternal beast. If the beast catches up, flight might save the Eight Mile Suspended Carnival, but not the man who made it.

SEVEN

SWEET SHELLS

I

Take everything apart and put it back together, but change the angles. Sort your possessions, get rid of the inessential. Mathematical process—the new map was based on principles of nature, light, the elements. No need to explain. Accept it as you might accept gravity. This progression—this relocation of attractions—may disorient you, but no need to fret. Your money still spends. Bring it over here.

Take everything apart and put it back together, but change the angles. Get rid of the inessential. There was a mathematical process on which Suspender based these exercises and the nuances of change, but he never explained his calculations. He did claim that the progression—the new angle or relocation of a tent after a drill—would disorient guests, and they would be more inclined to hand over their wealth. He never gave advance notice about the drills. He claimed the Crossing could come at any time.

Mim's first drill began with a rattle, which woke her from dreams of escaping skin. Her door opened. Suspender's voice bounded through the quiet dark. "Get up and get ready."

Outside, the real moon shone beside the Carnival Moon, which Tiger must have forgotten to extinguish.

"Go away," Cleopatra yelled from down the hall.

"Get your arse up." His voice moved away from Mim. "Now!"

Mim wrapped a blanket around her shoulders and left her room.

"No point!" Cleopatra yelled.

"What did you say?" Suspender sounded like a thunderstorm.

Mim went to Cleopatra's room. By then, Nelda, Lo-Lo, Smoot, and everyone else on that floor had gathered in the hall.

"You're all lazy! Get to work!" Suspender yelled, and went to the next floor.

Cleopatra closed her door, lit a lamp, and put on an uncharacteristically drab ensemble. "Shite. He's pixilated. He'll make us pack everything, only to unpack."

"What's pixilated?"

"He's drunk on grass juice, or crazy, or both. Just go get ready for some work."

Mim returned to her room and dressed in the pants and shirt that Lo-Lo had given her for painting.

II

Outside in the soft dark, Nelda trolled the Wishing Well's greenish water for overlooked coins. "Such fun," she said.

Cleopatra patted Nelda's back. "Leave it. I'll finish that for you later, dearling. I don't mind."

"If you insist, I accept." Nelda dried her arm on a rag and sat on her throne. "This man is going to kill us with his shite-storms. He doesn't see how hard we work, all the joy he takes from us." She began to cry.

Cleopatra hugged her and said, "I know. He really doesn't see. Sit and rest. Even the strongest divinity needs rest. Mim and I will deal with slime after we decommission the knife tent." She led Mim to a canvas tent, which the knife man had recently abandoned. They kept the knives ready, in case someone wanted to take his place, and to make the carnival seem more impressive. *Perhaps the knife man had simply gone off to relieve himself before the next show.* Cleopatra rolled the bronze knives in bundles and stashed them in velvet-lined cases. They moved on to her tent, turned the table upside down, packed everything into it, and folded it to make a giant suitcase. She sent Mim with bundle after bundle to the hand-wagons, where Tiger and Gnash managed what went where. A puzzle, the boxes and crates arranged by painted number, ropes here, detritus there, but if anything arrived out of order, they would have to start again.

Cleopatra also sent Mim on endless trips to the trash fire, lugging excess: old crates, torn clothes beyond their useful life as rags or stuffing, and trinkets carnies had made or collected but didn't need. "When you're done, see if Nelda wants more help."

Suspender amplified himself through the shout-horn. "Who knows the location of Anton the Elder?"

"Left three days ago," Anton the Younger yelled, not looking up from his work. "Left for Spurlock's."

"How did no one tell me?" Suspender asked.

The carnies performed their jobs like night-ghosts. Air mingled with task, made a dance like the flicker of moving pictures. Suspender horned on about how canvas must stay supple, to be packed easily. "Same with ropes and rigging," he said. They had to oil all the metal, smear each bolt, which consumed a great deal of the morning. As the sun rose, the parts were loaded, slick with ancient grease, into smaller crates with larger numbers, seventies and eighties. Mim looked at her hands, coated in grey fat. No rags would clean them.

Outside his construction shop, Suspender hung an intricate map: he required carnies to pile one part from each contraption into a colossal crate. The side of that crate, in tidy, small letters, said *Mother*. Cleopatra told Mim that each person was assigned to bring one piece. This assignment changed for each drill. Suspender counted and laid the pieces out like he was the Almighty creating the world. When something wasn't delivered, he would send Tiger to collect the missing part. This sometimes meant Tiger had to unpack the numbered crates. Tiger consulted the list, found the wayward carny that hadn't delivered, and slapped his face.

Words spun out, people muttered *pixilated*, again, a lot. Everyone looked tired and vexed. Mim recalled what Lo-Lo had told her, and stayed away from the Tower of Misfortune. Nipsy yanked laundry from the line, and bunged it in with the bedding. Late-afternoon, Suspender struck the bell in the center of the carnival, and people gathered.

"You've taken your time," he said. "Didn't jettison enough. At least one third of all current belongings must go. Next time, more speed!" He twirled a copper coin, part of his ballyhoo. "I have made a decision. Yes. I believe we shall remain."

Nelda spat on the ground. "You never let up," she said.

Lo-Lo stood still. Mim had never seen his face so uninhabited.

Suspender yawned and stretched. "Chef, what about some grub?"

"Make it yourself." Lo-Lo kicked through dust where the Wishing Well had been, past Nipsy who was quietly plunking on the xylophone, on through the gate, and out. In the breakup of the crowd, Mim followed Lo-Lo away from the carnival. He walked fast, and she couldn't catch up. He stumped toward the river, and flopped facedown by the water's edge.

Mim rushed to him. "Stay out of there!" she said. "It's poison."

"Who cares?"

"I care."

He spoke words into the mud.

"Are you okay?" she asked.

"Go away." He didn't move. "Might better be a Newfoundland dog fighting a wooden puppet in the shape of a demon."

"Why are you lying down like that?" It was hard to hear what he said for the river's song.

She perched beside him on the ground. "What's pixilated? Why aren't we leaving? Why pack and unpack?"

"To torture me." He turned his head and stared at the river. "A pirate's just a sailor with a grudge, as the song goes. I'll go. Back to Paladoona. Grand hotels where a cook makes troughs and troughs. Oysters luxuriate upon shells large as tea saucers! And the most exquisite samovar you have ever seen. Well, *you* haven't seen it but I have. You can imagine. I'll cook for those who don't abuse me." He pushed a curtain of hair from his grim face.

"How will you get there?"

He sat up. His face was a shadow. "I'll swim. I'll fly, I'll walk, I'll crawl, I'll work on the street. I've still got my health. Anything is better than this. Even slopping oyster stew at the night lunch wagon." He spoke to some vague apparition above Mim's shoulder, some bit of glimmer. A glinting cardboard sign, maybe a moon.

A new green leaf appeared from the stardust.

A half-moon, lit by candles, and a glowing red light above. A sitting room, every corner ornamented, red, and rich. There is a boy, a few years younger than Mim; it's Lo-Lo. An older man approaches the settle where the boy Lo-Lo is seated, touches the boy's hair, offers him a wedge of chocolate, big as his hand. Young Lo-Lo takes the chocolate, which smells sweet and bitter, and he squirms on the deep red cushion. Mim feels his thigh twitch. He bites into the chocolate, its flavor dustier than Mim anticipated. The man presses a heavy coin into his other hand, squats, and puts his face between the boy's legs. Mim senses bewilderment, tastes chocolate, and feels the coin in his other hand. The weight of the money and the melting chocolate join the quick judder, the judder she feels watching him, between his legs, the man's mouth around the boy's penis, soft, warm, but with an edge, with tooth, reminder of menace, the power of the man over Lo-Lo, and over Mim . . . the coin and the chocolate . . . and next comes warm wet spilling from what she knows *she* doesn't have.

Mim looked at Lo-Lo, who now stood in the shallow water. The river slithered past.

"I still have my health," he said.

Back at the carnival, Mim and Lo-Lo helped unpack and recreate. Part of Suspender's design was that everything was negotiable, so he continually revised the layout, the locations of everything. Annoyed the carnies, but he claimed it was good for their clock-brains, and provided more wonder for the guests. His mandate: keep it fresh, keep *everyone* guessing.

Never let our vigilance rest.

III

The carnival's new arrangement did stimulate trade. The scene was swinging. New guests came, strangers from beyond Wistmount, even beyond Astoria. They came by truck and car; some even came by horse, carried children in wagons pulled behind. All a big adventure! But mainly, the carnival was still a destination for adults.

One night, as she groomed Beatrice, Mim's body began to vibrate. Pulse and sound filled her. She mistook this sensation for the tomfoolery of her skin and wrapped her arms around her body to still it. But Beatrice must have noticed, too: she stopped gnawing an impoverished scrub plant and pounced at the ground, sought the source. A moment ago the world had been regular, flat, human, but was now ripped open by an unearthly droning.

Lo-Lo opened the kitchen's back door. "*Les cigales ont émergé!*" He sang to the pests. "Out you come, buzz-wingers, your sole song, oh dear dead and dying, blind and deafening! How crisp your shells, toasted, strewn atop our stew!" He ran off carrying a basket. Mim followed; Beatrice followed. He squatted behind the kitchen door, hunting.

"You ever eaten a cicada, darling?" he asked.

"I don't think so," Mim said.

"Then into the pot I'll stir air, and wishing! Especially for you."

The cicadas were everywhere. Lo-Lo and Mim gathered them; Beatrice ate hers, and licked her maw with her big grey tongue. Lo-Lo and Mim filled the basket with blind, shifting life.

Suspender grabbed a handful of shriveled shells at midnight dinner. "Best fried in bacon grease, and with plenty of salt."

"I ask: *Have you any bacon, Sir?*" Lo-Lo said. "These simple salted ones are good. You'll eat plenty worse in a lifetime."

"Lovely victuals, Lo-Lo," Nelda said.

"Yes, yes," Cleopatra said.

Mim took a bite of fried bug. It was nutty and crisp. Not unpleasant. Like a piece of popped corn, but richer, sweeter? She ate another, then took another and studied it, the shell separated from whatever had been inside. Her own skin quivered, and she was back at the spot where she had lain . . . scratch-land, before she knew this place, these people, before her own shell had been filled, by accident, really, by the world of the Eight Mile Suspended Carnival. Were these her people now? They were all she had, but were they *hers*?

If there were other people, a family, wouldn't they be looking for her? Wouldn't they care? They must not. Mim didn't even want to know them. If they even existed.

Examining the cicada shell, she decided yes. *Yes* to the Eight Mile Suspended Carnival. *Yes*. What was the alternative? No would not do. She bit into another.

"Wash 'em down!" Lo-Lo handed her a mug of wine.

The shells scraped against her throat when she swallowed, wine's smooth burn following it all down.

Just enough to keep the skin on, the breaths persisting. If you were offered a meal and needed one, you wouldn't complain. Intricate machines, the ones we walk around inside . . . and they need fuel to keep it all intact. To keep propelling you onward. To keep the species visible. Would you eschew a thing purely because it's unfamiliar? Discount its prehistoric charm? Get hungry enough and anything will make your mouth water. Anything will look like food.

IV

For several days, Mim would feel cicada-scratch in her throat, and whisper a secret to the dead bugs, to which she had said *yes*. And once, when that memory of the first cicada prickled her throat, a million bits in the air of her mind organized into one terrifying impression: The cicada she had eaten had been a girl.

The girl had been lost in the woods; she had been confused by the world around her. The world was fragmented, not unlike life through the metallic clang in which Mim lived, and the girl was only comfortable, only safe in her cicada shell. To the cicada, that young girl had also said *yes*. The girl cicada had been able to fly above her surroundings, unnoticed, invisible really, and the best part about it, for the girl, and for Mim, was that flying made sense of the world in a way not conveyable through words, but only sounds . . . sounds like the dent of a dish Lo-Lo was scrubbing right now, or the sound of Beede as he moaned and mashed against Mim, which now, when Mim considered it, sounded more like metallic chipping, a shovel on the hard ground. Someone digging. But how could Mim hear any of this? She had the sense, along with the cicada, spindle-tickle still days later in her throat, that some of this hadn't happened yet, wouldn't happen for decades. It was a different place, a different world, *but there was the girl,* who had once been (*would* once be) a cicada. As: sounds, like the songs of Lo-Lo, traveled forward and backward. Mim knew this. But beyond seeing people's memories, could she see what hadn't yet happened? When the cicada scratched her throat, was Time not tethered to place, to anything really, except possibly itself? Did minutes blow about on whims, cyclonic, ripped from their thin thread, how a string, a fiber could move, unskinned, unbothered . . . stirred, but not troubled? Just existing? Just a string?

But if Time is a string, how can we know anything? Can we only wait until it ends up wherever we prefer? Or can we grab it, tie it down, manipulate it like Suspender builds contraptions, a world of wonder, or more intimate things, the small-limbed person that Mim found in his memory, what she and he created (or *would* create, or *will*) in the rope room, that day when the Tobeys bound her and Suspender slapped the Tobeys from the room like a swarm of the wicked, naming her for himself? Something that hadn't yet happened. With Time, can we, *should we,* create an intimate that would someday be a person, like the future person who would eventually dwell inside Mim? Had that already happened, or was it still to come? A baby twitched in Mim's womb. An answer? Or was it only the baby of Cleopatra, which Mim had witnessed? Would that baby be a girl? Would she, someday, eat a cicada, and have the notion that the cicada had once been a girl, or rather the other way around, that a girl had once been a cicada, been *that* cicada?

When Lo-Lo had brought her some furniture from an unused wing of the hotel, she had ignored Cleopatra's advice, hadn't asked him to fix the hole in her floor. Instead, she had stolen a piece of broken potato crate to cover it. Down in the hole she made a nest: the book, the stone egg Beede had won. The small rope. Her diagram. Her secrets. A cicada shell.

Late in the night in her room, Mim opened the floor and put the stone egg in her lap and wrote what she had seen, each stolen memory, each story, and sometimes her own questions, in the purple-red book.

She wrote the story about the cicada girl.

EIGHT

SOMETHING PRECIOUS

I

After dinner one night, over chocolate tea, carnies listened to Suspender tell about the death pill factory. Not for the first time, but he decided to tell it again, for Mim.

"Some history and detail I owe to Timmy Zuzu," Suspender said. Timmy Zuzu, a line-puller from the factory, spent many nights at the carnival. Mim liked Zuzu. He had a wider vista than the other factory boys. She even liked the sound of his name—how, when she said it, her lips tingled.

"The current Spurlock was a rich orphan; his father had left him the factory. When he was a boy, some uncle ran the place. The boy's dead father, who had, in turn, been left the family burden by *his* father, was not what you would call a sensible man. To sell weaponry fuel is not a clean profession. You have to know someone who knows someone who knows someone, all very guarded and clandestine. It wasn't easy to light a fire in those days." Suspender lit his pipe from a candle flame, and smiled. He drank from his tea bowl. Why he used this fancy item was a fascination. Everyone else drank from metal, or occasionally, glass. Mim took a drink, and let the gritty cacao play on her tongue.

"The father of the father had never wanted to do anything more than set fires. Grandfather Spurlock was wild. Shocking, actually, that the operation

84

survived his years in charge." When Suspender smiled, which was rare, something delightful shone behind his face.

Mim watched chocolate flecks, tiny rafts barely surviving the swollen river of tea, but they would do, they would keep a person from drowning.

"The point is, Grandfather couldn't save himself from the powder. He roiled in it. Some say he slept in the powder house. The wife had no esteem for his career. One night, after she lit a candle, and the remnants on his clothes set their supper table on fire, she wisely left him. Least that's what Zuzu heard. Lit the supper table, along with himself, of course, and they had to call the medical doctor. Grandfather Spurlock's skin was burned; he liked that. That was the last in a string of acts this wife did not tot up as love, unless you include his blind love-o'-the-flame. The hot orange-white of the candle was never enough for him. Wife was sad, but he couldn't know that, couldn't see beyond ignition or its possibility. Back in those days, *that* place was the carnival. The factory! Because of him the factory went up, and they had to rebuild that first time. Scattered topography, as an approach, hadn't been obvious back then. One explosion, which led to the next, and so on, like hot, killing hiccoughs. Rocked the corpse of the building, all due to Grandpa's fascination and some alcohol. He lit a match for a hand-rolled cigarette. One spark started the whole disaster.

"But by then, the Special War was in sight, and the family, though they had money enough, saw potential to profit. Who remembers now which side failed and which prevailed? We've seen so many wars since. We don't believe in these pugilistic contests at the Eight Mile Suspended Carnival, friends. We just don't." Suspender stopped speaking and pointed at each of the Tobeys. "Listen and know it."

"What about Anton the Elder?" Mim asked.

Anton the Younger muttered, "He is like the dead to me."

"Defected to the death pill factory. Better he's gone, if that's how he leans." Suspender sipped tea, cradled the careful bowl. "Back to the telling. The family rebuilt. A passel of small buildings. Pain in the rump for those who work there, hard to get around in the rain, but it never rains anymore, and makes sense in a monetary-protection way of thinking. Which these modern Spurlocks are adept at, I might add.

"Yes. Grabbing piles. They tossed scratch around in Wistmount, built the town, a cathedral erected on death, the dance hall, the jail—what they call the Spurlock Hotel. That jail dangles above their heads now. Factory boys save up their foolish to spend over here, instead."

Gnash pounded his palm on the table and said, "That box maker who favors the Electric Trampoline says more than usual Wistmount coffins are half-sized lately."

"Everyone interrupts me," Suspender said.

Tiger continued on. "Less timber, but no less labor. Nobody wants to pay full price when they're burying a child."

"You say children are dying more often?" Cleopatra asked.

"Was this my telling?" Suspender asked. "Or am I mistaken?"

"'Tis river-swimming season," Tiger said.

"Babies swim in the poison and die," Gnash said.

Suspender continued. "Well it ain't ambiguous what they're up to, now you mention it. Downstream, any water will be fouled. You'll notice all Spurlocks live on the far side of Wistmount where they can access the pleasanter river. More than twenty miles from the factory. They can only smell the powder when a rare wind blows southeast, which is almost never. They knew plenty, building there, let me tell you. Nor do their progeny have to swim in our lowly river. You would guess they had real criminal minds. Puppet masters above the scene, placing things with care, to make sure their air was unstained.

"That contemporary master Spurlock you've seen over here, long brown linen overcoat, sweeps the ground. Hand-woven brown shoes, pristine, and other than that, he'll wear white. A slight lazy eye on him, if you look close enough, but that's no deterrent in a family of means. A man accustomed to leisure, time to think, beyond the rush of working people. Hands like seashells, washed shiny and iridescent, skin treated to the best soap, and little toil. Alabaster."

Alabaster. Mim touched her cheek.

Suspender held up and perused his own hands a moment, and continued. "I am not impressed."

"All those small coffins," Nelda said.

"True, fewer crumb grabbers pass through our gate, of late. I like that rhyme," Suspender said.

"Enough silly names and rhyme. You might show respect, even if you don't especially care about youth," Nelda said.

Lo-Lo said, "They're killing childhood!"

Suspender raised his bowl in a toast. "I have nothing against youth. Kill the next generation and there's no one to pay for your soup, friends. Too many Spurlocks have held the power of Divinity in their munitions work. Who will do the work, if they kill off the children downriver? Well, that's how the Spurlock machine thinks, or doesn't think. He's smart, but powder has clouded his vision."

"Oh, how I hate to ponder those pint-sized coffins; they haunt my dreams," Gnash said.

"We're none of us more than a heartbeat from death. No amount of money or featherbeds will change that," Suspender said.

"Have you ever seen someone die?" Mim asked him.

Suspender drank the dregs of his chocolate tea. The shadow of boy peered from behind his face.

"A good question," Cleopatra said.

"Read my mind and discover," he said to Cleopatra, but the child behind his man-face peeked at Mim.

The skin resides upon the skull as well. The skull, decorated in some cases with hair, works as a reasonably safe place to hide the stuff that really matters, the stuff we hide from each other. Some feel that names are best kept hidden. Does a name make a key to unlock what we carry? If so, protect yours well. If not, then we must continue to depend on skull, on skin. On a shut mouth. We can choose whom to illuminate with facts and yearnings, with our contents. We can choose where to donate our confession. And whether.

When I stare out at you lot, I see thin sheaths covering your mugs. That is: I am not impressed by your feathers and fortresses. You're always talking, always telling something. You have no idea how powerful silence can be. Let the other guess and fill in. Not only to serve the mystery that propels (for instance) guests toward a carnival on Saturday at dusk. No, not only that. In other words, it's not for mere sport that a wise crow will keep his yap shut. It's easier to taste the salt on the wind with a shuttered trap; it's a kinder spirit you will be subject to if you keep some of your own secrets in the vault.

You understand that is part of the commerce of this visibly revealed happenstance, this world you've sat down to peek inside, these pages.

(Peek, yes, please peek and pry. We won't deny your curiosity. Long as it's got the company of coins.)

II

Mim scribbled the Spurlock story. All this factory talk made her think of Beede . . . his face, square mouth . . . such a lovely cat, and his hands were crows, cawed at her, flew nearby, inside her dust. The fact of him became a drumbeat, calling her. She didn't fight. Why would she? Something happened. She accepted. She accepted that the rides, the carnival machines, would be there in the morning, that she would have a place, even a musty, uncomfortable place, but somewhere. She sometimes imagined sleeping through Suspender's early morning call to prepare for the Crossing. Huffish, tired carnies would pack up their lives, and she would wake, find only the dust of their absence. *But don't think about that, push it from the head, it needn't be there, it serves no purpose except to confuse and make skin peel off.* She needed that skin. Beede said alabaster, like something dear, like Spurlock's hands. Clean, but covered in death.

Many, many possibilities in the grope toward discernment.

Later, Mim knocked on Cleopatra's door. Inside, Cleopatra's grandness was spread generously across the bed. She rubbed a fringy shawl against her cheek. Mim sat on the armchair.

"Nightmare?" Cleopatra asked.

Mim sometimes came to Cleopatra after a bad dream. Like a child, but it calmed her. She never told Cleopatra what troubled her dreams, and usually, Cleopatra seemed oddly uncurious.

"No, I just can't sleep."

"What's the haunt, dearling?"

"I'm cold. What's alabaster?"

"Pondering Spurlock hands?"

Cleopatra tossed the fringe shawl at Mim. Could she know what Beede had said? Mim wouldn't tell her anything about Beede. She needed to hoard him as long as she could. Telling would dilute his essence like rinsing paint from brushes.

Mim needed an answer. "Alabaster?" She knew not to push. Cleopatra must believe she was leading; she would never tell if pressed.

"Alabaster is of the sea. No, of the hills. No, I'm not sure. Mineral, shell? I should know, but I don't. I know it glows pale and weak. Some praise alabaster, despite its anemia." She hesitated a moment, and looked carefully at Mim. "Your interest goes beyond a diction lesson. Beyond that Spurlock. Someone said it about you."

Mim began to understand what Beede had meant about her skin, its pallor. In her mind she took slices of ice and held them to her warm cheeks, to hide what rose there, so Cleopatra wouldn't see any more than the word.

Cleopatra peered closely, breath on Mim's face. "Who's haunting you today?"

"No one," Mim said.

"I should toss you a card."

"No, it's late."

"You see too much," Cleopatra said. "I know about hoisting that load. Seeing insides can unmoor a person."

Mim shifted in her seat, but suddenly couldn't get comfortable.

Cleopatra said, "Yes, one card. I must. Come." She hefted herself from her bed, and arranged the small table. Unwise to resist. The cards were slates, again, heavy in Mim's hands. And again, always, the Hanged Man.

"Constancy means it's true," Cleopatra said. "Means you're chewing on something."

"I guess so." Mim touched the card, which was cold.

"Waiting. You can wait a long time if you need to."

Mim let her head fall back against the chair and closed her eyes.

III

Ice melted, alabaster irrelevant. Work. Mim walked trash-eating Beatrice, stopped to watch the Electric Trampoline. Gnash pulled ropes, making the surface taught. He dropped a marble and it rolled, tentative, toward the left side of the metal frame.

"Three inches," he said.

Before it rolled further, he grabbed and pocketed the marble. With his leathery hands, he pulled one of the myriad short ropes that secured the thick canvas skin to the frame, dropped the marble again, and tightened ropes, following where it rolled.

He tuned the trampoline like a string-box, spent hours negating slope from its skin.

"Give us a hand, love," he said to Mim.

If the skin was level, people had a chance of staying upright, or if they fell, injury would be minimal.

The Electric Trampoline was among Suspender's more intricate inventions. It scared Mim more than some other rides, even more than The Ringer. The trampoline required skill. She knew the warning sign above it was hyperbole, but how could she trust her legs not to buckle, how could she trust that canvas skin? And most important, with the Electric Trampoline, you had to jump at exactly the right moment for your weight, when it was on the way up, and land similarly, or else it was possible to bungle, fall, crack open against the metal.

After reading the yellow and red warning, those who chose to jump had to swear by marking a piece of paper that they had no relation (neither marriage nor blood) to anyone in the legal trade. Then Gnash examined their breath for wine. If anything weren't right, he would follow their pupils and knock their knees with a hammer and tickle them under the arms to make sure their reflexes were prepared.

All part of the game.

Sleeping, waking. Who gets to decide? If you value truth or let's say *fact* of imagination, you would honor what happens in the clear sunshine, evidence, proof. If you value the wonder of invention, you would allow some blurring of that apparent clarity. The clouds might obscure our comrade Mr. Sunshine, and this would not trouble you. You would be willing to accommodate that temporary obscurity. You might be swept off your stable ground by the appearance of the edge of a leaf, the effusion of a yarrow flower's miniscule canopy, a crocus breaking through, how the sunshine illuminates, with its absolute light, the thinnest green foliage. That insignificant leaf edge, that light, that line may be enough for you, enough to keep your heart drumming in its cage. That's fine, and who am I to argue?

You present no challenge for someone in my role; you make me smile. But if you need that constant light—the sun—to break Shadow itself, you are where I trip up, you are what I cannot, in my path, swing away from. From you, I am always scratching an itch. You are a puzzlement. You I choose to examine, and taunt with queries.

Because without imagination, how does the drum beat forward? Or back? How do the generations exist, how do the small souls continue to light the world? How do I eat?

Without you saps, how do I survive?

And the carnival needs you! So down I reach to the dollhouse, the play-world of small soldiers at my feet (or I reach up from beneath the earth—place me where you will) and I push pieces around the stage, play with the locus of proscenium, *le papier mâché (en Français)*, the lens . . . it all crinkles and calls so beautifully.

We say play is for children. We limit ourselves with such hard finality. *Grow up, get to work!* You, you relic, you could reach for a dolly, too. The dolly waits for you, all you need to do is close your eyes and reach. (Keep reading.)

Needing to be touched, needing something real against her skin rather than that horrid wall of wind, her only full memory, Mim went to find Beede.

At the edge of the river, moonlit darkness tickled everything. All sound grew and stretched out of small scratching and the scratching grew into a greedy monster, tailed Mim, prepared to feast. She tried to ignore the monster and watch the other side of the water, working to find him, and when she found him, to touch him; she needed him to touch her like in Cleopatra's dream. The soldier. If Mim and Beede couldn't find a bed, the ground would do, the ground here by the water, even this ground. He could touch her. Make her know she existed.

But he continued not to be on the other side.

He was not across the water.

She would keep trying.

NINE

PROVISIONS

I

The town of Wistmount was fourteen miles west of the carnival. The carnies kept chickens and goats, and were resourceful humans, but they went to Wistmount for other needful things. And Wistmount couldn't resist the carnival, the yank of taffy and human imagination.

Before the carnies had eaten to the walls—cans, jars, boxes, bottles—Suspender announced it was time to go to Wistmount. "No putting it off, must provide, must get provisions," he said. "Can't eat dirt, can we?"

He was threading wire into a red metal skeleton about four inches tall, a gadget that he might build into a real ride someday. An idea from his brain, which was constantly cataloging, discerning which bits of detritus to use, which to discard. Not much discarded, usually. How could they ever make the Crossing? What would *he* agree to leave behind? He claimed he would leave anything, everything, but that must be a lie. What about that giant crate called Mother, one part from each contraption: who could lift and move that?

Nelda said to Lo-Lo, "Your turn. I have piles of fabric to fix."

"If I'm to go, give it over," Lo-Lo said, "*donne-moi d'argent.*" He put down the platter he had just cleaned.

Suspender took out his purse and gave Lo-Lo a stack. "Get me some wool, Clock. Color no matter." He called Lo-Lo "Clock" sometimes, and usually got no answer.

"Maybe someone there knows about me," Mim said.

Lo-Lo put the money in his pocket. "Be a lot better with company. Mim, you don't have anything to do. Come with. Maybe you'll find kin."

Her skin quivered. Would Wistmount help her remember herself? Would someone there know her? "Maybe," she said.

Suspender, Pelle, had been watching Mim a lot lately, like he was waiting for something. "Yes, you go with," he said. "Meet the beasties and critters and guests. Some you might recognize." Suspender stared at her. "Don't wander off."

She stared back, let him peruse her insides, find any detritus to salvage. What he might find useful, later.

The steam truck seats were dusty and cracked, like so much at the carnival. But Lo-Lo kept the truck's insides oiled and clean. "In case we need to leave fast."

"Why does he call you Clock?" she asked.

"Dashing needs a wipe," he said. He took a rag from his pocket and rubbed the controls, though he couldn't get at what lingered in the crevasses. So many dials, numbers and letters, fat and round—their pattern like a flower. Five finger-sized holes disturbed the smooth surface of the dashboard. The holes were full of grit. You could feel the same grit on your teeth in the morning. From one hole dangled a wire, strung with green pearls the size of marbles. The steam truck doors had no glass, only open space for windows.

"Hey windling, you ever ridden in one of these things?" he asked.

"I don't know."

He took a black ribbon and began to tie back his hair, but stopped, pulled a knife from his pocket, cut the ribbon in half, and handed her a piece. "Here. Don't need a nest of rats. It gets blustery on the road." He tied back his hair, and she tied hers likewise. "Delightful and pleasing," he said. He touched her cheek.

He spit-cleaned a pair of goggles and put them on. Like spectacles, but the sides were closed with leather. He cleaned another pair and handed them to her. "Strap these on, dear."

She liked the goggles, their pull, even how they yanked her hair and fastened her skull in place.

"Onward to the wistful mount!" He pulled the green pearls, and the motor started to churn and clang. He lit a saffron cigarette. Buttery smoke slid from his mouth toward his nose. "Want some?"

She tried the orange-tinged cigarette. It tasted like when his bean curry had waited on the stove too long.

He maneuvered the truck through the gate. "You look natural," he said. "Must have partaken before."

The road was built of bumps and gullies. Fast, fast, how the steam truck propelled them, though he cursed its sluggishness. She, Lo-Lo, and the steam truck became the wind. The sweet cigarette smoke filled the air above their heads, thick and yellow, flowing through the windows with the song of the miles, all wind and motion.

This shy wind, unlike the twister, didn't batter her, only offered a breath, a sigh.

The river was a ribbon, was a story, a snake mirroring the snake that was the road, now here, now gone, obscured by a swell of hill between the two.

She asked for another cigarette.

"Why not, I'll get more in Wistmount." He whistled a song he would sing at the sink or cleaning steam truck gears. "Might be a smooth drive," he said. "Don't be so quiet. Or what's the point of company?"

"I can be company," she said.

"Listen, about your origins. Those people in Wistmount are beastly unhelpful. Besides, where is anyone from? Does it matter? Don't let it upset you."

"But shouldn't we try?" She waited a long time, but he didn't answer. She pulled the goggles tighter. Did she really *want* to try? What if she found someone? Would she leave the carnival?

"Make some other talk," he said.

"Why does he call you Clock?"

He exhaled smoke. "Why does he call you Mim?"

Not fair. He knew she couldn't remember her name. "But why *Clock*?"

"Why does anyone do anything? Stop being such a strumpet."

"You wanted me to talk. What should I say?"

"Can't you sing, strumperlet?"

She whistled what he had been singing. He laughed. "I'm sorry. You're swell, but that's not singing."

She closed her eyes and let her body be carried on the jolts of the road. When she opened her eyes, she began to count the occasional trees, and remembered the barren edge of the river. "Trees," she said.

"I learned to sing from my ma," he said. "That's why I'm so good. She was good. The lady knew what she was doing. Of course my voice is innate, but she was no slouch."

"Could you teach me?"

"Hmm, not sure, with your craw. There are things that can and can't. But go on, try to hum. Like talking but close your mouth."

She tried, but nothing happened.

Gold flashed across the road. Lo-Lo punched the hand brake and jerked the string of green pearls, slamming their bodies against the seat.

"*Zut alors!*" he said.

"What was that?" she asked.

"No idea. Something out to kill us. A fancy something." He pulled off the road to park and removed his goggles. "Come on," he said.

Walking toward the flash, they burrowed through bush, dusty and sharp. A branch bit her arm, thorns everywhere. The woods wanted to eat her. Lo-Lo sped ahead.

"Wait!" she said.

"Gotta catch that gold."

She couldn't protect her arms from the talons, the grabbing briar branches. Why hadn't she worn sleeves? She expected a trip to town would be safer, hadn't anticipated such toothy woods. An aroma like rotten potatoes hit her, something dead, or dying. A glint. She caught up with Lo-Lo. He was leaning over, examining something gilded. Behind the thing, a small boy moved. Then wailed, like an animal.

"Shhh, okay." Lo-Lo said to the boy, "Where did you get that samovar lid?" He leaned over and touched the metal. "Oww, he bit me!"

The boy was wrapped in rags, or skin from trees. He growled and grabbed the metal again, using the lid to shield his face.

"Don't you want help?" Lo-Lo asked.

"Here, let me," Mim said.

"Watch it," he said. "Enjoys causing pain, *bestia*."

She crouched and waited until the growl softened to a faint purr, then waited more.

She whispered, "Are you okay?"

The shield moved; there was breathing.

"Can you hear me?"

Slowly, the shield came down. The boy's scowl was etched on his face.

"Get the wineskin," she said to Lo-Lo, who muttered something then headed toward the truck.

Mud-laden scabs swathed the boy's arms and legs. When Lo-Lo left, he seemed to relax a little, and stared at Mim.

Except size, this samovar-lid child bore no resemblance to children visiting the carnival, the infant guests, fat and sleeping every night in comfort. This boy's face held only vigilance and weariness . . . was he a child or an old man?

"We don't quite belong, do we? We're not like other people," Mim said.

She extended her hand, palm up. The boy watched her hand, his face a shield behind the shield. A large, flapping leaf appeared over his head.

Sunny red bouncy happy, jolty laugh boinky fun happy happy tickle, no tickle, there's puppy, soft warm funny fuzzy baby dog barky meaty breath, sunny fur, jumpy shaky fat fun. Mim smells the puppy's breath as the boy totters, arms outstretched, lumbering, a tiny monster, loving the puppy, needing to lick it back, finally tipping over, tumbling onto lush grass, green, bouncy glossy grass, grass of green, like a song somehow, yum, grass tastes like those crunchy green things I like, Mim thinks, but it is the boy thinking. And puppy breath, stinking of meat, warms her face, feels good, radiant, like love, but the smell, though sweet, sickens her, as she is hungry, and the boy is hungry, and Mim is hurled back into this scrubby brush, sharpness intruding into soft green memory, no grass now, only this metal scowl-shielded boy.

So much, she needed those things, those fireflies, those bits of memory, a past, warm puppy breath, or even leathery feet like the girl Cleopatra, even a home to escape. Even chocolate and coin in the young hands of Lo-Lo. Something that was hers. A lumpish stew churned inside Mim. Hunger for her own memories, a home, and an unreliable but persistent notion: she had never had a home. *Had* she never a home? Boards nailed to windows and doors, all closed, an archive to her lack of remembering? Was there no place waiting for her? No one?

Lo-Lo returned with the wineskin, which he had filled with water before they set out.

"Gotta figure what to do, yes, we need to shake it to get the grub in time, get back before dark. Come on now, fix it up, Mimsy. I like that samovar lid though. Like to find the rest of it."

"Shhh," she said. She extended water to the boy's unbroken scowl. "Drink." She showed him how, and again offered the wineskin. He reached out a paw and grabbed the wineskin, then his shield, and scampered away, deeper into the scratch.

"Oy now!" Lo-Lo said.

Mim chased the boy through the spines.

"Get back here!" Lo-Lo called after her. "We gotta scoot!"

The boy had shivered into the foliage, lost, chasing ghosts . . . puppy, home, a warm thing that Mim didn't have—had she ever? Would she ever? She sat on the ground and listened. At least the boy had something. He must have. She hated having nothing but other peoples' memories and what was right in front of her, which, at the moment, was Lo-Lo, quite vexed, plucking burrs from his hair.

"*Allons!*" he said. "*Le temps n'est pas notre ami.*" He pulled her from the ground.

"What about that boy?"

"Must have escaped the waifs' home. Parents die, or don't know what to do with offspring, apparently, so children end up at the waifs'. Sometimes they run off and try to do for themselves. They're fierce, some of them. That one bit me, you may recall."

"But he can't stay out here."

"You gonna ask Suspender to take in another stray? I'm not. We've already got you. That baby skell couldn't carny. At least you can take care of yourself, mostly," he said. "Beneficence, it's a good sentiment on you, looks pretty, but ain't realistic. *Natura fortuna* and so on."

She wanted to run in deeper, find the boy. How could he survive alone?

Eyes closed, sitting on the hard cushion in the steam truck, she could only see the boy. "My scrapes hurt," she said.

"Dung beetle took my wineskin. I'll have to get another in Wistmount.

Get you some salve, too." He lit a saffron cigarette, inhaled, and started the motor. "Liked to find that samovar carcass, though. Damn."

"What if I came from the waifs' home? Before the twister," she said. What if she had run off too, like that boy, and the twister plucked her from the woods; could wind have penetrated that thick, sharp place? Was that why her skin had been so scratched up? All she had were imaginings. How could she know?

Are you afraid of the dark? At night, tucked in your beddie, do you ever wake and feel the mystery push at you, does the night crawl into your gullet, get stuck there with its cold, cold whistle?

Some say night's cold whistle comes from the valley where the dream monsters live. The brutes mate and birth each other from minerals scraped off this spinning dirtball, from its deep, unyielding core. You know all this. You've heard it before even if you obscure it with preferable, sunshiny lies. That core line of metal, that womb of monsters is a truth you can't deny— the things you see around you, the machinations that Get Things Done are ancestors to these valley citizens who sometimes invade your dire imaginings, who jolt you from sleep with the gnashing of their fangs.

Your eyes aren't fast enough to see them when you wake, in palpitation. But you feel the stir of their bodies, so recently near your own.

II

They passed a constellation of abandoned farmery, like the bones of large, long-dead animals. Then buildings, shacks, clotheslines strung between poles, clothes dry or drying, all a similar grubby hue. Then houses with flowers, so faded, were they paper or real? Then a three-story brick building ringed with a tall, rusty fence. A man at the gate held a rifle.

"What's that place?" she asked.

"Spurlock Hotel. The slammy."

A line of men in dust-red clothing were being herded inside by a pale man who held a rifle. The pale man yelled at the last man in line, then hit the man with the butt of his rifle.

Inside a yard with a metal fence, dozens of children were running, screaming, fighting, spitting, and throwing themselves at the ground. Some were small, pants dragging under their feet, others were lankier, ankles exposed.

"The waifs' home?" Mim asked.

Lo-Lo nodded. "Welcome to Wistmount."

They drove into the center of town. Lo-Lo parked the steam truck near a corner grocery, and yanked the string of pearls. The engine crackled and stopped. Across the street, a clock tower loomed in the center of a public square. Everywhere were signs and words, and stacks of useful, bright items in shop windows.

He tossed his goggles on the seat. She took hers off, too. He smoothed his hair and retied the black ribbon. From the back of the truck, they took grab bags and unfolded a metal contraption with wheels. Mim looked for anything familiar.

Outside a shop with a red and white pole, a scrawny man in a white coat yelled to no one in particular, "Tops cut, get your tops cut!" A thicker man, dressed the same, stood beside him.

"Need a haircut?" the thick man asked Lo-Lo.

The scrawny man laughed. "Get your tops cut!" he said again. "Looks like we have a customer!"

Pointing at Mim, Lo-Lo asked them, "Does this youth seem familiar?"

"Like to say yes," the scrawny man said. "Mmm hmm. Pretty familiar."

The thick man laughed.

"Leech farmers, philistines," Lo-Lo said, but walking toward the grocery, he seemed less brave than his words. The white-coated men continued to sing at their backs.

Lo-Lo had memorized his list, alphabetically, and had recited it several times in the steam truck. This was how his mind worked. In the first shop, Mim was overcome by the many jars, the ceiling-to-floor shelves. She helped him carry corn and barley flour, rice, oats, and beans of all colors, some dotted, some striped, some small and wrinkled.

"What are those?" She pointed to the wrinkled beans.

"You'll soon see."

"They look like those frogs by the river."

Lo-Lo laughed. "Tomorrow we'll have frog bean stew."

The place smelled important, this mix of smells. *Food is important to people.* Maybe this notion was only about sustenance, but while they gathered items, Mim concentrated in case there was more. In case she could remember.

"Do you recognize me?" she asked the shopkeeper.

He glanced at her. "Nope."

"Are you sure?" Lo-Lo asked.

"These ain't frog beans," the shopkeeper said. "Damn carnies."

"Say?" Lo-Lo shuffled a bundle of cash.

"*Say?* I say you're pixilated," the shopkeeper said.

"Only the pixilated see pixilation in others," Lo-Lo said.

The shopkeeper glared at him.

Lo-Lo glared back. "Mirror-lookers. You want my money or not?"

"Give it," The shopkeeper said.

Lo-Lo paid. The shopkeeper followed them outside with each haul, wiping his hands as if to shed dirt. He cursed at Lo-Lo and drew a square around his body, a sign.

On the sidewalk, a man with alarming green eyes played a miniature string-box, and shook a can that was attached to his foot, making rhythm in metal. Lo-Lo dropped coins into his cup. The man said a couple words that Mim didn't understand.

"*De rien,*" Lo-Lo said to the man. "Must feed the buskers, bless 'em."

"Do you know me?" Mim asked the green-eyed man. She smiled but he didn't smile back.

"Come on." Lo-Lo pulled her onward. "See? I told you the mount could be wistful."

"Should I ask other people if they know me?"

"Do they seem friendly to you?"

"Not very."

He smiled. "There's your answer. Maybe next time."

Onions, potatoes, apples for sauce, cured apricots, five fresh oranges, boysenberry and wrinkleberry jam, but no canned peaches, not this time. Lo-Lo was vexed again, said he needed peaches. Square crates of dried figs, garlic, shallots, raisins, nuts, bacon, beef jerk, four grange hens, five hehens, all stiff and salt-cured—"the which I'll use for stock," he said. Wheels of reeking cheese. Fresh meat from a small animal carcass and ice for the crate to transport it. One pomegranate that he put in his pocket. After each shop, he sent Mim to the steam truck to pile it in, load it down, lock the canvas so no one pinched anything. Her arms itched, but it wasn't because of restless skin—it was the welts and scrapes, kisses from the woods.

"A new wineskin!" He came toward the steam truck.

"Where can we get salve?" she asked.

Shops, stores. There was a store with books and maps in the window. The sign said Oldfields. The books towered like a game of chance. Shops, and above that, windows: a woman with a baby on her lap; the woman looked cross and tired, the baby apparently sucking life from her breast. Had Mim lived somewhere like that? Did she remember a house above a store, or did she only imagine it, something to believe that might have been? The things below, maps, towers of books, plenty to look at when she got all-overish, when her skin began to roam. But had her skin always been so unruly? The wall of wind had done this. When she lived above that store, *if she had*, towers of books floor to ceiling . . . maybe books braced the floor above, maybe books were pillars on which to build a home, a life, a world, where she had real people who knew her, not these carnies with their concealed names, but a warm bed that smelled like live things instead of metal, strange mirrors, and deception. A warm bed that smelled familiar. Instead, all this grit.

Lo-Lo found salve and slapped some on her arms. She cringed as the thick stuff injured her again with its waxy pull. "Hurts like hell. I know," he said. "Think of something else."

"I have to pee," she said.

"Hades again. Me, too. Over here." He took her to the book & map shop. Oldfields.

Inside, an aged woman behind the counter looked up from a ledger and said, "*Bonjour!*"

"*Bonjour. Pouvons-nous utiliser le petit coin?*" Lo-Lo asked.

"*Bien sûr.*" The woman smiled, and nodded toward a curtained doorway in the back of the shop, past the antiquities.

"Thank you," Mim said. She went first through a kitchen that smelled of fish and clove. She found the comely little corner at the back, and relieved herself. While Lo-Lo used the little corner, Mim looked at a display of maps, all tinted shapes and spider-lines.

"Lovely, aren't they?" The woman pointed to a framed map. "Alsace, home of my ancestors."

"It's beautiful."

"I've never been there. There is something about a map that piques a person's fancy. Where are you from?"

"I don't remember," Mim said.

"It's a shame."

"I thought someone here might know me," she said.

"I'm sorry I don't. You're someone who should be known."

Mim smiled. "Thank you."

The old woman went behind the counter and retrieved a newsprint-wrapped package. "Read this. Every girl should. When you have privacy." She handed the package to Mim. "I think it will be a help."

Lo-Lo came out. "Refreshed for the journey. *Merci!*"

"*Au revoir.* Stop in again," the old woman said.

Outside the shop, Lo-Lo asked Mim what she had.

"The lady gave it to me," Mim said.

"Not fair! She never gave *me* anything."

Mim put the package in her dress pocket and cataloged Wistmount and all that she would later write down, all the new things to remember.

"*Allons*, we've emptied the bank." Back in the truck, Lo-Lo lit a saffron cigarette from a new tin. He offered Mim the wineskin, and she drank deep—she was thirsty—but instead of water, it was wine.

She coughed. "Salty," she said.

"That's not salty. *Dry.* We'll graze tonight and feast tomorrow."

Emptiness slid through Mim, searching for some small meal, but despite the provisions from Wistmount, the figs, cheese, and bread that she and Lo-Lo ate on the drive back, still emptiness. Emptiness moved, a snake, the dry hull of its skin scraped the bottom of her soul before leaving itself behind. Reminder of all that was not there.

"You've endured the initiation. Misty Wistmountery. Thou hath survived and thriven."

"What was that motion the shopkeeper did with his hands?"

"Hypocrisy lives in that place. They drink it straight from the water. Guile and superstition courses through them; it's how they live. They think they need protection, because they fear us so thoroughly. It's the small brains."

"No one there knew me."

"True. No one's hunting you. Maybe you came from the waif's home. But don't give up. Never give up when a thing is important."

III

By the time they returned to the carnival, it was dark and the air had cooled to nearly cold.

"What a queer summer," Lo-Lo said.

But for a few couples strolling toward the gates, the carnival was empty. Timmy Zuzu helped unload provisions. Mim and Zuzu organized dry things on basement shelves, meats in the freezer, and cheeses in the cabinet so they would keep.

When Lo-Lo returned from parking the truck, he said, "Hold out that cheese, Mim. Time for a nibble. You hungry? Say, Zuzu?" He brought out a board and knife.

All these hours, the motion in the shy wind . . . being company . . . and all in order to load up and make a circle. Good to be home.

IV

Mim went to Cleopatra's tent, which Cleopatra told guests was raised upon the ashes of a long-lost martyr. She didn't mention that the tent moved every so often after practice for the Crossing, with no unearthing of said martyr. Mim approached the tent from behind and recognized Beede's voice, saying something muddled . . . then *shore leave.*

Cleopatra laughed as if she were full of flowers, like the young ladies who came at night with beaux, did the Salty dance, one foot in, one foot out, and drank wine because their beaux insisted.

"Must keep those factory boys in line. You have no idea what my job entails," Beede said. "I get no rest. They work now while I take comfort here."

"But that's not why you're here. No, you have another particular reason tonight. Hunting someone?"

Mim watched shadows through the tent, distorted: Beede's hand in Cleopatra's, above the table. Cleopatra touched his hand, and the candle turned their shadows into flicker, like that couple in the moving pictures who swam and danced underwater.

"You're supposed to know everything," Beede said.

Mim wanted to tear down the canvas veil and be with him. He was for her, not Cleopatra; he was hunting, *came here* for her. Didn't he?

"I do know everything, you deviant," Cleopatra said.

He laughed. "A carny calls *me* deviant? That's rich."

"I find a name when it fits," Cleopatra said. "Do you doubt me?"

"I'm not that unwise," he said.

"Right," Cleopatra said.

Beede is for me. Mim was sure he wasn't a deviant, whatever that meant. She didn't like how Cleopatra talked to him, didn't like the soft crackle in her voice. Beede laughed, dropped a few coins on the table, and got up. He began whistling. The sound his lips made licked at Mim, found the hollow spot at the front of her neck.

Mim tied her hair back with the ribbon again and walked around the snake pit to intersect his path.

"Oh!" she said, pretending.

"Hello there!" he said. His breath tickled her forehead. "Not yet bedtime, is it?" he asked.

She laughed. "How agreeable to see you."

"You're sweet." He took her hand.

"But the snakes aren't," she said.

He laughed.

Head down in case anyone spotted them, she went with Beede through the gate, down to the river where the skiff was perched. Where he had come over. Hunting for her.

Things were different here at night. The river's sunlight gabble had quieted to whisper, drained down to those few secrets that no one tells another. Like memories that only Mim could see. They sat near the river, his fingers in her hair, heat beneath her skin, heat everywhere, despite the cool air, murmur of touch tickling each part, and she cringed.

"Alabaster, what's this?" Beede caressed a welt on her upper arm. "You've got some scrapes. Poor thing."

He kissed her. She wanted to curl inside this instant, which was the opposite of those thorns. This was a blanket of silk teasing her shell, licking with touch, with wanting. She wanted Cleopatra's dream; the heat that ran through her now needed fuel, needed more from him, needed to know he was for her. She pulled back and looked at him, his face, boxy lips, red-purple in shadow. His breath feathered toward her. She needed to slow down, know him, know his everything. She would keep secrets from everyone, even Suspender, who reconnoitered the entire vast world.

She needed his memories.

"What do you do in that factory?" she asked.

"Me? Little me? Security. Sure, they call Dead Louie foreman, but mostly I run the place. Have to keep our trade tight. Spurlock's got ideas and plans, and others want them. War's a top business, friend, and there are plenty of snakes out there—not your smelly carnival snakes—that want in here. I've got mundane duties, too. Taking the boys on shore leave. We'll head over to Wistmount for a few days. I chaperone the boys. Don't want any human machines to end up missing or dead. Last time, three men from overnight got shackled up at the Spurlock Hotel. No fun to be had in jail. So I gather."

"I've been to Wistmount," Mim said, casually, as if it really didn't matter. She touched the package in her pocket.

"I hear you don't know where you come from. Timmy Zuzu said you don't."

"I can't remember."

"I can help you find some things," he said. He raised his shoulders, making his body, like his mouth, more square.

"Can you?"

"I know lots of people, alabaster."

He could help her—he could. Could he? The snakeskin of empty memories coiled inside her body. *Beede, he can help,* the empty snake sang into her ears.

But then Beede said he didn't want to talk, no more stories tonight. Only his hands on her cheeks, down the sides of her neck, her arms, his fingertips outlining her skin, mingling with a tap-tap of fear, willowing her, all so new, then under, and inside, and each button was an earthquake as he undressed her, as if buttons were sewn to her skin, then clothes were gone, freeing skin to the summer-chilled air, skin of his parts touching her leg, his parts like insistence, hers unsure, wobbly, she suddenly became a strange newborn horse trying to stand. His skin between her legs unbuttoned her insides, seared warmth into her. She bit her lip with the pain, the sensation of him in and in, in and in until he shuddered and yelped and finally slowed and stopped too soon, before anything inside herself could explode: she was left with the absence, wanting and not wanting, and wanting again, through the illuminated pain, wanting that brilliance, Wishing Well, almost, almost, but not quite brimming, not full of water but gold, brimming with a million samovar lids, glinting and sinister in the midnight sun.

"Did I tear you bad?" he asked when it was over.

"No, not bad." Mim didn't know what bad was, being brave, and wanting, not wanting, wanting.

He passed his hand above where he had been inside her, touched her gently there, but even gently, it hurt, and she inhaled.

"It'll be better next time," he said. He traced a welt on her arm, kissed her mouth. When the kiss ended, he helped her up. They dressed. The package slipped from her pocket. "What's that?"

"Something from Wistmount." Mim put the package back. They sat together. She watched stars deck their midnight curtain and blur into lines, and everything had shifted, and she wanted, and didn't want, and wanted a next time.

TEN

FLOODS

I

And then you have the body. Bodies need to be acknowledged, we cannot sweep them, the fact of them, away. Hoist it, move it through the world, across these dusty boards. Shake it, taunt it, taste it. Delectify what you will. It can't stay still because of that damn river pumping through it, or maybe because of the wind inside us, keeping us upright and duping death. She knows all about it, the one inside. Not inside like the parts that merge and tingle, but deeper inside, inside the hidden cave of actuality. That tiny, shining part. But will the woman on the outside notice what she knows? Will she make what she can of the red pumping river, the twin windy skies-full inside her rib cage? Will she notice all that she has, all she can do and feel with this savory, momentary sack of meat?

On the dark walk back, reckless air lapped Mim's skin. By the river, she had watched Beede sleep for a long time, and now it was late. No one knew where she was—would they worry, or notice? She never felt alone, but always invisible. Except Suspender seemed to notice everything. *Pelle seems to see me.*

The stars went to sleep, covered by something thick, and blanket-tucked, they dreamt. Thickness snuffed everything. Thunder, closer and closer.

107

Rain? Rain. Rain slapped her shoulders, her arms. She ran through rain with ache between her legs, inside, where Beede had been.

She reached the now-locked carnival gate. In the dark, in the rain, in the lightning, the gate curved above her like a row of claws, the talons of a buried giant, grappling to become known. Rain enveloped her, snap-cracked lightning bisected, bled, whitened the sky. She grabbed iron bars and climbed. Bits of metal tore into her skin, skin wet with tears from the sky, slick now like birth, like when Cleopatra found her, like the kittens that slipped from the nethers of Nelda's cat before it died. She reached the top, eased herself over the sharp spikes, and climbed down the other side.

And ran past the sodden tents, the metal rides, and rain-silenced snake pit. Light cracked open the sky, contraption monsters lurched in the washing night.

Ran into the hotel, quietly, and went toward the stairs, but Suspender called out from the kitchen. "Whoever you are, a little help!"

The kitchen ceiling was crying. Cooking pots, bins, and barrels lined the floor, caught the invasion. And in the middle of the mess, Suspender.

"Where were you?" He adjusted the tall pot Lo-Lo used to stew bouillon frijoles under a braid of water.

"I went for a walk."

"At eighteen past three in the morning?"

"Earlier, but I lay down. I must have fallen asleep. The rain woke me." Ping-ping drop of metal catching rain echoed through her head, a hollow symphony.

"Working the overnight shift at the factory? I don't think you were alone."

Mim pushed drenched hair from her face and dried off with a dish towel. She had lost the piece of ribbon, probably washed away in the river. The rain wore stomp boots. Everything in her body throbbed.

"I know who you were with." He emptied rain into the sink and returned the pan to catch more.

His face reminded Mim of the boy behind the samovar lid. One of his faces was a boy, and one an ancient man. She wasn't sure which was his actual face and which was the moving picture, projected from some hidden praxinoscope.

"Damn roof!" he said.

"Why haven't you patched it already?" she asked.

"It never rains! It wasn't urgent!"

She emptied any basin she could lift, dumped water into the sink, splashing herself with cold. Why did he let the others sleep through the deluge? She didn't ask, fearing he would interrogate her. She really needed to go to her room and nurse the hole in her insides, which continued to swell, through wet clothing, through the pain, the memory of what had happened, which was now years ago. Time stretched and yawned, and wasn't itself anymore.

"Basement!" Suspender grabbed Mim's hand. It was the first time Pelle had ever touched her. His hand was smooth and warm.

"Crusty arse, we're flooded!" he said, "Go get everybody, drag 'em down here, go!"

Mim stared at the swirl of murky water.

"Gotta cut power to the freezer so we don't electrocute. Shite. Go!" Suspender shoved the word at her, shoved her up the basement stairs.

She ran to Cleopatra's room. The bang of pots sounded from below. She pushed open the door. "We're flooded!" she yelled.

Cleopatra rolled onto her back and snorted.

"Wake up, there's rain, the basement's full of water!" Mim shook Cleopatra. Warmth tickled between Mim's legs. What was that? But she didn't have time to check.

"Rain? When did it rain?" Cleopatra asked.

"Now!"

"Oh, hell." Cleopatra got up. She looked at Mim like a guest. "What're you full of? You've been with that factory man."

"We have to wake everyone!" Mim shouted at Cleopatra like Suspender had at her. Cleopatra went to get Nelda.

When Lo-Lo opened his door, Mim learned where Timmy Zuzu slept. Zuzu was snoring.

"Good morning, strumpy." Lo-Lo stretched. "Is it morning? What's the ruckus?"

"We're flooded, the basement, the food!" she said. She went to knock on the next door.

"Livestock!" Lo-Lo yelled. "Livestock!"

Cleopatra stomped down the stairs, shaking the chandelier with her keening. "Beatrice!" Her voice stormed through Mim's head.

Mim, Cleopatra, Lo-Lo, Nelda, and Tiger went out back. Three chickens were perched on the lean-to roof. Nelda handed a chicken to Mim and grabbed the other two, one under each arm. "Into the parlor," she said.

One of the chickens had drowned, the dumb one, body draped like a muddy rag. Lo-Lo picked it up. "I'll boil this for soup," he said.

The other birds huddled in the coop. The rooster, stronger than Time, had survived. They carried chickens into the hotel.

"Poor rattled babies! These birds won't lay for weeks!" Lo-Lo said.

Three goats were gone, Zlateh and another nanny, and one buck. "The other nannies' milk will dry up," Nelda said.

Once they had gotten all but two goats into the parlor, Cleopatra draped herself against Tiger. "Beatrice!" she said. "Beatrice."

"She's flown off," Tiger said. "She's crafty, she can take care of herself."

Suspender dragged in the last goats.

"Beatrice!" Cleopatra said to the goats. "Find her!"

"Not now," Suspender said. "Critters inside, good, now to shore up, then hunt. Basement next." He went downstairs.

"She must be terrified," Cleopatra said.

"Can't find her in this rain, best to wait." Tiger put his arm around her. "Come on now, old girl. Basement."

On the basement's bottom step, feet submerged, staring at the mess, sat Suspender. "Can't bail it. Get the expensive stuff. Get the low stuff. Get meat from the freezer. Get the freezer, too. Whatever you can hoist, take it upstairs. Make a chain. Hoist and crank!"

The carnies emptied low cabinets; the higher shelves of dry food would be okay for now. They balanced jars on their shoulders and heads. A few things slipped and broke against the steps: watery shards of baby shark; emblem-flower wine; jam with pine nuts; pickled goose liver. Many things fell but most made it to the top landing, which was loaded down and trembling—the items themselves feared drowning. Breathe in, out, in, out, move, carry, haul, rescue. Use arms, hands, legs. Behold the crate where Mim had found the book, the book she had saved from the sea that now gathered below.

All that mattered was rescuing what could be saved, keep moving, keep moving, this was all Mim had, these people, this dank home. No act was futile. The people, linked and cogged together, became a machine . . . until pumping items from the sodden basement made a pattern from the chaos. The carnies became one of Suspender's contraptions, and when he said,

"Get the Impossibles," Tiger labored with his old knees through the water to the huge crate of ropes and cracked open the lid.

Mim, five steps from the bottom of the human conveyor belt, looked down into the bin, from which Nelda and Tiger dragged first layers of dry then sodden ropes, no longer impossible from knots, but now impossibly heavy, laden with rank water. Saliva filled Mim's mouth, and her impatient skin wanted free.

"They're not impossible!" Nelda said.

Each bundle of rope was still coiled as Mim had left them.

"How? Well, drag it all up, anything that's dry, keep it that way!" Suspender said.

Mim passed bundle after bundle up the steps to Lo-Lo, who looked scrawny in his bed shorts, but one water-softened rope clung to her hand, wanted to stay. She stroked its fibers: rough, snaking. Lo-Lo grabbed the rope from her. She watched it move up the chain and wanted it back, but it moved out of her sight. The carny below shoved another rope at her.

"Pass it on!" Lo-Lo said. He looked like someone had gashed his cheeks with sadness. "All those victuals," he said. He was crying. "Zuzu, get the *jambon!*"

Timmy Zuzu supported the ham, which hung from a rafter, cut the rope, and carried the meat under his arm.

"Ropes will rot if you don't drape 'em up," Suspender said.

Once the carnies had taken what they could from the leaking kitchen, the Tobey called Rubyat suggested they drape wet rope across the attic rafters. "It's dry," he said.

"We'll have to shove some stuff aside, but it's a good idea," Suspender said. "Tobeys, carry everything on up. Tiger, you and Mim clear space."

In the attic, Tiger struggled with a pile of rope. "This bundle's too tight, can't undo it,"

"I can." Mim started to uncoil.

Finally, more ropes. She leaned over and undid end-knots, until all bundles were loose, then began unwinding, handing lengths to one after another of the men, who dragged rope over doorway transoms, tossed rope over rafters and hooks, forming a webbed ceiling.

"Don't cross them, don't want another sad, wild tangle," someone said.

"Could string up some food," someone else said.

"What for?"

"I don't know, I'm kind of hungry," someone else said.

That kinked rope Mim had taken when she undid the Impossibles, the one that widened like the head of a snake, the rope that still remembered . . . it needed her.

She went back to her room, took it out of the floor, and fell asleep in its coil.

II

Cleopatra burst into Mim's room. "Come hunt for Beatrice!" She pulled Mim from bed, and shoved boots at her. Downstairs they joined Nelda, Suspender, Tiger, Zuzu, and several Tobeys.

"I'm going to find the kittens." Nelda went outside.

Lo-Lo still sorted food, salvaged what he could. The kitchen was useless, and the food from the freezer had to be cooked before it spoiled, so he dragged a metal barrel into the lobby and made a fire. He or Nipsy had to tend constantly so it wouldn't smoke everyone out or set the hotel aflame. Lo-Lo opened a window for ventilation, but the wind kept changing direction, and rain poured in. Before the rescue party left, he pulled Mim close and kissed her mouth. *"Bonne chance,"* he said. He smelled like smoke, and his beauty hid behind exhaustion, hope waning, dreams crawling off somewhere to die. Her chest pinched when he kissed her; it was a sad kiss, like desperation, like a final breath.

On the porch, Suspender told each carny which direction to go. "Take five hundred steps, keep counting, keep looking. Look down, too. Then turn around and come back."

Into the rain they went, blind, groping . . . everywhere—water. Water poured down inside Mim's collar, despite the hat she had borrowed from Tiger. Instantly, she was soaked.

Her direction was the river. How far would five hundred steps take her? Light cracked the sky toward Wistmount. Where was Beede now, did he miss her? She lost track of counting. Why were five hundred steps important anyway? The sky had opened and was crying, bleeding, when would it stop, where was Beatrice, how could she manage if the beast needed to be carried? They each had a small rope to use as a lead if necessary. She wrapped hers round her wrist. If Beatrice couldn't walk, Mim couldn't carry her alone, could she? The rope was a wet, heavy snake on her wrist, but the snake reassured her, recalled her hidden rope. She walked through the ocean the air had become. Was that seventy-nine? Or eighty-nine? Step, look right, look left, up and down, both sides. Look for wet feathers. Poor Beatrice. Mim gave up counting.

Tiger's hat was soaked now, heavy and cold. She wanted to take it off, but the brim kept rain from her eyes. If she couldn't see, she might get lost herself.

There was the river. Across and downstream, the hulking ghost death pill factory visible through wavy air, snaky swell of water first, river, always water, but now loud and angry—had Beatrice been swept away? The factory buildings lurched in the rain, sighed and whispered, and if the structures had considered escape or refuge, now it was clear they had given up.

"Stubborn death pills," she yelled into the rain. How long had the factory been there? How long before the world would drown?

She stumbled in the chocolaty mud. The hat fell off and the rain poured on her bare head. She yanked the hat from the mud, held it in the river. Did water now cover where she had been with Beede, water and blood? River water washed mud from the hat but sopped it in a new stench, something nasty washed from the deluge, born of sound and loss. Death pill poison mixed in the rush of river water. Mim squeezed water from the hat and put it back on, pointless. If the river had gotten Beatrice, she was gone. Gone.

No one found Beatrice, but Nelda found three kittens alive, their hoarse mewling curled from a dry corner beneath the porch. She tucked them into her apron pocket and fed them soft sweet things.

Cleopatra bellowed out toward the drowning world.

Mim dragged herself through the unrelenting rain, became machine: feet stepping, body numb, eyes blind, only heart trusting that eventually she would find the hotel, and eventually she did, and in it, her room. She peeled off her wet things and sat on the bed.

On the bed beside her, there was the package from the old woman in Wistmount, which she had completely forgotten. Wistmount was years ago. Mim unwrapped the wet bundle: a small book, the yellow cover said *What Every Girl Should Know* above a shining torch. She opened the book to read, her breath slowed, and soon she fell asleep.

III

Rain, rain, rain, only rain. Rain, an accumulation of days, of nights.

Echo, clatter, and stomp throughout the hotel, even the ghosts of sleeping carnies sought the few dry corners. Rain and echo of rain until it rippled from inside Mim's skin. Outside her window, rain streaked the muted light. She imagined the rope-webbed sky in the attic and caressed her hempen rope, traced with her finger the three twisted strands. Together the strands made the lopsided snake, from narrow to broad, its end like the head of a snake, like a carnival attraction. She fondled the rope, remembering what Smoot always said about snakes: rub their scales in the wrong direction, and it's torture. Time goes in both directions, like snakes, but snakes only pleasure one way. The other is pain. Put your palm on a snake and keep still: does stillness balance the pleasure, the pain? Would it be only life touching life? Would it be, for an instant, enough? Mim tried stillness on the rope. But when she fondled the rope, both ways sensed pleasure, and pain, and prickled her palm. The weight of the rope-snake's head was stony and absolute. But its end was frayed, chaotic, blurred. She put the blur in her mouth. It tasted ancient.

She considered the tail, the head, which direction for pleasure, which for pain. The snake flicked its narrow end, the tail, away from Mim; its kinks flicked the tail, its memories, out of experience and habit. She would start with the head.

She unwound, and learned about ropes, scrabbled to untangle the feathery head. One, two, three. *Ropes have three parts.* She unwound more. The three spirals, an ancient puzzle, moved on their own, still memory, not only the kinked parts, but the tender insides of the curls, inside the coil, inside the twists, each ringlet sweet where it used to touch its sister strands.

She made children from the snake mother until three fringy piles of strand were separately born. Her skin whispered, hissed what it needed. She tied the end of one child around her right ankle, and wound it up her leg, then did her left. Covered them with a dry dress that reached to her ankles. Walked downstairs.

Carnies were strewn on chairs and settles in the lobby. After working their bodies, they collapsed from labor and despair. Nelda was curled around kittens, asleep. The runt was sickly. Cleopatra sat in a corner, eyes closed, and sent whispers out to Beatrice.

Mim went into the early morning rain, out toward the carnival, barely visible through the pour. She needed her rope wet; the weight would help secure her skin. But when she bent her knees, the rope chafed. Rain rushed, gnashed in her ears. She fought through the unseen gruel the air had become. The ghostly structures ahead bobbed like floats on the river. Had the river come to meet the carnival, lifted rides from stable ground, would the river whisk it all away? All this rain, the river must be high, the bank might be gone, everything gone. Had the rain washed away the river's memories? Its poison? Mim slipped and fell, her face pressed into the sponge of ground. Muck clung and sucked her down, saturated her dress, filled creases between the ropes on her legs, clutched her to the earth.

But hadn't this been what she needed, this gravity? She rolled onto her back and swallowed rainwater. Her eyes filled with rain and overflowed and the water poured toward ground, *where the rest of the rain goes.* This gravity, she lay inside it, thought of Beede, wanting and not wanting, wanting, and imagined his hands tying rope around her limbs, her torso, neck, all of her, whatever needed tightening, reassurance of gravity, existence. She wrote this sensation in her bones, so they would remember.

On hands and knees, rope bit her legs. She crawled, then stood. In the bash of rain, the hotel was a grey ghost, washed from sight by the ceaseless water. After many years, she reached the steps and struggled into the lobby.

Cleopatra still whispered toward her beast. One of the kittens had draped its slim body across Nelda's face. Others still slept. Mim trundled to her room, closed the door, and peeled off her boots. She fell into bed, legs still tied in sodden ropes. Who knew how much later, someone banged the door open and woke her. Suspender stood in the doorway, lit by hallway bulbs.

"Clocky wants help in the kitchen, says Nipsy's useless—he's in bed with the hives," he said. He stared at her rope-wrapped leg. "What in arse? Somebody tie you up?"

She covered herself with the blanket. The ropes burned against the back of her knees and itched everywhere else.

"Pixilated," he said.

A broad, green leaf hung above his head.

Rope. He is being trussed. He's young, the lion-maned boy he had been. Pelle. A smaller, tremendously cruel boy—together, Mim and Pelle name him Orphan-Monster—ties young Pelle to a pole, the pole is surrounded by a patch of farm near the woods . . . the pole is taller than the house that lurches nearby; the pole leans toward a barn. Wooden buckets ring the ground at Pelle's feet. And something stale. He and Mim peer into a ragged hole in the ground, a grave the Orphan-Monster dug for Pelle's hand-forged contraptions, now smashed, burned, buried. The Orphan-Monster, mouth shaped like a box, is tying Pelle's hands.

"I'm gonna get in your meat-house!" Orphan-Monster yells. He grabs two handfuls of Pelle's hair, holds on, forces him, and Mim, to look into his face. There's that shadow again, heavy, swollen, swaying as if in a breeze. Is it suspended from a beam? Orphan-Monster laughs and lets go of the hair. Young Pelle is panting: Mim feels his throat, sore from screaming. His is fire and so is hers—a memory within a memory finds her, being slapped by that other hand, that small monster with a square mouth, like Beede's.

This boy now doing the tying, Mim remembers, as Pelle remembers, had previously beaten Pelle till he had yelled everything out, till he was quiet: and now breath is only for breathing.

From Mim's hotel room doorway, Suspender said, "Get down there and get to work."

"Fine-it." Mim found the knot on her ankle, untied it, and pulled rope from her legs, leaving damp snake-bundles on the floor. She dressed and went downstairs, but couldn't let go of that Orphan-Monster, of who he might be.

ELEVEN

KISS

I

Stain, clang, drench. Beauty and filth mud-colored the carnival.

It rained for a week. It rained for two weeks. Longer. Hung over from persistent muck, work, drink, the carnies traded an indolent headcold. Even their breath was waterlogged and slow, as if their breath, too, wore turgid leather boots to slog through the mess that, each day, inched higher.

Mim's hands became bloated fish from the constant chasing of water. Suspender wanted to salvage what they could of his rides and machines. They made a mountain of debris, trash heap of lost hope. They kept finding dead, blue-white snakes everywhere. No one found the eyelash viper.

"Never knew we would need to keep water snakes." Suspender laughed.

Things weren't staying true; things shuffled like Cleopatra's cards, abandoning the fact of simple plane and stretching against nature, sprouting hair, teeth, and playing go-go, hiding in the folds of the Eight Mile Suspended Carnival.

Think to your past. Recall my oratory about the need for play? We think of play as a child's game, as fun, but it's never that simple. Sometimes it's a mirror trick.

No one had slept a full night since the rain. They nodded off where they stood, or fell over anywhere for a couple hours. Sometimes Mim would open *What Every Girl Should Know* and read; soon the letters of the words coiled, linked arms to describe the body and spirit of the growing female, and danced her to sleep. Mim's eyes were layered with varnish. Sometimes the scene before her appeared to be painted, a backdrop, like the Camera of Illusion. How long could a world stretch into sinew and mirage, foist on the watcher the suffocating seduction of sound, light, beauty when it's been sold for too little, or too much?

If the world was not the world, but only painted in front of her, what would that signify? A façade, like the sign now drenched in rain and nearly invisible in the downpour—*The Eight Mile Suspended Carnival*—still flying, if you can call it that, still boasting words stretched on rotting canvas across the maw of this world which was possibly only daubed in front of Mim's weary eyes. The moon? The moon next to the sign had been forgotten.

II

Mim stepped in the puddle that was everywhere. Pits and rocks and valleys that hadn't mattered when it was dry now woke to foil movement. Lo-Lo unpacked his *grandes jambes*, the stilts, for moving through mud, but despite his expertise, the mud was too thick; several times, he fell. Mim lugged metal ride carcasses to pile atop the mountain. Better to be rained on than drowned in standing water. Better tickled than submerged. If you squeeze your toes as you walk, your boots don't get caught in the mud. Who cares that your calves ache?

One morning, or afternoon—who could tell?—Lo-Lo accosted Suspender. "Fix my kitchen roof," he said.

They had hauled the freezer up to the kitchen and Suspender was performing a delicate reanimation, because it had suffered from the flood.

"Fix my roof! I need no drips," Lo-Lo said.

"Keep it dry and I'll do, just to shut you up."

Lo-Lo and Mim rigged a tent above the leaky roof to keep Suspender from the rain while he welded flat scraps to cover the holes.

III

After the first two days of rain, water had slunk in everywhere. As for the basement, folks, open that door and all you see is bad luck. Bad luck. A sick, lurching pool of loss. Suspender rigged a pump, but there was so much water everywhere, it just seeped back in.

In the hotel, Suspender made a concoction of grease, and carnies boarded up windows and sealed cracks around jambs. The grease coated their hands like tar. They marked time by *when it was dry*. But no one talked about whether it would be dry again. They might silently hope, but no one said the words.

During early flood days, Mim could exile thoughts of Beede. Navigating air that had become water—working without drowning—required her complete attention. Complication surrounded each physical act. But then Beede crept back in. Where was he? Timmy Zuzu couldn't cross back to the factory, so he played carny and bailed out their world like everyone else. What was the situation over there? The death pill factory stood on a hill, up from the river. Had Beede sung of alabaster? Years ago, at the river, Mim had bled after he burrowed inside her, but now all her blood was gone. She held the stone egg and missed him. Considered blood, and *What Every Girl Should Know*. Considered the other boy, the Orphan-Monster in Suspender's memory, how square his mouth was, and deliberated on what she didn't or couldn't catch with words. Vibrations in her head. She carried the egg in her pocket, and remembered Beede's story.

IV

Then, one morning, the sky was not the thick ugly color that went on forever, but pinkish grey. Slowly, while they ate breakfast, pink shoved lethargy aside, and all became quiet. The taps on the kitchen roof stopped.

"What's that?" Lo-Lo asked.

Suspender growled, and kept eating.

But by four o'clock, sun sliced through clouds. Brightness stung Mim's eyes, and everything, even the steeping structures they hadn't been able to rescue shone in the sun. Some carnies laughed, and some of them cried.

In the sun, Suspender's face was a leather boot, discarded in a root cellar. Before the flood, Mim had seen a boot like that, why one boot alone, she didn't know. In the basement, in a crevasse near a pile of ancient, sprouted potatoes. The boot fascinated Mim: whose foot? Where was its mate? That imponderable boot was the same hue of rain-Suspender's face. During the deluge, no one had bathed unless you count rain. Who could think of such frippery; everyone was covered with dirt. But Suspender's face had been replaced with that boot, unsure why it was abandoned, wary to trust the blushing sun, this new attraction, the sun—.

The waterlogged nightmare, how long had it been? Sleep was an unreachable memory, and Time stretched and shrank like an inchworm, like a snake, and days had yawned into weeks, and so much had washed away.

Mim, as Mim, hadn't ever had much, but she had her body. Which ached from bailing, hauling, craning to stay dry, which didn't work but was involuntary; humans react, no choice, bodies react to an impossible rain, futile. Clammy, lost, missing Beede but unable to recall his face . . . maybe he had fled . . . the roar of rain drowning everything but the urge to salvage what could be lifted, sheltered. *Save remnants of a life that was already nearly nothing.*

Sun on her head. Because she was human, and bodies react, her eyes and the corners of her mouth moved upward, toward the kindness.

Lo-Lo gave everyone a glass of wine, yes, even before dinner. "Special circumstances," he said.

The carnies sprawled on the hotel porch, speckled in pinkish light, and the wine tasted salty and bitter but after the second sip Mim's tired muscles relaxed, and giddiness flooded her gut like freedom. So good not to be pressed down anymore! People smiled. Even those who had cried now smiled, laughed, located their forgotten hearts, unnecessary for a while— hearts cannot bail. Tiger hugged Suspender. They ate dinner early, and slept until they were full.

———————

In the silence, there are actually heaps to hear. Train your ears. Slow your breath until you glean what's left. What's been missing. The exhalation. Feel your shoulders drop. Everything you've ignored during The Disaster hasn't disappeared. Even if it's in the river and snagged on a rock, been taken captive, or submerged in mud, it's still there, still out there somewhere. Maybe sleeping, maybe waiting. Maybe it's only the bones.

Maybe the next thing that happens is: whatever's waiting wakes up.

V

It was time to begin again. Slog, sort, and make sense of the bedlam.

At breakfast, Suspender told Mim to repaint the banner.

"Already? Isn't there other work first?"

"Gotta remember our name, right? Banner confirms we're still here."

Suspender told Rubyat and a couple others to lay out plywood under a ladder on the swampy ground. Mim lugged leftover paint to the plywood island. She mixed the stiff paint. Probably good it had thickened, because the canvas itself was still damp from rain. After she had painted a word and a half, she put down the brush, and looked away from the banner to stretch her neck. And saw Beede. Walking toward the carnival, leading Beatrice by rope, her mouth muzzled with leather straps.

"Oh!" Mim said.

"Oh to you!" Beede said.

All the damp burned out of Mim when she saw his square mouth, but she couldn't do a thing about it. "You're alive."

"Yes, darling!" he said.

"It's Beatrice!" Mim yelled toward the hotel, and a chain of human echoes delivered the news.

Cleopatra peeked from where she had been airing her tent canvas, saw the animal, and rushed—sobbing, wailing—toward the gate, enfolded Beatrice in her arms. Mim's knees wanted to collapse on the climb down the ladder. Hearing the rumpus, all the carnies within range came to see.

Beatrice. Thin and dirty, flank feathers missing.

Cleopatra grabbed the rope. "Why are you strangling her?" She removed the straps.

"Got skittish. Bit one of my men," Beede said.

There were wounds. Beatrice barked, shimmied from Cleopatra's grasp and sped toward her pen. Cleopatra caught her, and gave her some sugar.

"Kind of you to bring her back," Suspender said to Beede.

"No trouble. Well, a bit of trouble. Part of the bridge washed out. Needs repair. Lucky we are—an undamaged boat turned up after the storm, so I could return your friend."

Suspender watched Beede.

"Where did you find her?" Lo-Lo asked.

Beede kept looking at Mim. She compressed what had woken inside her body and didn't return his glance.

"Night that rain commenced," Beede said, "there she was by the river on our side, right? Honking and barking. Must have swam too deep in the river. I was down there,"—he glanced at Mim—"and it started to rain, and that one had a hurt foot, maybe stuck under a rock, maybe a branch, I don't know but anyhow, there she was. Naturally, I yanked her out. I meant to bring her back sooner, but with all the rain . . . "

During his reportage, Beede puffed up, stood tall to tell his story, but he was still a head shorter than Suspender.

Suspender stared at Beede for a while. "She must've chased the goats."

Timmy Zuzu, who had been burning dead snakes, joined the crowd.

"What-ho, Zuzu," Beede said. "Wondered where you were."

"Got stuck over here just before the flood," Zuzu said.

"Guess you did," Beede said. "Boys and I were dry across there. Some of the boys got spooked by the deluge, and took off. Don't guess they made it too far. They'll be back. We sheltered your creature in the dormitory. Couldn't stay out in the rain, busted paw and all. Wouldn't let me look at it, and wasn't pleased with our lodgings. Spit and fussed when I tried to help. After a couple days, she took some bread soaked in milk and whiskey. Must have been hungry."

"Wouldn't we all," Lo-Lo said.

"Name's Lucien B. Dunavant." Beede offered his hand to Suspender.

Suspender didn't reciprocate. "This is my place," he said.

Beede rubbed his hands together. "So I gather. Carnival, how'll you do? Looks a bit of a mess."

"Once it dries up, we'll be alright. Or maybe we'll be on our way," Suspender said.

Lo-Lo chuckled.

"I don't need a reward for returning your kin, but wouldn't turn down an ounce of beverage," Beede said.

Suspender nodded toward Timmy Zuzu, who filled a metal cup and handed it to Beede.

"Thanks kindly." Beede raised the cup.

"You didn't happen to find three goats, did you?" Lo-Lo asked.

"Goats? You keep goats?"

"Yes. Lost exactly three goats. One of them a snowy." Suspender watched Beede swig wine. "Beatrice usually traces their whereabouts. I'm astonished she went off without them, flood or no flood."

"Goats. Now you ask, one of the overnight boys mentioned he saw a white goat near the river. Broken neck. Ugly business."

Lo-Lo groaned. "Poor Zlateh. Could have brought her back for the meat. Was it still fresh?"

"Didn't think to check," Beede said.

Nelda laughed quietly. "Chefs, grabbers of cadavers."

Beede scowled at Nelda. Mim thought back, his word *coon*? Coon? Means what exactly? How he reckoned about people because of skin? So much about Beede was tarnished, bent up like a bad wire. Could a bent wire be reworked? There was sometimes that closed, flat look in his eyes; he knew everything, had *decided* about everything, but he decided bent up and wrong.

"You don't speak shoddily," Beede said to Nelda. "But someone must have taught you the tongue."

"What? What makes you assume that?" Cleopatra asked.

"Tell me, how does she talk so well?" Beede asked Cleopatra.

"How do I talk so well?" Nelda said. "Am I not standing here? Why not address me? You speak around me. I am not a child."

Suspender spit at the ground, then spoke to Beede. "It would appear that Spurlock and your pack over there are not enlightened on humanity, are they?"

"Never mind, meant no offense," Beede said.

"Fling an arrow, but watch how it strikes," Nelda said.

"The river gives birth after such a rain," Anton the Younger said.

"What?" Cleopatra asked.

"This talk of arrows and cadavers!" Anton said. "We must go catch fish."

"We can't eat poisoned fish," Mim said.

"Why poisoned?" Beede asked.

"Offal drains into the river from your factory," Nelda said. Cleopatra smiled.

"Any fish up river from that factory will perform delicious on a plate," Anton said.

"No, thank you," Lo-Lo said. "I'll add my own salt."

Suspender took his ballyhoo coin from his pocket, spun it. "The rain will have washed things clean enough. At least until death production resumes. Wait till the silt settles. Silty fish is bad luck. Anton, go consider the bridge. Perhaps I myself can patch it."

"Death production? A fairly cold term for our work, sir," Beede said.

"Am I concerned with the temperature of my words, Dunavant? Many trade in cold words."

Beede looked at him. "Didn't catch your name."

"No, you didn't. Maybe you missed it. Or maybe *I* spoke shoddily," Suspender said, and carnies laughed.

Beede grinned, but looked unhappy, like he had lost a game. He finished his wine and wiped his mouth with a handkerchief. "High ground at our factory. We'll be up to production again soon. All's well, beyond missing Zuzu here." He handed Zuzu the empty cup.

"Crafty, to built on a hill," Lo-Lo said.

"Well now, we've got work to do," Suspender said.

Beede looked at Mim. "Some mighty fine people you got here, sir," he said to Suspender.

"Boy did we hunt for our Beatrice," Lo-Lo said. "Thought she had perished!"

"Thought she had been washed away in the river," Mim said. She touched the stone egg in her pocket.

"I can see why you would think so, miss," Beede said, "One swollen river that was, bawdy torrent. A punishment of rain." The sound of his voice heated Mim's body, the parts he had kissed, the parts he had entered. Too much, turned sour now. He pulled up his sleeve. A black ribbon circled his wrist. Was it hers, the scrap that had restrained her hair from the shy wind? "Zuzu, you coming?" It wasn't a question. Zuzu gave the cup to Lo-Lo.

"Yes, well, we're all glad now the rain's stopped," Suspender said. "Too bad our Beatrice is so wounded."

Beede tipped his hat, and he and Zuzu went toward the gate, and out.

Mim held the egg and tried to quiet her body, which, like any other human body, generally reacted to the changeable world surrounding it.

VI

Cleopatra and Mim took turns sitting with Beatrice. Mim gently touched her velvety cheek. Beatrice didn't flinch, just stared at Mim through bloodshot eyes. Mim touched her snout, soft and wet, like something hidden in the river. A turgid leaf floated above Beatrice's head.

. . . Blur of feather, fur, motion, sound . . . power . . . jumbled engorgement of thoughts . . . screams, a hurricane of Luna moths . . . bashing against *la vida dura*, to release all misery, all pain and pointless flight . . . only a week to live anyway . . . cannot escape the cycle . . . only breed and move through the mash of voice and soul . . .

. . . And alongside the colors and musky smell of Beatrice's rage and fear, Mim swoops into the wind again, and the rope-wind uncoils around her, then burrows into her soul, and into Beatrice's soul . . .

Not like seeing a person's memory, but in her bones Mim understood what Beatrice had survived: taunts and beatings from factory men, being strung up, whipped, fighting against the urge to give up and dangle, like that shady form in Suspender's memories, faint, but always there, an echo of something corrupted and terrible.

Beatrice's jaw shuddered, then she exhaled at Mim. Mim could see that Beatrice knew what Mim had witnessed. Beede had let it happen. Had *done things*, too. Beatrice nudged Mim with her swollen nose-beak. Mim kissed the velvet, luscious, heart-busting.

Mim tried to fix into solid what she had seen. The panic and rage, the voices . . . and Beede. Was it Mim's fault somehow, for going to the river, being with him . . . was there something she could have done to stop the death pill men from hurting Beatrice? Beatrice had survived. Maybe the animal would forget somehow, someday. But how could Beede have hurt her? Maybe she was mistaken, had misread. Could Cleopatra help her decipher? No. If Cleopatra knew he had hurt Beatrice, she would kill him. The carnies disbelieved in war, but revenge was different. Cleopatra was strong, and loved the creature too much to ignore such a thing.

No. He *couldn't* have done it, not Beede. But . . . his foulness about Nelda. *Fling an arrow but watch how it strikes.*

Cleopatra came to the pen where Mim was reading *What Every Girl Should Know*. The scent of fenugreek surrounded her, and ginger, and maybe nettle. Living so near the apothecary, Mim recognized this perfume.

"I hope she can rest." Mim closed the book.

"I wish I knew what happened. It's so cloudy," Cleopatra said. "What about you?"

Mim shook her head. "I didn't see anything."

Cleopatra took the book from Mim. "What's this?"

"An old lady in Wistmount gave it to me."

Cleopatra opened and read some pages. "Interesting. 'Every girl should first understand herself: she should know her anatomy . . . ' Yes. Useful. Nelda would appreciate this, too."

Later, Cleopatra braided Mim's hair while Nelda read passages aloud, her voice rolling over words like they were bodied in her mouth.

"I like this bit: 'The girl of wealth, of the so-called upper class, can beautify herself and adorn her body with the costliest jewels and fabrics. All eyes are upon her in admiration of her exquisite taste and attractive appearance. Yet this same manifestation in a working girl is condemned. Any attempt on the part of a working girl to give expression to the desire to be beautiful is considered *dangerous to her welfare*; is spoken of as her *awful desire for trinkets*.'"

"I adore trinkets," Cleopatra said.

"Me too," Mim said.

"Exactly!" Nelda turned the page and continued to read. "'A craving for beauty and pleasure, dancing, music, singing and laughter, which comes down to her from primitive woman, together with a burning desire for—and love of—romance, characterize the adolescent girl and often remain with her far beyond the adolescent age.'"

"We need something to make up for our indignities," Cleopatra said.

"And our misunderstood charms," Nelda said.

A narrow leaf twitched above Nelda's head, then spun, as if caught on a tiny twister.

Mim is with Nelda, who is barely a teenager . . . an infant strapped to her back . . . found in the field last week, an infant, a life Nelda has to take care of, an infant who will not keep quiet. Baby strapped to her back while she chops at the dirt with a hoe, high grass scratching her legs, a snake slides past her foot, grasshoppers jump everywhere like the ground is spitting them out . . . Mim feels the sweat that covers Nelda's body, wet baby squirming and whimpering on her back, how a human needs to do, how even this young, we must keep moving. Nelda crouches and so does Mim, unwraps the baby from her back, shushes and rocks him, brings him to her breast but nothing comes out, he's not from her body, but he is from her bones, no idea which mama left him in the grass, or whether the mama was even still around, or alive. Mim's eyes fill as Nelda's do, the burden and boon of this life she has to keep alive, free but not eased, free isn't so simple as the small word sounds . . . free but still beholden, free is not fine and easy, free drains you dry even in this drenching heat, with the yelling boss and the few pennies at day's end. And the baby strapped to your back, so small, all lung and tears until Nelda puts her breast to his mouth, and he tries and tries but she has nothing, so though she no more calming herb to add, she feeds him rice water from a bottle, she feeds him on rice water and love and sweat, nothing more to give. She is crying in the grasshopper field, still enslaved though her mama was born "free", fucken freedom isn't a beacon, it's a lie, a few pennies for a day of toil. Through the dry grass Nelda and Mim hear a body move toward them, swish and footfall on dry ground. Nothing left to offer, but unwilling to give up, Nelda straps the baby back to her body and runs, and runs, until she and Mim can no longer hear the man back there in the grass, and into the trees they go, where the air still suffocates, but at least there's no sun, and the trees cool her fire.

"Nelda, you never ask me about seeing things," Mim said.

"What should I ask?"

"*About* it," Mim said.

"Do you want to tell me something?"

"Nothing particular."

"I'll leave your mystery alone. It's not hurting anyone." Nelda smiled at Mim and resumed reading.

Where did Nelda find this acceptance, this peace? How is such tranquility possible? The voices of Mim's elders were a comfort. She drifted off to sleep.

VII

After the rain stopped, after everyone began to sleep again, they compared flood dreams. Carnies told of being submerged in buildings, drenched in fields, or subsumed by the river; everyone had a different fear, but it was the same dream. One morning, Willie climbed onto a table and performed a recitation:

> "Day after day, day after day,
> We stuck, nor breath nor motion;
> As idle as a painted ship
> Upon a painted ocean.
> Water, water, everywhere,
> And all the boards did shrink;
> Water, water, everywhere,
> Nor any drop to drink."

Suspender applauded. "Thank you ever so, William. And Mr. Coleridge. Now. The boards, our boards, did they shrink? Must test things out, see what works. Must pay respect to the HydroWheel."

Somehow, the HydroWheel was undamaged—and had, in fact, gained strength from the flood. Suspender summoned everyone to the moving picture tent. "A little fun won't kill us," he said.

"Fun? How fun!" Nelda said.

"Me, I shall pop up some corn," Lo-Lo said.

Inside the moving picture tent was rank like everywhere. Thin, grassy fuzz masked all surfaces at the carnival.

"Looks like moss," Suspender said.

"Moss can sleep for decades," Cleopatra said.

"I have an idea," Suspender said. "We'll hunt club moss by the river."

Mim caressed the tent moss. While everyone settled onto wooden benches, Suspender took the motor from its shelf, and plugged it into the air wire. He fed the reel into the praxinoscope, and flipped a switch. The machine sputtered, flickered. Then pictures. Lo-Lo brought the roll-cart, laden with pans of popped corn, and carnies grabbed handfuls into their laps. "All hail the Maneri method!"

"All hail the Maneri method!" the carnies yelled.

"Oh, what glory to be entertained," Nelda said. "And fed."

A sandy beach, palm trees. A boat on the horizon. A music hall full of drunken cowboys. Ten ladies on seven bicycles. Carnies watched and laughed, relishing the break.

"How about another?" Suspender again fed the machine.

A woman with lace over her head danced with a man in a beaded jacket. The carnies watched in silence.

"Poor Desiree," Lo-Lo said, finally. He took another handful of popped corn.

"One cannot toy with suspension. She knew that," Suspender said.

"Who's Desiree?" Mim asked.

"Turn it off," Cleopatra said.

But Suspender left it, and the dancer spun in a circle, while several other men surrounded her. She laughed silently in the choppy light. She began to undress, but the film ended before she had finished.

"Show's over." Suspender took the reel from the machine and tucked it back into the crate. Everyone else got up to leave, but Mim stayed.

In the dark, between stale canvas folds, she closed her eyes. She was never alone at the carnival, even in her room; all through the night, she heard floorboards creak. Always someone busy doing, stirring, snoring. Here in the tent, it was quiet. Memories of the flood, new memories, washed over her: clean, bail, and wait for the rain to stop. *Pink sky. Exhale.*

Eyes still closed, she conjured Desiree, exquisite flower and lace, and danced with her; Mim wore the beaded jacket and, still in loose mucky boots, she stomped her own small feet on the eroded marble floor. Desiree smelled like sweet dust-spice underneath. But Mim soon was surrounded by men, pushing her away so they could get closer to Desiree.

"You sleeping?" Suspender stood where the moving pictures had been. The light coming through the tent door had changed.

He took out pieces of praxinoscope, dusted them with a red cloth. He opened boxes of strips, and held them up to show her. "Indestructible. These will still haunt. Good. You know that man, don't you?"

"What man?"

"That Dunavant from the factory who wrangled Beatrice." He studied the strips.

Mim didn't know how to answer, sensed he would be angry if she said yes, but angry too, and moreover he would know, if she lied.

"He knows *you*. How he watched you."

"I didn't notice."

Suspender laughed, all gag and choke. "You noticed. You were with him at the river, the night the flood began." He hadn't asked her anything, so she kept her mouth shut and waited. "That man is not what you add up."

"Because he flung arrows at Nelda?" Her throat tightened around the words.

Suspender put the strips back and came closer, sat beside her. He stroked her grimy hair with a grimy hand. His face was swathed by the grey twilight that had tiptoed into the tent with him.

She didn't pull away.

He traced the line of her mouth with his finger, whispered, "Look at you."

A new thing inside her made it hard to breathe.

He kissed her. Surprisingly clean. "You're going to work. You're going to lure him; you'll be my shine. My ballyhoo." He laughed.

"What do you mean?"

He moved his hands in the air as if holding something, making something. "The plan is still arriving."

A swaying leaf shuddered above his head.

The small lion-maned boy he used to be sits in a chair by the window, leans toward light. Pelle's mother is gone. In the early morning, he holds long steel needles, tying knots, Mim thinks at first, but then her hands, along with his, aren't tying but knitting thin grey wool. The wool smells damp. A shape has yet to come forward. Each loop is an empty mouth, silent, silent because mother always told him to be quiet, said her head hurt, said she had to go to town, said *get off me, don't cling, you're not a baby anymore*. She taught him but she'll never know how well he knits, how careful he is with every mouth-loop, feeding each need. How silently he works. He and Mim smell his mother's powder. When she left, she forgot to take her scents, the faint, sweet bergamot. Her boy believed she would come back to get them, but she never did, and now he knows she never will. Every morning he wakes and Mim wakes and every morning together they remember again that his mother is gone. Every morning in this elusive light he knits before his father gets up, and Mim knits with him, every morning, feeding the hungry mouths, dropping stitches and going back to catch them again.

Had Pelle gone? Mim's skin, easy and still while he was close to her, now trembled, itchy, impatient. She sat for a while more, pressed hands against her arms, strove to calm her skin. Alone in the moving picture tent, she recalled the Luna moth of Beatrice's fear, the futility of a life lived simply in order to procreate and die. Her mind chased clouds: what did he mean? She had *been* working, but his command about Beede was different. And he had kissed her. It meant something.

Different from Beede's tongue pressing in, which now would taste bent up wrong, like what he said about Nelda, would taste like hurting Beatrice. Different from the sad kiss Lo-Lo had given her before the hunt. Suspender's kiss was a stamp, but more, and gone so fast like fluttering, light and pure and wordless like the Luna moth. He took his time with things. He understood ropes.

Ropes.

Mim slid from the tent and back to her room, quick and quiet in the pinkish-grey twilight.

To her bed. To the rope she had shed, the tangle she had shoved under the bed, where she hid her inheritance.

The rope hurt her hand; the fibers crawled and tingled, but she caressed it, forcing herself to feel the texture, full of spiteful purpose, the texture she wanted, didn't want, wanted, wanted around her, to contain her, capture the rough rubies of heart and body, places even Beede hadn't visited. She took rope and unwound, unwound, hitting knots and bumps and kinks and seeing the path to each undoing, her own secret Impossible, which had mingled with her wayward skin, that stuff that didn't want her, that stuff that wanted to run off and away, back toward the wall of wind, back to wherever it had been before that. Where had her skin and the rest of her been—did her skin have a memory to find?

131

Mim needed weight and magnitude, a word oft used at the carnival. Twists of snaky rope pulled her from herself, toward herself, out of her head, into her body. Into what mattered. The rope conferred with Mim, and aligned against the rebel, her skin, pale as the sad milk Lo-Lo drank when ill . . . *skim off the layer of cream,* he said, *save for later, stir into the cream char-spice and paprika, bits of color, stir, drink it down.* That thick stuff smelled foul, like soap, but Lo-Lo claimed it helped the gullet. Soon friend rope coiled around her nakedness. It was better naked, more real, and the weight of her tether, its bodied texture, would save her. She wound rope around her chest, her breasts. Frustrated, trying to balance her needs, she unwrapped and tied it again, looser, but snug enough, and on her tender nipples the rough tongue of rope licked, and she touched the soft parts between her legs and she moaned and moaned, and wonder flooded everything.

PART TWO

TWELVE

THE SPIDERWEB

I

The heavens weep and decant themselves. Scratch-land becomes sponge. Flooded shrubs turn green, and a fringe of moss covers the world. Spines glisten around the Tower of Misfortune, exhausted by rain; wet metal wonders *will it ever dry?* Mildew rewrites history, ponders whether trees will rise, and creeps among the layers of paint that once again proclaims *The Eight Mile Suspended Carnival*. Treasures are brought by the current. Carnage, chaos, borders upended, shattered, reformed. What life gives us, we must harvest, be it good or ill.

The return of green refreshed all other colors. A new day. The flood reshaped the contours of the carnival and everyone in it. Snakes drowned, people survived but moved differently through space; water transformed everything. Mount Detritus became Moss Hill. Some Tobeys left, and new ones came.

Suspender wanted to see what they could salvage. Anton wanted to fish.

"Refrain from eating silt, I beg you," Suspender said. "Wait another day. Set your angle on the jumbles. Wash things clean with underground water at the hotel." He organized a reconnoiter. Carnies dragged a wagon as close as they could to the river, brought boards along in case wheels got stuck.

Lo-Lo transformed his *grandes jambes* into poles to pull things in with. Jars, wire, bones.

Two canoes had washed ashore, one in pieces, one intact. The rotten dock had been reduced to a single piling that caught a baby carriage. Suspender wrenched from the muck a brown object, larger than his head, and lifted it to show.

"What *is* that?" Mim asked.

"Want it?" He handed it to her.

Muck-covered, foul, and heavy. She rinsed it in the river's gush. A skull. Lower jaw gone, but the teeth on top were huge and shaggy. It was ghastly, and full of primordial power.

"Can anyone discern the origin of that species?" Lo-Lo asked.

Mim held out the skull. Anton the Younger touched the contours. "Horse," he said.

"That's no horse," Lo-Lo said. "I've seen a horse head."

"Haven't we all. Look at the nose. Too stubby for a horse," Nelda said.

"Sharp teeth, or they were," Anton said. "Maybe polar bear."

"Polar bear skull! What do you say, carnies? That'll play well," Suspender said.

"Give me that polar bear," Cleopatra said. She wrapped the mess in her bindle.

In the dim water, something undulated, like a child's body. Mim extended her pole to pull it in. A swath of silk wrapped around branches. Crouching at the shore, she untangled and wrung out the silk . . . its embellishment included a tear, a hole a hand could fit through. Could be washed and mended. It was cold. She wrapped it around her neck and tied it twice.

The carnies hauled stuff to the wagon to take back and sort. Nestled both canoes into the river landing, in case. They might be useful someday. All else would go to the fire.

Later in the bathroom sink, Mim scrubbed the silk. So delicate, but so strong . . . she washed grit from the fabric, but between each thread, silt made muddy-beige what might have once been pale yellow, like Cleopatra's wedding dress. After the water ran clear, she wrung it out and took it back to her room. The scarf dried quickly, the silk's embroidered flowers now weeds, filaments of floss torn and dangling. She mended what she could and tied it around her neck. Its compression helped her skin. But she needed more.

She needed to be tethered, contained.

Rope has secret ways that have nothing to do with words. Rope is all body, the heft of fibers wound around each other and around Mim. She stared at the fibers in the light in her room, unwound them and put them back together. She had studied this substance and it told her its stories, and so she knew.

II

Everyone thinks about what's there. A body, a structure, a well-cooked tenderloin on the plate. It exists until you eat it. But as before, I train your gaze toward the importance of boundary, line, edge. Toward negative space. We wrap ourselves into neat or sloppy packages, spit-comb our hair, chew a handful of mint leaves. Make all this meat acceptable. Hide the rot. But really the borders are invisible. The borders escape notice, and keep us tidy. Irrelevant, the presentation, the spit-comb. Your wig does not concern me! You can fall all over the place and still, I will hesitate before I let you in, let you touch me.

Sometimes our armor comes from where we don't expect. Sometimes our armor is conveyed down the river and into our waiting arms.

Each day when she rose, Mim tied on her river scarf and wound daughter twine from mother rope around her legs and arms. Containment suited her, kept her from flying away. She tried different ways to wrap: sometimes she had to adjust again and again before she could dress and begin the day. The result was worth the effort.

While Mim helped Lo-Lo and Nipsy wash and put away, Suspender dropped a stack of paper notices on the kitchen table. Said he drew them up himself. The work, and the rope wrapped round Mim's limbs warmed her skin, but this sensation was almost familiar now. Nelda sat at the table and stitched three pockets into her green dress. Tiny emerald bedlets, to hold one kitten apiece.

Suspender said to Lo-Lo, "Ready to hunt provisions?"

"My feet are still dehydrating," Lo-Lo said. Some other carnies had abandoned their boots to liberate clammy feet.

"Wistmount won't mind if you're unshodden," Suspender said.

"I have doubts," Lo-Lo said. "And surely the road's a failed soufflé."

"Road might be bad, but you don't have to cross any bridges."

"I want to go, too," Mim said.

"Did I request the help of a strump?" Lo-Lo asked. "What I really need is to cut my hair."

"Hair can wait. We need stuffs," Suspender said. "Put up these notices. Reopening Saturday."

"You droop me," Mim said to Lo-Lo. "Of course you need help."

"Thou shalt not sing," he said.

"Smart boy." Nelda fed the kittens bits of jerky but the runt wouldn't eat. "I've heard you sing, Mim. It ain't attractive. Even the string-box can't cover that mess."

Then a leaf above Nelda's head.

Nelda wraps a few belongings of the boy who used to be the baby on her back, and some of her money into a rag bundle, and takes the boy's hand, and walks, quick quick, looking down; Nelda and Mim and the boy walk with purpose toward a building at the corner of a quiet street. A store, crates of vegetables and fruit in the window; Nelda and Mim hand the boy the bundle, and put a coin in his hand, and together they tell him, "Go buy a peach." The boy does, without question—says yes to who he calls *Nenna*, and steps into the mouth of the shop where Nelda knows that a kind woman works, a family who might shelter him, or find a place that will. She believes this. It's the only way to know he will survive; she has no mother's milk for him, only her dust and the urge to roam. If it doesn't kill you, you're stronger for it, she once heard someone say. The Lord in whom she has never believed won't give anyone more than they can bear, but the burden of this boy isn't hers, and she can't carry it any longer. *He survived this long, he'll be okay*, she thinks, and Mim thinks it too, and Nelda and

Mim watch him buy the peach, and abandoning him, they run down the street toward the train, each step forging Nelda's new lightness, nothing but her own bindle on her back, to find work, to find a way, even through wet eyes.

In the hotel kitchen, Lo-Lo tied back his hair, and left to prepare the truck.

Nelda petted the runt and closed her eyes. Mim went to Nelda and rubbed her shoulders. A sound came from the kitten, but it wasn't the kitten. It was Nelda who did the purring.

Mim and Lo-Lo strapped themselves into the truck and drank fermented frog bean liquor. He had been experimenting.

"This is terrible!" she said.

They drove through porridge. "Have you heard the legend of the spider queen?" Lo-Lo asked.

The river lapped beyond its edge with the love it had for itself, full of rush and burble, meeting the stream of story that came from his lips. She listened and caught pieces to write down later in her book.

"The spider came from the cracking of an egg. You would never know it to look at them, but the first spider was born when the first egg broke."

"That's not true," she said.

"Don't interrupt!"

"I can speak if I want to."

"Anyone can do anything! I can fly this truck into the sky, but right now, I can't be bothered. You're an unscratchable itch today."

"You, too." Mim poured her frog bean sludge out the window.

"Waste and you'll regret it," he said. "The spider didn't know she was a spider. Only knew she was no longer eggshell."

"She wasn't eggshell?"

"Of course not! The egg fell somehow, hit a stone, I don't know. It was a long time ago."

"What kind of egg was it?"

"Maybe the kind Beatrice came from, but smaller. I wasn't there. Listen up, even that spider didn't ask all these questions. *Well, since I am no longer egg nor shell, I must make a buffer, somewhere for myself and all these legs to dwell.'* She didn't even think about food, to start. Thought about what she wasn't, and thought about shelter. Years passed, and she got hungry. Who wouldn't?"

"I'm hungry," Mim said.

"Too bad you dumped those frog beans. You'll eat in Wistmount. The spider didn't even know what she wanted to eat. She had no menu, no chef. No garden. She had a web, cold shelter it provided in the wind— what the arse demon possessed her to make a house flat and fine like that? How did she know she had silk? Not exactly the first thing you would puzzle out, once you cracked free of the shell of a *don't-ask-me-what-kind-of-beast* egg. Would you? Spit silk out yer bum? But she had this flat fine home, and because its substance had escaped her arse, it was sticky. And in stuck a fly."

"This is starting to make sense."

"Make sense? Nothing makes sense. Rain and rain that won't stop, *that* doesn't make sense. This place, this whorl in which we live, none of it makes sense. I'm only telling a story. Don't ask me please for sense."

Mim laughed and first, Lo-Lo frowned. Then laughed too.

By the time they arrived in Wistmount, Mim was dizzy from hunger. There were folds inside her that would never have opened if she hadn't arrived at this carnival, what her friend called 'this whorl'. She was changing. She was a woman, and she had no reason to know whether this was new or old—before here, had people loved her, had people found her lovely? And was she? She was younger, but less substantial than Nelda and Cleopatra. Not counting guests, three and no more females worked at the carnival. She had noticed how some of the men looked at her. Sometimes they looked hungry, but perhaps lacked a sticky web to catch food.

"Spiders are funny with food," Lo-Lo said, somehow sensing her notion.

Past the jail, past edges of town that had been completely washed away. Downtown, near the clock tower, people shoveled mud from walk-paths, and tended burning piles of debris. Things that had been dusty were now clean, but the ground was still a sponge that might never dry. Moss overspread the past here, too.

He parked the steam truck in the usual spot and pulled the green pearls.

"Where can we get some food?" she asked.

"Spiders eat as much as they can, when they can. Gluttony. Some churches in Sackfort speak against it. But do they clear cobwebs from the choir loft? No." He slammed the door.

"Is it strange if I ask people?" She trailed him toward the stores.

"Ask them what?"

"If they know me."

"I wouldn't. Answers might break your miniscule heart. Remember last time. If someone knows you, they'll speak up. Just show your lovely face, that's all."

At the grocery store, the man behind the counter said, "You carnies didn't get washed away."

"No, sir," Lo-Lo said. "Neither did you, apparently."

"Well, then."

Many usual provisions were gone, but Lo-Lo found what he could, paid the man, and handed Mim a package of tack. "Carnival's to open back up on Saturday. Mind if I pin a notice outside?"

"I do not," the man said.

"I appreciate it. And spread the word, if you're inclined."

"Sure."

"We'll be off then."

The man didn't do the curse this time, only nodded and stowed the money.

After they loaded the truck with necessities, they went to the public square to pin up more notices. Several men were unearthing a thick rope that appeared to be rooted in the mud near the clock tower, like a giant's pull-toy.

"What's that rope for?" she asked Lo-Lo.

"Zuzu said Spurlock once tied up a man who stole his pork crop. Tied him up for a week."

Tied up for a week, trapped, unable to move . . . she needed rope, but not like that.

Wistmount memorized the flood, and would not forget for a long time.

RETURN OF THE EIGHT MILE SUSPENDED CARNIVAL!

All ye who have survived the downpours,
your drought of diversion has broken!
The MAGNETISMS that pull you to our wondrous gates
have been reinstated
& WE ARE READY!

With new WONDERS to unfold!

CURIOSITIES of NATURE and beyond!

Wishful thoughts will wash the bitter
deluge from your well-tuned palates!

First FIFTY people through the gate,
half price and FREE REFRESHMENTS!

We'll see you on SATURDAY night!

Do make the effort—it hasn't been the same without you.

The notices worked. Saturday night, the carnival brimmed with guests, and Time sprinted toward midnight.

After dinner, Mim unwound her rope skin, and Cleopatra came in without knocking. Quickly Mim pulled on her robe, but Cleopatra saw.

"That's unusual," Cleopatra said.

"Helps me feel . . . stronger," Mim said.

"*Sante*." She lifted her jar of wine. "Little runty died."

"Oh, no," Mim said. "Poor Nelda."

"It's terrible. She's valiant, but it's so terrible."

"Nelda loves so well."

"The fates would please me if she could keep a little sunlight. Maybe time alone will help. She plans to hibernate awhile. Makes sense. But the shade is everywhere: you should have seen my guests tonight, pitiable souls. One wail after another. Death in the family, stunted crops, drowned babies, heartsick, boils, suffering up to here. Makes me passels, but I hate nights like this."

"Did you tell them the truth?" Mim asked.

"The truth?

"Their bad news."

"You know I never lie. Well, I might coat a bitter bit with sweet. Don't want to scare them off completely. I only tell them what's physically bearable. In walked this young man—still sick from the last war—he was the saddest sack of all, and buckteeth, too. I'll tell you about that another time. My words are empty. I need to recline and quench." She did both.

Something rushed between Mim's legs. She looked down, saw a gloss of red. "The moon."

"Well, that's a thing to celebrate." Cleopatra raised her jar and drank. "Go, make ablutions, I'll be here."

Mim took her pad with the ribbons to the toilet room, trying not to make a mess. She washed herself and secured the pad.

Back in her room, she coiled her river scarf around her head as she had begun to do at night. She lay down and listened to Cleopatra hum. And sing. "Oh my dearling, no one has given you a baby this moon. Do not go back to that Dunavant."

"I don't know what you mean."

"You *do*. Do not go to him. He is covered in a skin worse than death. Wear ropes if you must, but do not go to him."

Mim tugged the river scarf down to cover her eyes. "Poor Nelda."

"Truly. Poor dearling Nelda," Cleopatra said.

IV

Because of the rope, Mim's skin became numb in places, vibrated unlike its usual rebellion, its wanderlust. Her shell tried to wake, but couldn't. Mim liked this. She tied loosely around the tender spots. The ropes made her skin heavier. It would stay attached.

One evening, a couple of weeks after the carnival reopened, she sought Cleopatra at her tent because Beatrice had regurgitated dinner, and Mim wasn't sure which digestive remedy to give. Near where the snake pit used to be, Rubyat and three new Tobeys approached. One short, one tall, and one with a top hat.

"Come with us," Rubyat said.

"Why?"

"Fortune-teller said."

"She needs you to get something," said the tall one. "In the attic, said you would recognize it."

"But I need to ask her about Beatrice," Mim said.

"Later. She needs the doohickey right away," Rubyat said.

Mim told Beatrice to wait there for her, but Beatrice trotted off toward the Tower of Doom.

The Tobeys herded Mim to the hotel and up the stairs to the attic, where the freed Impossibles still webbed the rafters, left to dry and forgotten. Mim had checked on them once, but at the time they were still damp. You don't want to store damp rope. What did Cleopatra need from the attic? Ropes had been woven into a set-up dangling from the web, like an intricate seat, but with too many strands to make sense. Rubyat grabbed her arms. She cried out.

"That's a bit rough, no?" Top Hat asked.

"It's only a game," Rubyat said. He tore off her dress, and she stood in only rope, cool air shocking her exposed skin. They circled around her. "You want rope?" Rubyat asked. "Rope we have."

"She's pretty. String her up," the tall one said.

"I bet she can fly!" the short one said.

"I bet she can make this fly." Rubyat pointed between his legs. All except Top Hat laughed.

Mim rushed to break away but Rubyat grabbed and held tight. She wriggled and yelled, "Stop it!" To Top Hat, she yelled, "Make them stop!"

"Too rough," Top Hat said.

Mim yelled and yelled.

"Everyone's at work. Yell all you want. No one hears you," Rubyat said.

"I love tying them up," the short one said.

"Best part," Rubyat said. "Leads to the even better part!"

"Don't seem right," Top Hat said. "I'm leaving."

144

"More for the rest of us." The others held her. Rubyat unwound her ropes and river scarf, and dropped them on the floor. She thrashed, naked, but they pawed her parts and hoisted her into the seat. His breath was horrid, like burnt basil syrup. The others climbed ladders, pulled and tightened ropes, and the rope web opened like a maw, grew teeth, and bit into her parts. The men pushed her, swung her, and laughed and laughed. As she swung, the wall of wind pounded, filled her head with clash and trouble, choking, cackling, creating for itself a face, a soul shaped by the burning cascade, wind in her eyes, her irrelevant eyes . . . the wind's wicked face spun her in circles . . . spinning, shadows, Tobeys . . . then there was Suspender . . . Suspender's mouth moved in the asymmetrical light but the sound of his voice was an orphan. She disintegrated into wind and throb and beat and heart and pulse and terrible, lost skin. As she spun, she saw Suspender throw the tall Tobey to the floor. A thousand years later, he lowered her. The wind was gone.

"Get out of here, you lot," Suspender yelled. "Experiment failed, get out!"

"Just having a game," the tall Tobey said.

Rubyat kicked the tall Tobey.

"Hey! It wasn't me started it!"

"Get out!" Suspender yelled.

Mim could no longer feel her naked skin.

He untied her from the web and piled canvas scraps into a nest and helped her lay down. Covered her gently. "That Tobey Mason was supposed to go fix the Slanting World but I saw him leaving the hotel, so I asked what the arse was going on." His face floating above, he sheltered her in a swath of canvas and her river scarf, the scarf a river where she floated. Inside the wind's darkened womb, there was no buffer of water, no fluid where real babies are held safe. Her only cushion was the wind's internal strife: one wind pushing against the other. It could have been anyone, but it wasn't; it was Mim. Inside that womb, wind had pressed into all physical vacancies.

The color of brown-thick air sickened her. Shadows flew past, bumped into something, but how can air have heft? Air took shape as life and broke her from whatever she used to have, used to be. *Is there a shape to hold? Does anyone miss me?*

The river scarf was all of eternity, flowing before her, beside her, beyond. The scarf was Suspender, was Pelle, the boy he had been, and who he was now, who he would be in the moment his breathing ceased. *Back, back, back, and forward.* The scarf was a way to keep time, a way to hold it in place, a way to mark and a way to survive.

Pelle was crying.

"Water," she said. She noticed strings attached his head to his shoulders. "Your neck isn't made of string."

He looked down at her. The leaf that appeared was silver as a ghost.

Pelle's small head beneath his lion mane, a boy, again a boy, and he is in the barn and he is trying not to see the swaying shadow. The shadow is the shape of something that once lived. To keep his mind off the shape, he makes a miniscule man from pieces of things; a coin-sized wheel for a head, and other parts strung together, delicate metal, a toy. Making this toy calms him. Parts of the body dangle, and Mim feels the thrill of its fine string limbs, and with the boy, she pulls gently so the arms, hands, legs twitch to life. Piece by piece they move together, ordered: a bantam being, a creation, and Mim smiles as Pelle smiles, pulling arms and legs to walk their creation across the dry ground.

Mim focused on the creation, and her body quivered again. Air licked her bare skin. The rope web behind him made a sky; his saddened face was the world.

"You made a person," she said.

"How do you know?"

"I see other peoples' memories." Safer for him to know. Necessary. Why had she waited so long?

After a moment, he wiped his face. "Tell me what you saw."

She did.

He whispered words that she couldn't hear. Maybe they had to do with metal, and rope, and the tired, tired dreams that must still live inside his body. She both knew and didn't know that, as he uncovered her skin and gazed at her naked body, his dreams were released into the air of the rope room. And it was what she held inside her skin that released him. He knelt and held her. Kissed her.

His kiss tasted clean, like before. Full of life. Gentle wind moved from his mouth to hers, buoyed her. She needed him as close as possible, would climb inside his skin if she could. His face was made of candle wax in the dim evening, warming, softening.

"Take those off," she said.

Pelle removed his coveralls, buttons clumsy; bulge between his legs tented his thin under-layer. His ballyhoo coin fell from his pocket. He picked up the coin, lowered himself next to Mim, and laid it in her palm. On the coin was the image of a dog.

"This is beautiful," Mim said.

"Nothing compared to you." He took the coin, pressed it to her lips. "Open up."

She did. He put the coin on her tongue, its flavor mineral, clean. Gently he climbed onto her; his weight on her skin snagged her breath, but she didn't swallow the coin.

"Sorry." He held himself above her, his body forming a contraption, becoming logic, a series of lines and beams and gears to spare her skin. The mineral in her mouth, his penis touching between her legs, and the push of him inside her eclipsed the pain of burning skin, calmed her like his kiss. His machine above her machine, the flavor of their metal, the two became one machine, invisible strings pulling them together and apart. She moved her hips to meet his, whisper-touching, making a box of limbs. Skin inside of skin. The coin's terrain across her tongue, the stillness of the floor beneath, then sunshine inside her as they moved together and apart, sunshine all rosy like when the rain had finally stopped. Suspender paused above her, quivering, his face tight, and didn't breathe, *why did he stop like that,* she pulled up to meet him, she wanted to share insides again. "Don't stop," she said. It was hard to speak through metal. He held himself there, not breathing above her until she pulled him back, brought him inside her again. She didn't care that his weight pushed her now; his breath on her skin was the remedy for everything. The sun broke out again. Through coin, she moaned and moaned, and he put his hand to her mouth, said *shhh,* but she couldn't keep quiet, moaning, loving, and inside, the sunshine spread everywhere.

They slowed down. He rolled onto the floor. His absence hurt. He touched her mouth, parted her lips to reclaim his ballyhoo. She closed her eyes, held the clean taste of him. After a while, she heard movement and looked up. He dressed, and paced the room.

"Pelle," she said.

"No one calls me that," he said.

"What's wrong?" she asked.

"Quiet, I'm thinking."

After several circles, he stopped at a window. One benefit from so much rain: the windows, those that still had glass, were washed clean. But now it was late, past closing time, so there was nothing to see out there, just the night.

He began to map something on the glass with his fingers. "I've been stuck in this mud too long, no story, no plan, only hunger. A beast, my famish blinding me. Vengeance blocked the need for a good plan. Something was missing. I knew it wouldn't work, wasn't ready. When I draw the constellation now, there's a gap shaped like you. How could I be so dull? Who dreamed you up? The twister knew. I had my reasons to stay but that dry twister *knew*. Brought you here, to me." His hands danced, fingers outstretched against the glass, then the fronds of his hands wove together, like tree roots intermingling.

Mim gazed at his hands, at all of him under his coveralls. She had seen and touched his shell, parts he hid from the day. His tremble and beauty almost killed her now. He turned toward her and stared. Then walked closer, and pulled the canvas over her.

"Thank you. Stay here." He left the attic.

What else would she do? Her skin was quiet. Between her legs shone, she supposed, because of the sun that had been there. She needed that again. She needed to be what was missing from his obsidian sky.

THIRTEEN

OCCASIONAL IMPROVEMENTS

I

Shapes are always negotiation. A line, for instance the idea of Time, drawn across the page: past, present, future, a fixed order. But Time can also be a spiral, can become plates—stack as you like. The order is up to whoever does the stacking. If Time is a spiral, does it really matter whether the spiral becomes a channel, a tunnel forward or back? Let's say you find yourself spun like a windblown spider in a room full of ropes, and there you find an idea, a delicious and sticky act, and the act becomes a constant, a star, the sun. Does that affect what happens next? Does its light bear down and open you up? Are you thereafter forever changed? Can you accept the sun for what it is, a star? Or are you burned, ruined by its light? Or something else, some third door?

If something excavates the contents of you, and, even through mystery, illuminates yourself, your whole self, why not simply enjoy that bright bit? If you are the shape that has always been missing, does that mean you get to exhale?

Mim was startled awake by footsteps. Were they going to tie her up again? She clutched canvas around her body and curled into a ball. But when the door opened it was only Suspender. He stared at her. "You still there?"

"I thought it was them."

He said, "No. Only me."

"What we did, can we do that again?" She smiled.

He laughed. "You're hurt, you need a bath. Get up." He helped her rise, wrapped her in the torn dress, and tied it closed with the river scarf. "I'll take this." Around his shoulder he looped the rope she had been wearing, what Rubyat had torn off her.

She was still on that rope; her skin left its scent, its impression. He was taking her with him.

He helped her walk down to the baths. The muscles above her knees were made of water, of nothing. Though she knew her legs were still there, they didn't feel like it.

In the room, the closest tub was almost full. He swirled the water with his hand. "Salt bath. This should help."

She untied the river scarf and dropped her dress on the floor. He looked at her, then away.

"It's okay. It's okay if you see me." She didn't care that she was naked. Let him see her skin. It was good to be seen, good to have this new responsibility, this gift from Pelle.

But his face wasn't soft like a boy anymore; he had regained his mask. He gave her soap from the sink. "Wash up. I'll get the fortune-teller."

She got into the water. "It stings!"

"Give it a minute. Soothing, if you give it a minute." He was right. Soon, the pain subsided and the water was silk. "Better?" he asked.

She nodded and exhaled.

"Good." He left.

The world's fierce wind had blown her here, to this moment of breath . . . submerged in liquid silk, lost from whoever she had been . . . but now, found. The water held its own substance, was protection, was a whole body . . . couldn't unravel like rope, like Time. There was something in her eyes; she was crying.

Cleopatra rushed in with her leather bag of remedies. "Those fucken Tobeys, arseholes, torturing you like that! Oh, poor dearling." She sat beside the tub and stroked Mim's head.

At Cleopatra's gentle touch, Mim folded, and sobbed for a long time.

Cleopatra whispered comforts, tenderness, until Mim grew quiet. Then she took out vials and jars, mixed a salve. "This will help your skin. Can't

150

let it fester. You can't do this anymore. No more Rope Girl. Skin needs to heal."

She held Mim's hand. "Shite. Such a broken world. You already knew that, you didn't need them to prove it on your body."

Would her skin peel off, and fly away? Keeping skin was the whole point of the ropes. Now the sun was gone, and she was raw where the ropes had been, and worse where the Tobeys had tied her. Mim sunk her head below the water and soon, the broken world was muffled and quiet.

Resting later in bed, slathered with salve, a word dangled on a string above her head. *Alabaster*, it said. Everything breaks. Why was Beede so concerned with skin? Maybe Beede had forgotten her. Maybe she should forget him. But Beede and Suspender were *both* inside her skin, now their mixed metals clanged. The sound of Beede was sharp, demanding, and distracted her from the lower, steady echo of Suspender. Pelle. Pelle was clean, kind to her, careful with her sore shell. He salvaged, gave her sunshine. And now he knew what she could see.

But Beede told her stories, traced her face, won the stone egg. Whispered *alabaster*. Too much about skin. He gave her lies. Spat on Nelda. Spewed shadow across the beauty of the carnies and what they believed. Tortured Beatrice, betrayed where Mim had grown fond. How could one man hold such filth hidden for long?

II

Mim woke, stiff and ragged. Only the bed was safe. She recalled a dream, a room full of rusty parts that she was supposed to shape into gold. The pile had been impossible to sort; bits tumbled endlessly to the ground. There was no rope and no wire. She heard steps outside. Someone opened the door and chucked in more parts. She had to keep building but couldn't find the piece she was looking for, or anything to make attachments. Metal edges bit her skin, left splinters that burrowed inside.

She took a deep breath and got up. Her arms began to quiver, then shake . . . she couldn't stop the shaking . . . her whole body . . . a sound was outside herself, then inside . . . her voice . . . an animal . . . a fanged beast, shaking, shaking, shifting until her broken pieces were released and found each other and melted in a fire, like the fire that wakes life from dust.

It was pleasure, it was power . . . this flitter, this light, and the feeling dropped her onto the bed.

Not a dream, but this: flying in the web of ropes, the wind, Suspender, his body careful above hers. *Pelle.* Their sunshine. The ecstatic contraption they had crafted from human bodies.

Lo-Lo arrived with a tray. He pulled the chair beside the bed and sat. "This broth will help." He kissed her forehead, and handed her a cracked green mug. "And a few bites of dinner."

"Thanks." She sipped the sour broth.

While she ate, Lo-Lo read amusing magazine stories aloud. Being a friend. His company made her happy, glad to be his friend, like nothing had happened, no ropes all over, no Tobeys, no rent in the fabric of her skin. *Maybe I should love Lo-Lo,* she thought, but quickly let that idea go, too tangled; already her insides clashed with two kinds of metal, the first and the second—and the second echoed forever.

He finished the gossip and put down the magazine. "*Dummkopf* Tobeys. Good riddance. Suspender miserabled those skells. Out-and-out brawl. He unhooked Rubyat and that whole lot. Decent fishers, but they won't uphold Rule Number Seven. No smooth relations for them. Kicked them straight out of the carnival."

The sunshine returned. She wasn't invisible. There were consequences. "Good," she said.

Later still, Mim propped herself against the pillows. Cleopatra was reading a newspaper. Mim didn't feel like getting up, but sleep had helped. A raw spot on her arm brushed the blanket, a tingle . . . she recalled what Lo-Lo had said, how Suspender exiled those Tobeys. How would this new day be, if, truly, she were no longer invisible? She laughed, and drew a circle around the wound with her finger.

Cleopatra held up the newspaper. A photograph of a lady with short hair. "Look at her!" she said. "How shiny she looks! Let's cut our hair. Just like that. Yours first, then I'll do mine."

"It looks so odd."

"Lighten the load! Occasional improvements! Change your luck!"

True, she could use better luck. "Can hair do that?"

"Come on."

Cleopatra helped her out of bed. She dressed slowly, legs still weak, but stronger than before.

They grabbed towels and scissors, and went to the baths. Out in the hall, each step took a year, longer . . .

Cleopatra filled a sink. "Bring that chair over here." With her pocket-knife, Cleopatra scraped soap into the basin, and mixed it with her hands. "First we need to wash your hair. Tip back." The sink bit into Mim's neck, and the wounds on her backside and legs recalled that awful flight.

Cleopatra rubbed Mim's scalp with soapy handfuls, dusty rose, tingly with rosemary. "No use brushing till it's clean." She stopped rubbing and stared at Mim. "Wait. Something different about you. You're full of something new."

"Why don't you wear rings?" Mim asked.

"I prefer other decoration."

"But why no rings?"

"You always buzz me about that. Okay. I once knew a student of palmistry. She never wore rings. Why? Didn't want to restrict her possibilities. Makes sense. Of course I have grandmother's mourning ring on my neck. As you know." She resumed washing Mim's hair.

The water had lost its warmth, but the rubbing made Mim's whole body relax.

Cleopatra said, "Something is changing in you."

"I don't know what you mean."

"Of course not. I'll keep studying." Cleopatra drained the sink and rinsed Mim's hair. "There, clean. *Allons-y*, as Clock says."

Mim wrapped a towel around her hair and squeezed.

"Bring the chair over to the mirror so you can see. Brush it out. I'll cut some of the snarls, but it's better if it's brushed first," Cleopatra said.

Mim brushed and brushed until it hurt too much. Cleopatra held the open scissors beneath Mim's left ear. A slice, and in the mirror Mim watched two feet of wet hair tumble. Cleopatra cut and cut and hair fell. A breeze found Mim's neck, and her head floated upward. Cleopatra was right, the load lightened.

"Well," Cleopatra said. "Touch! Give it a shake!"

Mim shook her head, put her fingers through her hair, and giggled. "Just . . . look!"

"I know!" Cleopatra dampened her own hair and cut a hank. "I can't see the back. How does it look?"

"Want me to do it?" Mim asked.

"Sure." Cleopatra handed Mim the scissors. They giggled.

Cleopatra's hair whispered, like rope. Mim caressed the whisper, searched for the children in the mother. She would keep their hair, make something.

"Go ahead!" Cleopatra said. "Cut it."

While Mim cut, striving to make it even, Cleopatra speculated about what the guests would think. "We'll start an epidemic of cropped hair!" When Cleopatra was satisfied, Mim put the scissors down and ruffled out loose bits.

"Oooh," Cleopatra said. "Delicious!"

"I'll keep the hair," Mim said.

"Yes, gather it all up. We should bury it."

"Can't we save some?"

"If you don't let anyone else touch it."

Mim swept the hair into a pile with her hands and wrapped the pile in a damp towel. Something *had* lightened. Walking didn't hurt as much. On the way back to their rooms, they met Suspender in the hallway. "What happened to you?"

"We needed a change," Cleopatra said. "A little cheer."

Mim giggled.

"Alright, well, how's Mim?"

"I'm fine." *Why didn't he just ask her?*

"Questionable," he said.

Cleopatra linked arms with Mim. "You still need time to heal. But skin learns fast."

Mim thought of the red places on her skin. Red bits, like the occasional bits in chicken eggs. What Lo-Lo had fed her, soon after she arrived at the carnival. Whenever he broke an egg and saw red, he proclaimed it lucky.

"Now we've got lucky hair!" Mim said.

The next morning, Mim pulled leftover hair from the towel and made two piles. Cleopatra's hair was thicker and longer. She laid her hair out lengthwise and took about half. She found thread and tied one end of the hair, and separated that hank into three sections to braid. It was hard to work with. With a smaller amount, she began again. She clamped the thread-tied end in her mouth and braided down toward her lap. She pulled it up to look. Progress. She braided awhile and finally pinched the untied end. With her other hand, she took more thread, cut it in her teeth, and began to tie the end. Someone knocked on her door. "Just a minute!" she yelled, quickly finished tying, wrapped the braid and the remaining nest of hair in the cloth, and shoved it under her pillow. "Come in," she said.

Suspender. He handed her a mug. It smelled like what Lo-Lo had brought, with more salt and dirt. "Clock mixed in some shite he said was medicinal."

Mim took a sip. "Terrible!" She searched for the child behind his face, for Pelle. "I feel better. Can I come down for dinner tonight?"

"No one stopping you," he said.

"You stole my rope."

"A person doesn't need rope like that. Come down for dinner if you want." He turned to go. The door creaked, and a wet leaf rustled above his head.

The boy Pelle, so small, hears his father come into the house. Through the boy's untamed hair, Mim and Pelle look at the father, thinking maybe he's hurt bad because of how his face looks, like when the thresher chewed up his shirt, which had been tied round his waist. (A hot day that had been, so luckily he had taken off his shirt, and the machine only ate fabric.) But here now his body doesn't look hurt. Only his face. With a rag, he wipes his eyes.

"Martha?" he says.

There's stirring in her room, a warm sound. She's been packing. The boy and Mim know this. They peer through the crack, the dim line where hinges no longer creak because the boy's father oils them every morning, quiet hinges for her headaches. "You don't know how much it hurts," she always says. For the boy, and for Mim, her pain eclipses everything else. Quiet, mother says she needs quiet, so she's leaving them, in search of quiet.

Pelle looked at Mim. "Just now. Did you see that?"

"Yes," she said.

"This will be interesting," he said.

In the kitchen, a few carnies were grumbling about bad seats. Mim had never understood these intricacies, but to a handful of people, especially Tiger, seats were crucial. Some people wanted to sit near Suspender, some, to sit as far away from him as possible. Lo-Lo was dashing around, pouring cream into pots, grinding in a stone bowl a dry paste comprised of what looked like glassy insects.

Lo-Lo said, "Ooh, saucy! I love your hair. Love it." He handed her a pitcher and pointed at the smaller pots. "Pour about half into that first one. And some in each of those, too."

She was glad to help. When she had finished with the pots, she sat beside Nelda, who had entered during the cleaning; Mim hugged her. "Sorry about runty," Mim said into Nelda's neck.

"Thank you." Nelda pulled back and regarded Mim. "Look at you." She smiled.

"Eat-up," Suspender said, in his shout-horn voice.

They did. Nelda fed tidbits to the two kittens that were ensconced in her clothing, and sometimes stroked the empty pocket.

"Three cheers for Clock!" Suspender said. "Victuals taste extra fine tonight."

"A bit of praise doesn't hurt!" Lo-Lo raised his cup. "Butter, butter the doom-drum!"

Carnies clunked their vessels.

The food was good, and scoured fatigue from Mim's mouth and belly. Even in the short time resting, she had missed these people. Unexpected— she still wasn't sure she belonged. The missing felt warm. Carnies drank, voices swelled: laughing, fighting, complaining, competing. Mim inhabited her new hair, her belonging. Did anyone feel lonely here, in the motley puzzle of the Eight Mile Suspended Carnival? Despite the filling food, she realized something *was* lacking. She was unforlorn.

Suspender stood. "Hear, all of you. Direction since the flood points upward, but we can't assume anything. We've naught new to offer guests, aside from that washed up polar bear skull. As you know, four Tobeys including that skell titled Rubyat hath departed, as commanded by myself.

Please remember: whoever can't abide by the rules will be dismissed. Know it. I've learned that pugilism has many facets."

Cleopatra said, "Oh, and Smoot retired last night. Can't do much with a tangle of drowned snakes."

"I was getting there. Friends, our Smoot recognized the gap between the impossible-to-ignore macabre and the simply rotten unappealing. To give in when the celestial clock declares it's done, that's one sign of grace. Sad to see him go. Time to grapple at new fabrications of delight. I found some club moss; we'll start a spark show or summat. If you're inclined toward the pyrotechnic, meet tomorrow after breakfast. In addition, I'll pursue money by way of bridge fixing. Will see Spurlock and company about same," he said, talking really to himself. Then he said, "We'll have acts better than back in Plowjack when that Pfeffer boy's father used to get on stage at the Majestic and pull a fruit-cart with his hair!" He spoke as if he held the shout-horn, telling guests. "Yes, human oddity is never enough, friends, here we display the delectable boundlessness of human ability! We are not a freak show, oh no, oh no. Our people reek with talent."

"Even the snakes reek with talent!" Tiger said, and some carnies laughed.

Nelda punched his arm, then she laughed, too.

Suspender laughed and said, "More to come!"

"Welcome back, Rope Girl," Anton the Younger yelled.

Suspender was still. Then he raised a glass. Others followed.

"Welcome back," he said.

Lo-Lo kissed her shorn head.

III

Skin is, indeed, remarkable.

After salve and some time, the wounds on her arms and legs shone with new skin. During the healing, she didn't feel like going outside much, so worked inside the hotel, sorting debris left by previous inhabitants. Like her dream. Suspender said some parts might be useful, but hadn't yet taken the time. He told Mim to save metal and wood, but torn bedding should be burned. She shoved gray, stained fabric into hallway corners to haul, eventually, to the fire.

When she wasn't working, she wove miniature ropes from the remnants of their hair. As ropes, they were slippery and only about a foot long, but she loved them. She gave one to Cleopatra and kept the others tucked in her pocket for luck.

One morning, her door opened and Cleopatra came in. "Still among the vibrant?" she asked.

Mim didn't feel like getting out of bed. Had she slept at all? Light slunk through the window. The water cup on the chair beside her cot blurred in the lamplight. She curled into herself. "I'm so tired."

"I see you. You miss that friend of yours, from the factory, that Dunavant," Cleopatra said.

"It's Beede."

"No, now that I look closer, it's not him. Here." Cleopatra produced her cards.

"No cards," Mim said.

"One card. I'm your proxy. You like an uneven cut." Cleopatra split the deck on the crate table. "Always! *Le Pendu*, again. How do you always find it? But this time, it's for renewal." Cleopatra's stare hurt Mim's bones. "You're not alone, are you?"

"You're here," Mim said.

Pale sunlight's soft toes crept across the floor, toward her rope pile; the fibers sharpened, clarified in light.

"The Hanged Man. The fool who's no fool . . . sitting quietly, wrapped in ropes, barely moving, maybe resting, appearing to do nothing, a shell to show off the hempen skin of the Rope Girl. Everything passes by, drunken guests, children shuddering at how tight they imagine the ropes must be, everything moves, Time, the world—"

"And wind," Mim said.

"Yes, wind. Then those Tobeys meddle with fate, become actors in *your* play, string you up, until proverbial coins fall from your rope pockets, tumble to the ground, and you see them as merely bits of metal. Yes, a coin. Something about a coin. Everything you named as *real* is on its head. Dangling between worlds, uncovering mysteries . . . and oh, what mysteries you do uncover, you flimsy thing. But you *are* getting curvy. Shedding childhood, stepping into that next, voluptuous world." Cleopatra leaned over and whispered to Mim, "And you don't even know it yet. Everything will revolt; what you think is sturdy and sure is about to change. If only it were as simple as being underwater, or illuminated like ropes in the sun, floating . . . but right now, for you, poor fool, it *is* that simple . . . you'll learn in time, when this suspension has passed, and you've fallen from the sky again. And again. And again. I'm only giving what you can handle. Wait." Cleopatra took Mim's hand. "It's not Dunavant. You aren't alone in that sad skin. What've you been about?"

Mim took her hand away.

"Too late; I caught you. I can't believe I hadn't sensed it already. I'm always right about this, friend. You've got another in there. It's not your Beede. It's Suspender! I won't peep. We'll take care of you, baby and mater."

Mim knew inside her body, knew what she had done with Pelle in the rope room. But the knowing clashed against the letters of the words. Baby, *baby*, what mothers have, and how could she be a mother? She recalled the mother that nursed the baby in Wistmount. That mother looked cross, more than cross; that mother had faded, disappeared in the vastness of her baby's need.

"How could I be a mother?" Mim asked.

Cleopatra looked at her. "Any cat can be a mother. I told you how things happen. You've read *What Every Girl Should Know*."

"But they don't always happen. Not every time."

"No. Watch out for Suspender."

"What does that mean?"

Cleopatra stroked the picture of the Hanged Man. "Death surrounds him, too. He steeps in death like bitter tea."

"You've read him?"

"He never let me."

"But you did."

"Indirectly."

"What did you see?"

"If the locomotive of a human is need, that man's engine is death."

"You think everyone is death," Mim said.

"Everyone *is* death."

Mim tried to think what that would look like, death as an engine. She imagined Beede, moving forward, always moving forward, like a train.

Death. Cleopatra said death was Suspender's engine, but she couldn't actually see him, not like Mim could. Mim stretched her tingly limbs and stood. She put on her loosest dress, nothing beneath, draped the river scarf over her shoulders, took the stone egg from its place in the floor and dropped it into her pocket. Twined thin hair ropes around each wrist, made sweet.

Her head was light and unburdened. She shook her hair, still so new.

After midnight dinner, Mim stayed up with the others. Wine and stories about antiquated carnies like Sweetine, Zadie, Molge, Garbage Jack, and Smoot's grandfather, also a snake-handler. Gnash told stories on everyone, including himself. And the remaining Tobeys were louder than usual; Armand, Anton the Younger, and Leslie took turns punching each other in the face. Eventually they toddled off somewhere for more drink and outdoor mischief. Suspender sipped from his near-empty tea bowl and turned his sunshine toward Mim. She smiled at him as the carnies continued to outdo each other with their tellings. He smiled back.

Now that she had rejoined the vibrant, she itched to find Beede. How he looked at her, wanted her. He was horrible. He was a splinter she needed to remove and yet wanted to leave be.

Timmy Zuzu came into the kitchen; Lo-Lo yawned. "Hell. I deserve a holiday. Nipsy can clean up in the morning, and gather the eggs, too. I'll sleep late tomorrow."

"I'll clean up now," Mim said.

"Pixie dear, if you insist, I accept." He kissed the top of her head, and he and Zuzu went upstairs.

She picked up dirty kitchen wreckage, but Suspender said, "Come over here. You heard Clock—Nipsy can finish tomorrow." He took a bottle of wine from the rack, and sat down across from Mim and Cleopatra. Between them, wax pooled at the bottom of a candle, a thick river of insignificance. He poured them each a glass, and filled his tea bowl. Everyone else had gone to bed.

"Wine tea?" Mim asked.

"On occasion," Suspender said.

"To the point, sir. I grow yawny," Cleopatra said.

"Our young friend here can see things. Actual memories that are not her own," he said.

She was naked again now with these two, but instead of skin, her interior was exposed. Relief, then a rush. Things would change somehow, were new and shiny like her healed skin. But the change meant she could sit at the table and discuss her secret, not be invisible. Could sit with them, not hide her true capacity.

"Really," Cleopatra said.

Suspender looked at Cleopatra.

"Of course I knew. Soon after she got here," Cleopatra said.

"And didn't tell me? Neither of you?"

Mim dipped her finger in the wax, which hardened into an uneven cup. She popped it off, but her finger still throbbed. The wax cup rocked back and forth on the table. Cleopatra drank wine, took the wax cup, and began to craft something else from the candle drippings.

"You must tell me things! Don't hide behind that feminine façade. No one tells me anything." He said this quietly, like a puzzle only he could see. "That's the problem. But Mim will learn some secrets."

"It's not like that," Mim said.

"What's it like?" Cleopatra did not look up from shaping wax. "I can see from the outside; I know plenty from my seat. But *inside*, what's it like?"

"I always know when it starts. I see a leaf."

"What kind of leaf?" Suspender asked.

"Why does that matter?" Cleopatra asked.

"Just some kind of leaf. Silvery, or dry. Always different. Then I see the things. Sometimes it's just a moment, sometimes it's big. I see it happen. I feel it happen, from inside. Like it belongs to me."

Cleopatra said, "She's seen me. She's been catching leaves and she's seen me. She's seen you, too, or you wouldn't have found out. I can't fathom and don't want to know what goes on in your brain's rust-heap."

"I can't make it happen; it just starts," Mim said.

Cleopatra handed her the wax creation. "An offering, a poppy. A gift for a gift."

"Quit all this sport, this candle-waxing. You two will figure how to *make* it happen," he said. "Mim, you sit in her tent. Start tomorrow night. Sit and watch, and see what you can. Think of a leaf, put your mind on it, maybe that'll work. And you," he said, looking at Cleopatra, "See what you can bring out."

"Meaning what?" Cleopatra asked.

"If you see something big, tip the guest off balance. Use your nature."

"I refuse to upset my guests unnecessarily."

"Okay, trumpet-mouth, you do what I say, or go find another home."

"Against my better humor," Cleopatra said.

"Does anyone else know?" he asked.

"Nelda," Mim said.

"Of course," he said. "Thieves and females stick together."

"Yes, we do," Cleopatra said. "And Nelda is a vault."

"Well, I hope so," he said. "Don't tell anyone else. Not Clock, not anyone. Don't even tell the quiet dark in your beddie-bye. But report back to me. See if you can compel guests. Then try carnies. I need to know who I can trust."

A thought buzzed nearby. Beede. *Beede. What had he done?*

"What's all over your face?" Cleopatra asked Mim.

"I don't know what you mean."

"There's something you know . . . sitting right there on your face. Something you want to say. Needs to be pried off your face. What is it?" She leaned toward Mim and squinted.

Heat scorched Mim's bones. She had to tell. "It's not only people. Beatrice, too. Not clear, like peoples' memories. The factory men beat her. I saw. It wasn't the storm."

"Was it that Dunavant?" he asked.

"But Dunavant brought her back," Cleopatra said.

"Doesn't mean he didn't hurt her," Mim said.

"What do you know?" he asked.

Mim put down the poppy and recounted all she could.

"Shite," Suspender said.

"It was just . . . knowing," Mim said.

"Why didn't you tell me?" Cleopatra asked.

"I'm sorry."

Cleopatra grabbed her arms and shook her. "How could you keep this from me?"

Mim pulled away. Cleopatra began to cry. "I'm sorry," Mim said. She began to cry, too.

After a while, Cleopatra wiped her face and picked up the poppy. "You'll have to earn me back," she said.

"Dunavant," Suspender said. "Violent and unnatural."

"Yes," Cleopatra said. "I believe Beatrice. I believe Mim."

He said, "That poppy smells of something beyond wax, smells of more. Amazing."

"Because I'm magic," Cleopatra said.

"It reeks," he said.

"Reeks with talent," Mim said.

Cleopatra laughed. "Okay, you. I can forgive. But never lie to me again."

Mim promised she would never.

FOURTEEN

FINDING THE GOATS

I

There were a million waking insects inside of Mim. She couldn't go to her room after the others left. She boiled water, mixed in cold, and scrubbed pans. When she finished, she went outside, past the menagerie, toward the river . . . could she read Beede? Could she learn more about him, surprise Pelle, like untying the Impossibles?

The night uncoiled, full of twinkle and husk-singing insects. Beatrice sometimes troubled her fur, going after thingies that would burrow and otherwise, Mim supposed, drive the beast mad. But these night bugs were more like carnival contraptions, not specks to bother a person, but ineffably important, meeting to conduct miniscule business via scrape and whirr. The skiff was gone, but there were the two canoes washed up from the flood. One, unfixable, was still upside down with broken ribs. The other, Suspender had mended, and carved for it a paddle.

Mim pushed the canoe into the water and began to paddle. The work was hard, but arms were for work, backs were for work, bodies were for work and other things impossible to push from her mind. *Her* body was for seeing things. And being with her men. Wasn't that a kind of work, though, all the in and in, and the roiling . . . pleasure but not leisure? It tingled like her skin, but went deeper. Bodies were for that, too.

She approached the opposite shore. Powder permeated the air. She breathed in, filled her body with that pong, a tiny experiment with death. Her shoes sodden from pulling the canoe onto the muddy bank, her dress sweat-stuck to healing skin, she started downriver toward the factory. No night bugs over here, or maybe they just didn't dare peep. Maybe they were dead. As she went up toward the factory, the waiting silence pressed in.

A smooth voice sang, "Gone, gone, my baby's gone." From behind a building came a man, whistling and singing.

Mim stopped, and the man stopped. He pointed a shotgun at her.

"Who's there?" His voice bit into her. "Identify quick!"

"I'm Mim." The flavor of bullets returned from what she had seen inside Suspender, dusty and mean. She didn't want any.

"Like a rabbit with a split ear. What're you doing out here, huh?" He kept the shotgun where it was.

"Looking for a friend." She spoke loud because it made her feel braver.

"Anyone in particular?" The man kept the gun pointed at her. He stepped close enough so she smelled his body's milky odor.

She stepped back, needing distance. "You know Beede?"

The man laughed. "I know him. Whaddaya want with that scallywag?"

"Who are you, anyway?" she asked.

"Who am I? I'm the one with the arsenal. You're the one with no threat. You want Beede. I won't ask why. He's in the pit." The man pointed at a building up the hill, much larger than the hotel at the carnival. "Go on up there, don't be scared. Don't know that he expects company, but go on. A twig like you can't hurt nothing."

Mim started up the hill.

"Tell him Randall sends his regards!" the man shouted. She walked faster.

She found a door, knocked; a dull sound echoed behind it. She tried, but it wouldn't budge. She went to the other side of the building, away from the river. A door opened and some men spilled out. She backed into the shadow beside the building.

"Come on now, give us some of that gypsum weed, boys!" one of the men yelled, and others laughed.

Nearby, three other men in boots and helmets walked toward a small building across the compound. "Oh yes oh yes oh yes," someone sang through gravel, and the others laughed. Their laughter sounded weary, and soon transformed to coughing. "To the job!" someone said. One man leaned over and spit. His spit sounded like the grinding that moved the rides at the carnival. But this cough and spit was not meant to amuse. This performance was a mandatory machination of the body, like Mim's willow-skin that now crept from wrist to shoulder, around her back, winding her torso like a ghost of the ropes she yearned for. She stepped from the shadow and pushed the door open.

A dark hallway with light ahead, air stale and pungent like the snake pit. She approached the light, hearing slap rhythms. Men lounged on sofas, chairs, the floor, and clustered around tables. Some she had seen at the carnival. In the center, a circle of men yelled and howled; some laughed, gagged, and coughed. Plenty of noise. She couldn't see much, but from the center of the ring, sparks flew up. Men jumped back. Heavy boot-stomps from the center. She smelled burning, foul and devilish.

A man on a sofa stirred, said, "I gotta whiz." He came toward her, poked his finger at her. "Which ghost are you?"

"Is Beede here?" she asked.

"Hey Grover, a visitor for Beede!" he yelled. Another man turned toward them. The yelling man pushed her further into the room, then went toward the hallway.

"Remember ring-handed Jake!" someone said.

From the center of the ring, Beede emerged, buttoned his pants. His face and bare torso were covered with soot. He smoothed his hair. The men who weren't passed out watched him approach Mim.

"Well, if it isn't my pal! Boys, this is Mim." He smiled but seemed unsure what to do. Coming closer, still smiling, he said, "What are you doing here?"

"You haven't been to the carnival," she said.

"She missed me, friends, see what happens when you bust a chickadee's heart, see how it goes? Oh, I'm just making conversation." He smiled at the men around the room. "Return to your evening, gents, nothing to specu-late about." He strapped a leather bag across his chest, like a wineskin, but oblong, with a fancy latch. He pulled her toward the hallway.

"What were you doing in there?" she asked.

"Vegetable sulfur, that moss, its dust being highly flammable. Thriving since the flood. Carnies and swindler-mystics aren't the only ones with tricks!"

Beneath the bright moon, he led her toward a shed, held her hand, which started to hurt. He kicked open the door, and they went inside. Counters, tables, trays with dents and holes. Crumbles of metal littered the floor.

"Not the safest plan, but it's entirely fine to see you. How did you cross?"

"Canoe."

"Someone stole your hair, darling."

"Oh, we bobbed our hair."

"Well. How unexpected. I look a mess, too. Pardon my disarray." He wrapped charcoal arms around her waist. When he pulled her close, his skin scratched hers; she gasped, still tender to touch.

"What's wrong?" he asked, but didn't wait for her to say. He shifted the wineskin to his back, untied her river scarf, pulled the neck of her dress open, and touched a breast. "Sweet alabaster." He kissed her.

She inhaled his burn, and wanted, and didn't, and wanted more; she drank singe from his skin, and sparks swirled in front of her, found a passage deep inside, a passage to all of her, to a part that she was only now meeting. The part of herself that resembled Beede, the part that lived to feel alive. Her legs quivered and she leaned back against a counter.

"I missed you," she said. She needed his insistent clank, needed to contain his sound in a sweet box and hold him forever, with sugar and amber honey, even though it tasted bitter and sickening, needed to own him; he was hers, he was for her. She wished she couldn't see all that. She had so little in this world. When Nelda and Beatrice came to her mind, she pushed them back out.

"I missed you, too." He nuzzled her neck, said something low. His mouth found her breasts, his tongue lapped at each small darkness, and thrilled; she moaned, held the back of his head, trying to think in words. The whole world radiated from that tip of her. Was it the memory of ropes or smoke, or something else? Her nipple fiery, she grabbed him, his burnt skin. He laughed, and bit her nipple. It hurt, and was good, having him ready between her legs. He pushed inside, ground into her, skin clashing against skin, between her legs, shiny and soft, and the grind inside was like that on her skin, but more, and he lifted her onto the counter. Bits of metal scraped her behind. "You like me, don't you?" He bit her nipple again, and she yelled but he laughed, then moaned, and the metal ground into her behind . . . like Beatrice's pain . . .

"Stop," she said.

"Can't stop. MMMmmim," he said, voice invisible and slithering through the field of metal.

She almost didn't see the leaf.

Beede and two other factory men shove three moaning goats toward a darkened shelter near the flooded river. As they cross the spongy ground, Mim feels a goat bump her leg. Zlateh. Under the shelter are some tall wooden ribs, several buckets, and a pit. Each man straddles a goat, takes a long knife from his belt, and slits the animal's throat. No more moaning. From the wooden ribs, they hang the goats to bleed. Red pools beneath the bodies while the men laugh and tell each other bullshit lie after lie for minutes, hours, years . . . until Beede breaks the talk and the dripping hum.

"Time to skin those goats, cut 'em up, boys!" The men pick up their knives. "Clean 'em up, ready 'em for the pit! Take those bits, though; stuff your pockets if the buckets overflow, but don't leave 'em for trash, they're tasty!" Beede is all shine, all laugh.

The skin comes off; it just comes off. Work, sure, but pull and pull until it comes off. Mim implores her own skin: *Stay, stay! And don't be pulled away!*

There is sweetness about how a dead body smells. And the men cut and cut while the skinned, emptied goat bodies balk with each strike as if still alive, as if grasping to hold on. And into the bucket the men toss the unctuous repast that comes from the bellies.

They hoist carcasses to the giant spit. Beede has prepared wood and alcohol, stones in a ring; Mim knows he made it ready for the burning that's about to happen. And toward the coals they go, flames born above sodden ground from a tall wood fire burned down now to orange coals, and the goats sizzle and cook, and the scent is the extinction of all vibration, how things die in finality, not simply an insect stepped upon, but a heaving, yearning end, how one world folds over into the next, and into the bellies of the men these goats will go, piece by piece, Beede's offering to the flood-heavy men for keeping the goats alive while it rained, and they all fall like beasts upon their beastly meal and lick greasy lips and drain cups of thick beer, and Mim's belly gurgles, hungry, then rejoices in the feast. Beede sits back, eats slowly, controlled, not a gorge but bite by bite, careful, watching the dirty men and their glossy faces, and Beede in his deepest reaches knows, as Mim knows, that by this feast, he owns these men just a bit more.

Nausea waved through Mim, seeing Beede now in the bouquet of metal bits, her gut full of goat meat memories, but actually empty, and despite having eaten at the carnival, hungry. And with things thusly twisted up, she knew that by this memory-feast, his lies about skin, and torture of Beatrice, she owned Beede. Just a bit more.

And inside her body, the not-wanting murdered the wanting.

II

The sun rose weaker than last night's moon, and Mim slunk back to the carnival. In her room, she dropped the river scarf, peeled off her sticky dress, and slept until she heard breakfast preparations. She put on a clean dress and the scarf and went downstairs.

"There was an ultimatum, but we nifted it away." Lo-Lo sang and stirred the morning sludge.

"Good morning," Mim said.

"Hi, Mimsy, you cleaned up good last night." He put down the giant wooden spoon and turned toward her. "What happened to you?"

"What do you mean?"

"Grimed up your face?"

She looked in the glass on the cupboard. Her face was charred from Beede. Why, why had she forgotten to wash? "Don't tell anyone," she said.

"What would I tell them? I know nothing. But strumpy? Unsavory? What have you been at?"

Before she could decide whether or what to tell him, it all rushed out. Everything but the goats. Lo-Lo took food seriously; food was sacred. And he loved Zlateh. If he knew about the goats, he might go kill Beede. And the nausea in her body locked the slaughter behind a door.

After her cascade of words, Lo-Lo stood by the stove, stirring, staring at her.

"What should I do?" she asked.

"Wash."

In the baths, the whole room assumed the color of moss, like the living mantle that emerged after the flood. So much green. Flood-rain had awakened the dormant green. In the room of moss she turned the faucet to fill the last tub on the left. She didn't want soap, soap meant the brown nub that everyone used, or waking Cleopatra for good soap, neither of which appealed.

She put her clothes and river scarf to soak, and slipped herself into warm water. The part of her body that Beede had opened, thirsty, took water inside. She tried to relax. The porcelain, smooth and cool, calmed her skin. She leaned back, drowned her hair in the water. Perhaps she fell asleep.

Then came a hand between her legs, and before she opened her eyes, she knew it was Pelle.

"Clock said you crossed the river," he said.

Damn, damn, damn. "Yes."

"What's that Dunavant up to?" His hand between her legs, water slicking down her hair, tightness and expectation everywhere. Pelle said, "He doesn't remember me. But he and I have a Crucial History." He slid his finger inside, and she realized *this* was what she had needed, water hadn't been enough; she needed Pelle. Not Beede, not like that. But she could use them both. Two kings, different metals, and clash, clash, clash. Something opened the slaughter gate.

"He killed our three goats. Had a feast," she said.

"He told you?"

"I saw inside him last night."

"Detestation." He removed his hand from her, from the water, and rubbed his ballyhoo coin, brought it close to his face, studied its contours. "Some believe goats carry illness away from a place. Load them up with poisoned ideas and send them onward merrily, rid a place of disease. Fine. We'll be cleaner for it. Those goats will only bring strife to the bellies that partook. Their sacrifice will carry to those skells what they deserve. But there's more to do." He put the coin back in his pocket. "I'll send Dunavant to the Spurlock Hotel. If he survives my plan, of which there are three possibles. Which is an *if* and not a *when*. If he survives whichever plan, I mean. You're my lure." Pelle pulled her from the water, which held her like perfect skin.

She said, "I will if you explain how, and why."

He held her behind, and pulled her, dripping, to the window and kissed her. He let go and undid his coveralls, pushed into her. Simple: that was all she needed. Him inside, for inside was all she had.

170

"Yes," she said.

III

More inside each of us than anyone can name. In this case, the clang was caused by parts knocking at each other, the byproduct of the inside, She Who Knows. Even when metal's fully twisted out of shape, it still has the opportunity to choose, to say Yes. When metal gets bent till you can hardly recognize it anymore, even then, it can still chime in about its predilections.

In other words, the lady knows her mind. Knows her body. Or so she thinks. Invites all this shadow and light into the shelter of her skin so she can fit somewhere. Only to see that she fits, has a place. Only to find where she fits.

She knows she can see things. Maybe she can see things if she tries.

On the first night in the tent with Cleopatra, Mim saw nothing.

On the second night, nothing. And so on, for a week and a day. Each night, after closing, Suspender asked, and she replied *nothing, nothing.*

Until one night.

Outside the tent, a slim, quiet man studied his boots. Mim had seen him before; he came here to imbibe. Why, on this night, hadn't he gone straight to the wine tent?

Cleopatra welcomed him. He sat and removed his brown cap. She put her hand on his. "All will be revealed, if you choose to proceed." She arranged the cards.

"It's my mother," he said, but Cleopatra lifted her hand to stop him.

"Don't speak."

"Sorry." He looked as if he had broken something irreplaceable.

As with all guests, Mim studied him. The weariness of his body, its apparent weightlessness. If you looked away, he might float off.

"Cut the cards," Cleopatra said.

Mim recalled each leaf she had seen before, how each was different. *This time, first see the outline, then architecture. Think leaf, leaf, leaf; sweep everything else aside. Think leaf, leaf, leaf.* Above the right ear of the man who might fly away, a spindle of green.

171

"Can't they see me," the man says, and Mim says it too, feeling his corporeal lack of substance even on the boulevard. He enters the wine tent, and Mim slips in with him, and the hushed chaos of the candle-lit tent envelopes them both, and they are warmed by the smell of beeswax and the prospect of that drink, which is soon in hand despite his invisibility, and soon in his mouth. Mim feels warm grapes trickle down her throat as he drinks and drinks, simultaneously trying to stretch it out and get the heat he needs. He takes more coins from his pocket; Mim feels them in her hand, and puts them down for Lo-Lo, who ignores Mim, and ignores the man, but pours another glass. In the cunning mirrors, bottles multiply, appear more like blood than wine.

"Can't you see me?" the man and Mim ask Lo-Lo, who looks up.

"Sure, I can," he says, and someone else plunks down money, and Lo-Lo resumes dispensations.

In the fortune-teller tent, Cleopatra told the man about his woes. He nodded; he knew them already. His mother.

"Do something with those tidy facts," she said, "Do or do not, but now the truth is yours. You own it, as it owns you."

He paid and left.

So much sadness in the world, such unmet yearning. What could Mim do with these glimpses, do about the mess that lives inside each of us? She had hollowed herself out for Pelle. There was only question and air. What more did he need?

IV

Mim wandered the carnival, sleepy, ravenous, ate what Lo-Lo offered, seconds, thirds, more pulled bread than any of the other carnies. She had begun to feel thick, and slow. One day, getting out of bed took more effort. She moved not through air but something soupy that blocked progress. Time stuttered. Her body clashed with natural laws; the light from the window—its edges were different, more insistent. She wasn't able to move like light anymore. A contraption was being wired between her hipbones. Somewhere suspended inside, a small toy began to spin. A curio, an invader made of bodies: hers and Pelle's. Where did she stop, where did it start? She was not alone. There was a tree or something growing inside her, with

172

roots and parts that would make a person. How lunatic it all was, how unlikely, how frail. How useful, these actions that sometimes floodlit the body and heart. How useful the push and pull of two humans, the ability to create life inside another person, inside Mim, to carry on after the vessel no longer lives. There were machines that could make things, could hang things upside down and bend them backwards, make boxes, containers.

The woods toward Wistmount, that child behind the samovar lid. Each child at the carnival, how much they ate and needed. How would she fill such a gorge of need? People were made, then born onto the dry crust of the earth, and somehow were kept and nourished, or were forgotten and dried up like pulled weeds, like husks. How do you water a baby? Beatrice needs food, we all do, but a baby needs life. A baby takes all you offer, but needs more, and cries, whinnies, balks against mother, face red and breathless, keeps living somehow despite the hard curls of world that batter and bruise such a small green thing.

Was that living, to depend so completely on another? When would it become aware of her? It was distant now. The idea of a baby, of life, was as vague as anything from before the carnival. The carnival would be her place to live, the carnival her backbone. The carnival was more real for Mim to be growing inside of, not this thing inside her, a person who would be born into the world, a future-person. The carnival was now *her* womb, and also her interior, what she would breathe and swallow and act out. She was the carnival's toy, its baby, its marionette. A life inside her made no more sense than anything she was in the midst of, no more sense than a sprout busting through dry scratch-land. How could life happen in this parched then flooded game?

But how could it *not*? Generations of people used to sing the songs of Lo-Lo. Who would sing these songs in future, if not more lives? His was a voice in a thread of other voices, she was a vessel in a thread of mothers, a safe, wet interior where some man put himself, and she welcomed the putting, the in and in, and it wasn't even considered that she would have a baby, that her body could do that. To have a baby. But even that was so far off. She was still barely with child. It wasn't real yet, and when she did consider it, when the idea of how it would rope her to a man, that man . . . when that idea lit her up inside, it seemed like someone else's memory. Impossible that it could be hers, instead, was she seeing inside another? She wasn't convinced it *wasn't* someone else, another, mirror Mim . . . a body who looked and smelled like her, but wasn't actually lost, who had a home and a place and that certainness people are allowed when they actually belong somewhere, belong to a set point in the world, to a family. *That* Mim knew what it meant. That Mim regarded this Mim, and this Mim saw the other face wasn't hungry, wasn't lost. *That* Mim's face was closer to beauty.

To stop pondering babies and need, Mim applied herself to Pelle's projects. There was always dry muck to clean from machinery, gears still laden with memory from the flood. Mim's hands were as fully stained now as her desire to run off at night, escape the carnival. The privilege of having a place to belong.

After Mim was finished seeing things, and Cleopatra rolled her tent door down, Mim filled her cavern with leftover porridge crust, sugar-beans, and figs. Full for the moment, she slipped away to the river, her own Crossing. To move the canoe required a hero's effort now, and she paddled, exhausted from the day, but somehow full of energy. Maybe it was the baby. The sinew and shine of Beede's naked form, strapped with his strange wineskin, all for her, drew her across the water, called, *Come and take.* And through the thickness of her disgust with him, the swell of her torso and her job as lure wouldn't allow her to ignore that voice.

Knowing Beede had butchered the goats, tortured Beatrice, and scorned Nelda, she could avoid loving him. Instead, she would use him, consume him. She lost count of days, nights, and sometimes her need for skin on skin was stronger than even her need to sleep or eat, feeling within her the baby, that imp, a moon-sprout in darkness, glowing, growing . . .

FIFTEEN

THE TREE THAT WASN'T THERE

I

Mim spooned out a third bowl of midnight stew. "Leave some for Beatrice," Cleopatra said. She scraped carnies' leftovers into a bucket. Since her return, Beatrice had been needy and hungry.

"There's more in the pot," Mim said.

"Not bloody likely," Lo-Lo said. "Not with your appetite."

Nelda came to Mim. "Visit my suite when you're done."

"I need to digest."

"Digest *chez moi*. New moon."

Mim was exhausted. Her feet hurt, her belly thick. Somehow heat had mixed with dust and they both shadowed her. She needed a bath, but it was new moon.

She went up to Nelda's suite and knocked. "It's me," she said.

Nelda opened the door. "Welcome," she said.

Mim stepped inside. She hadn't seen the suite since before Nelda's hibernation. During which time, Nelda had re-covered the furniture in many shades and textures of green. "It's gorgeous," Mim said.

"*Merci*," Nelda said. "Help us set things up."

From a crate, Nelda pulled out red drapes, a blanket, some pillows patched with burlap. She arranged pillows on the floor. "We found new adornments."

"But I haven't bathed," Mim said.

"Make your nest," Nelda said. "You can bathe later."

Cleopatra handed Mim raspberry tea in a metal cup. The three of them settled into their nests. Nelda took the blanket she had made from scraps of costume, had embroidered vines surrounding each piece, and wrapped it around her body, like protection.

"I don't want to move," Mim said.

Nelda laughed. "You don't have to do anything, just rest here." She began to massage her own feet. "I'm so good at this."

"Just be here with us," Cleopatra said to Mim. "Being here is enough. It makes three."

Mim closed her eyes. Dark night. She heard small insects sawing away at their legs, and then it came to her, quickly. The intention was clear. "I want to remember."

"Wanting isn't enough." Nelda moved her hands to Mim's shoulders, down her arms. So good, to be touched like that, so melty, even with the heat that willowed through her bones.

Cleopatra lit a candle. "How do we speak purpose? How do we request what we need?"

"I need to remember," Mim said.

If what's burned off and left charred behind you is still there at all, the skeleton leaves, the rib cage of desire unmet, if there is detritus behind you, why would you want that?

It's something to hold onto, Mim heard the voice say. *A tangible thing in the world, material, not air. Not fire, but fire's remnants.*

Her whole life ahead, Mim would never have a circle like this again. It would burn behind her, red and glowing but not charred, not like the carnage of her obscured past. This fire would continue to burn, and burn far into the reach of Time. When she closed her eyes sometimes at the new moon she could see her sisters. Making a circle in Nelda's suite. Nelda's deep strength and heart, whole and fortified by the miles she had trod with that babe strapped to her body, then later holding his hand. The search to find somewhere safe to abandon him. And Cleopatra's blood, the tiny life she had once imagined and always missed . . . her body a rock of memory and wisdom, but also, sadness.

These women were part of Mim's armature, her sisters. Even after they were no longer together, that circle would burn, a sisterhood intact, open but unbroken. Each was stronger for their bond. Sometimes the ring, the fire circle would leave the floor, would begin and begin and begin to rise.

These circles Mim would remember until her last breath, beyond. She needed her own memories, these new ones, after the *ruin, collapse, release*. This circle of fire: three women. Each with stories inside, stories new and old, their bodies the carriers of stories. Stories carried out into the world, ashes back to bone.

After the circle that night, Nelda asked, "You okay? Sure you had enough to eat?"

"I had plenty." Mim wrapped her green silk robe around her body and snuggled beside Nelda on the pillows. The hem danced a few inches above her ankles, the silk supple and cool. She ran a finger through a penny-sized tear in the left sleeve.

"Here, something redolent with history." Cleopatra produced from the crate a wisp of a baby's gown. "It was mine. I was wearing it when I arrived at the waif's home. Always kept it. I knew someday there would be a reason. For the babe."

Mim looked at Nelda.

Nelda said, "I heard a rumor. It happens sometimes. This is why she and I avoid intercourse. Not always easy, being the only women in this company of shite. Until you, of course."

"True. Avoidance needs cunning." Cleopatra smoothed the baby gown. "But it's worth it. I've got all I need, here in my own meat sack. No matter how much that yellow book condemns pleasuring oneself. To wit, 'Perhaps the greatest physical danger to the chronic' . . . I can't say that word . . . *person who pleasures herself* . . . 'is the inability to perform the sexual act naturally.' I disagree."

"And who gets to decree what nature is? Naturally, I reject those pages," Nelda said.

Cleopatra clapped. "Absolutely! Those are pages to reject! Although I accept many other pages. For instance, the call to rest during our monthlies. We make a circle. If we don't want to tell the carnies, at least we can secretly slow down. The moon's visit droops me."

"Yes! Slowing down is bliss," Nelda said.

"I don't get tired when I bleed," Mim said.

"Well, be grateful. And one benefit of your situation is the break from bleeding." Cleopatra handed the baby's gown to Mim. So fancy, rosettes round the neck and hem. Through the fabric, Mim could see her hand.

"It's big for a newborn, but will serve her for a while. If she makes it. Not all of them do." Cleopatra subsided onto pillows.

Mim wasn't sure what she wanted. Children who came to the carnival, the fat, shiny ones—there was something beastly about their grabbing and whining, the clinging to mothers, the fear and need. Would this one be fat and shiny, would it cling? And what about the child in the woods, that boy with the samovar lid? What would make a person leave a child to survive alone like that? Or had he escaped the waif's home? Sometimes a woman would come to Cleopatra's tent, fully swollen, wondering if her man was true. Cleopatra never lied, but she would speak vaguely when needed, always focus back on the bundle. But a bundle grows into a person, and things get thorny. As Nelda well knew. A person needs so much.

Cleopatra took cards from her pocket, and Nelda stretched across the bed of pillows.

Mim watched the cards, always the cards, *they tell us everything, all we need to know.*

"Cards are vessels, vessels like bodies. Cards nourish how food cannot. Cards nourish the imagination." Cleopatra repeated what she often said to guests. "I'll be honest with you. But always with discernment." The fortune-teller handed guests these big true things, what was needful to know, what she needed to tell. Though Cleopatra said she discerned between what people could and could not propend. Like Pelle, Cleopatra created worlds and made limbs move, "Because if you tell people things they can't propend, they might take no action, wrong action, or worse. Knowing what they know, might blame themselves when, for instance, the money, food, or love shrivels. It's no good. Which is why artists of intuition must tread with care."

Now she put her hand on Mim's middle. "Still soon to tell, but I sense a girl."

"You can't know that!"

"Oh, she can," Nelda said.

"Besides, you are a vessel for a girl. And you're voracious, not only for food. That says girl. Or is it the other way around? But wait." She stared at Mim like she was a card. "Do you even want this bundle? If not, there are ways . . . preparations. Methods. Death is everywhere. But, caution—that's a lot to carry onward. So I'm told."

Cleopatra didn't know that her training hadn't worked: Mim could still see her memories, but hid this fact. Now a crumpled leaf rose above Cleopatra . . . pain . . . burning, tearing . . . young Cleopatra on a bed, blood spreads across grease-cloth, and she clutches her soldier's metal pin, sharpness biting her palm; Mim feels the pinch amidst the hot, raw pain, tink tink in the background. A woman sits beside Cleopatra, holds her other hand, and something else—a long metal implement. The brother of her husband is there, too. Just outside the door. In Cleopatra's tight hand, the grey dust from the pin makes a pattern, lacy, somehow scenic, like a metal leaf, the charcoal outlining its shape on her hand, the live blood searing, boosting the pain in her hand, a pain actually located in her heart.

A baby. But no, no baby. Only this pain, this shadow, what would have been inside Cleopatra, something complete and alive and inevitable, broken, surrendered. If Cleopatra had wanted it to end, fine and fair that would be. Her body. But nothing is simple and Cleopatra hadn't wanted to it to end, not really, had wanted it to stay, for life to leech what it needed from her body and rise into this sharp, clear world. To breathe and survive. Wanted the warmth of that other soul to feed with her body, to share the fragmented cosmos with her. To be kin . . .

Now sadness, a deluge.

"You wore this gown?" Mim asked, to veer from what she had seen.

Cleopatra exhaled. "Apparently. Now, about your situation. Physics. Understand them. The body understands. Things fall, things tip and gather. Things move toward, or away. When something's lacking, something else tumbles into the void."

Mim saw Cleopatra's heart close. "I don't know what that means," she said.

"How can I explain if you don't understand? You were empty, then someone filled you up. How the twister changed things, you forgot your own but you see the others. With the exception of me. Your body, like your memory, was empty. Now there's something there."

"A baby isn't a thing," Nelda said.

"You know what I mean," Cleopatra said.

Mim hugged a pillow. "Should I tell Pelle?"

"No one calls him that," Cleopatra said.

"Suspender," Mim said.

"Good question," Nelda said. "It's up to you."

Cleopatra spread cards on the floor. "Behold the majesty."

Mim had never looked at them in a bouquet like that. Ornate lettering, depictions, their color shrouded by time.

Cleopatra said, "Each card holds an infinite story. Regret. Fear. Victory. Destruction. Here's something for you." Cleopatra lifted a card that said *La Force*. A woman holding open the mouth of a lion. "Strength. Yes. Open the lion's mouth, but *understand* it's a lion. Use any calm intellect you find inside yourself. Release, or don't. Tell him, or don't." She turned the thick card over and over, and looked at the wall. "Decide what you want to live with."

Nelda laughed. "That's a heap of deciding. There's a lot of life out there." She reached over and rubbed Mim's scalp. Such freely given beauty could very reasonably tear Mim apart.

II

In the morning, iridescent light trickled through Mim's window, became floodwater. Residue, what was left of the night. But with something new. Light whispered in like air, between the glass and the pane. There was energy in the light. Mim rose, hungry for food.

Some carnies slurped Cleopatra's good coffee and others drank tea. Most had already eaten. Mim filled a cup with coffee and sat beside Cleopatra. Suspender told whoever had eaten to go finish the flood cleanup. "I'm full of muck," he said. Between his teeth, a tin toothpick wiggled when he spoke. He took it out and examined it. "Scour, scrub, get in and get it done."

Above his head, a leaf like a piece of jewelry, small, sweet, and covered with silvery dew.

He is in the rope room, after their coupling, walking the perimeter. He peers inside her. Sees a new life. *He knows.*

And that simply: she, herself, was inside a memory. Not merely there to watch, pulled into someone else's time. She belonged. Someone remembered *her*. She existed? She existed. And, for Pelle, the shadowy bulk again, the burden, swinging.

Above the dishes, above his head: another leaf. Not showy, but perfectly symmetrical. She looks down at herself in the rope room, feels her shoulders inside his shoulders, and he eases down into her, and she is loving herself; after they are finished, the feeling in his ribs is the feeling in her ribs.

They are making a person.

Mim was going to have a child; they were going to have a child. The child (the girl?) would survive.

"Did you see that?" Pelle asked.

She nodded. Curlicues whittled inside her bones; *should I tell him? Does he know?*

Pelle drank tea, to hide a smile.

Lo-Lo spooned out breakfast soup for Mim. But everything smelled like oil or tin. Mim had lost her hunger. Her head was full of dishes, noise, tin toothpicks. She tried to push these things aside so she could think, but Lo-Lo intruded.

"Stew for the Mim." Lo-Lo scooped a dollop of fonse cream to sweeten, and said, "Makes the frog bean stew rounder to the buds. How is our Rope Girl?"

"Fine," she said. She didn't think Lo-Lo knew, and she didn't know how to tell anyone. Or if. What words. It didn't happen every time with the men, with the skin on skin. Only sometimes, depending on the moon. Now Mim knew about the contraption built from two bodies, and sunshine. And maybe Cleopatra was wrong about Suspender.

Maybe he wasn't all, only, death.

III

In the construction shop, Mim trailed a finger over an iron plate, feeling its patina, listening to Pelle's hammer. He ignored her; she ignored him, too, but craved proximity, yearned for his memories. She would consume Beede, milk the power of his attraction for her, but she would crawl inside Pelle's head, inside his shell. She wanted to be there. There was so much metal in him. If she were to open his door and step inside, she would find a universe of discarded treasures, full of use and fancy. He probably sorted

181

his interior according to function, like in the shop. Here, flat pieces stood against the wall, a variety of walls themselves, ready to be chosen and cut, chiseled, shaped into something new. Inside his shell, he would store useful things in prominent places. The bizarre would be hidden, cast aside—but kept—for you-never-know-what, purpose not obvious, not *yet*, but still, hoarded. Most people would look at Suspender and see utility, function, the boss of the place, but Mim knew his strings and whirligigs, metal, maybe even mud, fragile bits that had dried in the sun after the flood, his memories, his life and liveliness.

Not looking up, he asked, "What are you gawking at?"

She hadn't realized she was staring at him.

He said, "Start with the carnies. Lo-Lo first. Don't try to read my mind. There's enough of you in here already."

He wrapped heavy wire around a wheel, weaving, fingers like birds, hands nimble and sure.

"What are you building?" she asked.

"Need to finish the *punctum*. Each of these must wound somehow, or people won't care. This one, for instance, the floor can't be too square, or it won't do its job." He knocked the wheel against a tall wall of iron, and it made a hollow echo, like tuning an instrument, like when Nelda plucked birdstrings on her V-block.

"All those parts you collect in that huge crate. What are they for?"

He laughed. "You're a question machine."

There were holes in the metal: ragged, absent polka dots. He looked at her through one of the gaps. "Wish I could find more of that club moss. I could use the fire."

Mim rested her forehead against the top of the polka dot. "I love what you make."

He smiled. "You haven't seen the best of it."

"Show me."

He stared at her forever through the polka dot. Then he ducked around to her side, took her hand, and led her through a hidden back door. Outside, he let go of her. They passed one of the surviving kittens, Nelda having finally released them from their green satin pockets, and walked toward a tall wooden structure. Closer, it looked like a tree, but twice as tall. Made of wood, but not alive. Holding a tiny house.

The tree was the color of the house marooned in it, a color that blended so well with the browns of the terrain that it was possible to believe no one had ever noticed it. Certainly Mim had not. A small door was carved into its side.

Inside and up a spiraling ladder, up to the house that leaned invisibly against the wooden tree's limbs. At the top was a platform, a porch that barely fit two people.

"You built this?"

Pelle began to open the door's lock. He performed seven distinct steps. "Ritual," he said. Inside, they maneuvered through the sea of models that hung from the rafters. A slab of slate leaned against one wall. On it was a chalk drawing of a contraption. Mim recognized several parts harvested from other carnival rides: parts on the list for the Crossing. "What's that?"

"Special project." With a rag he erased chalk lines, leaving ghosts. "If I live a thousand years, I still wouldn't be able to make all this full size," he said. "But attempt is important. Stretches the brain-pan. Helps solve problems."

"Like untying the Impossibles," she said.

"Not impossible anymore."

Energy flooded her body and words came out. "Cleopatra says I'm going to have a baby."

The boy behind his face stared at her. "Why would she say that?"

"You know how it happens?"

"Course I know." He went to the slate, pressed and swiped his cheek across the board and made a new ghost there.

"Are you vexed?" she asked.

"*Denouement.* Clocky claims it's French, means the untying of knots. Knots are everywhere. Sometimes they can sneak up."

"I guess we sneaked this one up ourselves," she said.

He grabbed and kissed her. Then spun intricacies, wheels, pulleys, and delicate fan blades no larger than spoonbeds. Soon the whole room undulated like a flock of crows in the wind. "So you want to do some real business for me?"

Seeing the wonder of this hidden place, what, given infinite time, he would create, she felt she would do *anything* for him. But she didn't want him to know. *Anything* was a lot. Anything might be too much. "I need to show *you* something," she said.

She took him to the hotel, to her room. She lifted the board that hid the book. "I found it in the basement, near the Impossibles." She handed it to him.

He ran his finger down the spine, opened it. "What is all this?"

She explained.

"It makes no sense, I can't make it out."

She sat and tried to decipher her notes for him.

"Read to me." He stretched across her cot.

She read most, kept some back. She skipped details about him, and closed the book.

"What about Nelda? And the fortune-teller?" he asked.

She pondered those memories as if they were scenes in the Camera of Illusion. "No. There's nothing you would mind, nothing about this place. What's inside my friends are old things. Not for you."

Pelle frowned. So familiar, his frame draped on her cot. "Guess I have to trust you. Can't read it myself."

"Trust me." She told him about Lo-Lo and the man, and the chocolate . . . the boy they found in the woods, and many other things she had seen.

"What's it like, to see my memories?"

She closed her eyes. One word would not leave her mind. "Sad," she said. The hanging shadow that hounded his every memory swung in her mind, no memory attached this time, only that heavy, dead shadow, a cloud that would never dissipate, would never forget its cruel promise.

"That's what it's like for me, too," he said.

They looked at each other, inside the hush.

"You don't even know if you have anything to be sad about," he said. "What is that like, not to remember?"

"Quiet. Like at night, when the carnival's empty, no wind, and all you feel is the air press in, like cotton, or like nothing."

"You can be sad," he said. "I think you have reason to be sad."

She went to the cot and curled into his body, which wasn't as warm as she had hoped for.

Know how some spritely fools will see a flower, let's say a daisy, and write a song about it? Those suckers who don't know better? Or who say they

184

have given up on the world and its platitudes, yet still hold a drop of child wonder inside, some part they never quite shucked off, still willing to believe in magic? Say I speak against that crust of disillusionment, just for a few moments. Uplift, the flutter that taps inside a prison of ribs, that sunlit moment. Maybe it's hope, maybe it's love. Call it what you want. Sometimes it's hidden until another drop of wonder falls and finds its twin.

How she wanted warmth, it was some kind of yarn like that. And why not? What could such stupefying trifles possibly hurt?

Let's see.

Later, Mim crossed the murky river, careful not to touch the water. She repeated aloud the instructions Pelle had given her.

The sentry, Randall, leaned against a barrel, asleep. His shotgun leaned, too. Mim ran past him up the hill, toward the large building. Raucous ban-joletto music came from inside. Gravity works harder on a banjoletto than anything else, she had heard carnies say. Inside, men stood in a circle around where Beede had stood before. A pile of grey and orange coals glowed in the middle, a scent like burned meat. Someone from the ring approached Mim: Beede, covered again in soot, that leather bag again strapped to his chest.

"Missed the first act, sweetheart, but you'll catch the second. Might be too hot to stand close, but you can listen back here."

"I'll wait outside."

"No! Stay. Men, tip your hats. We have a visitor."

The men ignored her.

"Pretty, isn't she?" Beede said. "Tempting. But she's otherwise occupied."

He works so hard for their attention.

"Don't take it bad, Mim. They've lost their drive toward the ephemera, the fair sex. Here at the works, all pretty urges get ground out of 'em." He touched her breast.

"Okay, students! Time for edification," he said to the men, then pushed into the center and began to recite.

"Who lost track past midnight at Spurlock's Trap, near-river, 1917?
Oh yes Oh yes Oh yes

What you're to see, boys, you dirty cads, you
seen plenty spark here, what else, you're thinking
you constitute yourselves of solids, you're commanding
gentlemen, can take some things, maybe you've traveled, say
Illinois, Illinoise, farther, it don't take ambition
to see the world, just a slick hand and some loose pocket. Rust is
    everywhere—
Davey knows my language.

Who hasn't done some time, all we got is time in this vast
bum's end of things. I've spit up wet gobs of coal, we're all the same
just don't get caught.

Once saw a man dangle from a shagbark hickory, by his neck, all of it,
tree bark and scales
fallen from those eyes. All I can say: use the brain-pan,
don't get caught
and you won't end up with any fallen scales.
Don't laugh back there, it wasn't all
that amusing to see that man dangle, the weight of himself dead
meat. He didn't have much luck.

But you've stepped up here, all of you,
to wait for that kiss which makes us all breathe in, every crusted
    morning
for whatever long years we've got, a kiss humid and lovely like that
    lost mermaid,
she's got curves, wait another day and maybe you'll find that luck
somewhere. Factory life got you groaning, you're thinking anew,
    ambitious,
ready for this fire?
Let me take off my shirt now. How I do it, you won't even see the
    spark,
just watch.

Lucien B. Dunavant will show you the light.

You count your breaths; I'll count mine. That old sack granddaddy
    Spurlock
has not *one* thing on me.

Ready, boys?"

Some men applauded, bellowed. Some didn't. Beede spit on the floor as
if in triumph, bowed, and went to Mim. "Arms to bear, to lift, to grab." He
wrapped his charred body around her, then pulled her to a door and out
into the night.

"What's that?" Mim pointed at the leather bag.

"What, my bota?" He lifted her skirt and tickled behind her knee. She
laughed. His smoke-tinted torso shone and pulsated; he looked like a
monster.

She moved his hand away. "Show me where they make the powder."

"She wants to see all!" he said. He twirled her into the darkness. A three-
sided building appeared, lower on the hill, near the water but set aside from
the rest of the buildings. The fourth wall open to the river.

Sourness leeched out; layers covered the ground nearby like tar, or something slithery, dampened by the lumpish forms that circled the building.
Rain barrels? An exquisite pulley system, with a track and many buckets,
ran from the river into the structure's mouth. The art of Suspender.

She pointed to the track. "What's that?"

"River pulley? Your boss made that. To kill small fires. Say some overnight nincompoop forgets where he is and decides to have a smoke. Crank
the lever, pump up some water, and lug it over. Big fires, not much you
can do about them, not quickly enough, anyway. We need the river for the
grindworks, but also for putting out flames. When possible."

She walked toward the dark building, then through its mouth, and
something sharp bit her shin.

"Careful, darling. Can't exactly light a candelabra in this place." He followed her inside, stood behind her. "One of the boys was talking about
you. You're famous. Are you still from nowhere?"

She turned toward Beede. Her belly rippled. "Everyone is from somewhere. Me, I don't remember, that's all."

"Nothing at all?" His face crowded hers in the still, pungent darkness.

She hadn't wanted Beede to know too much, though all a person could know was her loud, wind-wail emptiness, the unease of her skin, more common when she wasn't wearing ropes that remembered.

That, and the seeing.

Adjusting to the dark, she traced his mouth, its succulent squareness full of sour death. She ignored the stench and kissed him, a distraction from Pelle's instructions. *Find the powder house, find the sparks,* he had said. Pelle's intent was still unclear, but her affection for him eclipsed this fact.

She needed to study the powder house; that's how Pelle had put it. *Learn the contours, in the dark if you can, makes it easier to set up.* But she had to be casual, merely curious, like a guest, maybe.

She kissed Beede again, using their shared commerce. "Show me everything."

He took her hand, and pulled her deeper into the room.

"All shifts on duty, working their sad arses off. We need to make more 'death pills' as you carnies call them, for the big Gatlings."

"Gatlings?"

"There's more war coming," he said. "No time for inferior powder. And Spurlock is making a new something, oh yes. The whole world will change."

The foul powder met them fully. She coughed but had to finish the job. She wrapped the river scarf over her nose and mouth and studied the place.

"I've got summat important here," he said. He unzipped the bota and pulled a gleaming lump from a velvet pouch. About the size of a child's fist. "It's the real thing. New material. They say people will go mad for it. War is about to get a lot more interesting, I promise. Lighter than metal, stronger and sharper. Better for battles. They hain't even named it yet. But I got a piece! It fell from the box and those bigwigs didn't even see it. I aim to get the plans for it, too. After the last shore leave, they invited me to the Engineers' to give a Report of Security, and I saw where they keep the formula. Saw the plans. I'll sneak up there and learn them some night, real quiet. Take 'em if I can."

"What'll you do with them?" She memorized the room.

"Don't worry about that. All kinds of people will want something this useful. But enough talk of business." Beede whispered into her neck, "You really don't remember anything? Neither Mama nor Bapa? No impudent big brother with Christian name, no Matthew nor James? Truly nothing?" He held her breasts. "You're blooming," he said, then lifted her dress. She let him; she nearly needed him, despite having to breathe foulness. Even as he disgusted her. He moved, pushed her forward. She hit another sharp metal edge.

"What's that?" Hard to talk, hard to breathe with him behind her, inside. He laughed and made lots of other noise, but she was distracted.

He finished and buttoned up. "Curious cat, aren't you? That's the 'Will Rack.' One of the grinder steps. The grindworks run by water, so sparks are unnecessary. Mmm: perhaps your papa was in munitions. You are a curious cat, that's true."

She didn't see the leaf over his head, but saw what followed.

Beede, square-mouthed boy, with that other, younger boy, with wild hair . . . the boy Beede . . . panting, sweating, grime on his hands, grime on his neck, and the younger boy stares, both of them, all of them stare at what's heavy and dangling from the rafters, a body, *his father,* the younger boy's father. In the killing air of the powder house, the spark of the death pill factory, confusing past with present, Mim sucks in dusty ancient air of memory, and the younger boy, Pelle, the one Suspender used to be, vomits all he has inside. Mim knows it is all he has, and the boy Beede laughs the laugh of a crow, a choking caw, and though she oddly can't feel it, he also seems unable to breathe, no one can, and especially not the man, the father, who hangs from the rafter by his neck.

She didn't fully understand Pelle' plan. He had said that he had three possibles, and some things to build. But now she knew the Crucial History. Now she would be one hundred percent lure. Now she understood why.

IV

At Sunday breakfast next noon, the sun licked every surface smooth, candifying the world. Suspender whistled and announced another drill for the Crossing.

"Empty even your minds of anything not essential. Machine your bodies, do the work. Faster you go, sooner you'll rest. You have twenty minutes to eat, then get moving."

Nelda leaned toward Mim and Cleopatra. "Lest we forget how to perform the pointless."

Cleopatra laughed.

During the first step, disposing of trash and anything obvious, Mim went to Pelle. "Dunavant stole a chunk of something new from the factory. The bosses don't know he has it. Something they invented. And he means to steal the plans."

"What's the chunk?" Pelle shoveled flood-moldy hammocks and canvas into the pile.

"Something dangerous. For the war."

"He's a thief. Even better for us," he said.

They set the trash on fire. Mim delivered her assigned part from the Electric Trampoline to the crate outside Pelle's construction shop, then began today's main job: helping Nelda de-rope tents, starting with the east and working west toward the river.

PART THREE

SIXTEEN

THE VESSEL

I

Innovating, copulating, creating. Wire and metal, muscle and bone, the material you choose is nearly irrelevant. The matter, the carbon, is only an excuse. An opening. A way to clear your throat. *It was there, staring at me; I had to do something.* The energy, what we cannot see, the invisible part is what's alive. Maybe if you watch, with patience and care, you'll see a glimmer, your eyes will tell or trick your mind there was something there, just now, did you see that?

More like a song, more like a flame, barely visible, but watch for its quiver, its dance, watch for the moment it leans toward you. And wakes.

Pelle was crafting the body of a small mechanical person, an automata that Mim was to install in the powder house. This contraption, coupled with one strong Impossible, would cause the bucket system to suck water from the river, to flood and ruin the Spurlock powder.

"No explosion necessary," he said.

"Sounds simple," she said.

The idea was to arrange things so Beede would be blamed. "As if he had overlooked summat, some element of security. Or better, that he himself aimed for sabotage. Punch that rattlesnake with his own venom. And slow the inevitable doom-drum, slow the killing." Pelle wanted to wait another week, until the powder house was crammed with the stuff of death. Beede had explained to her their production and transport process. Waiting would increase Spurlock's loss. Waiting would also leave time for Beede to steal the formula. "We'll make sure his arse is in the fire," Pelle said.

Mim now understood why the carnival had stagnated so long. Without intent, she had bloomed between brother enemies astride the river. Her job bled out from that water in both directions. *The river tells a story,* she thought, the river divides and unifies. We all need water, we all need power, and she needed to move back and forth between the wills of these two men. Inside her body, she held one of them, and with her skin, she held the other. Both men bent up the world where she existed, both had fashioned the natural world, the earth and the sky, both twisted their missing pieces in her direction, each knowing only part of it, but she knew it all, knew the full world they had made, the three of them. With this life growing inside her, the four of them. Her part was the sinew, the vine that allowed motion. She was the river between creation and destruction; she was the edge, the damp dirt, the borders that allowed water to flow, from before to after. The river was Time. As the damp dirt along the edge of this world, her keenest need was met: she was part of Time. She belonged.

More than belonged. Maybe she had never existed before the fortune-teller found her. Maybe she had been born there, through the wall of wind, which had nearly destroyed her, but was her only mother.

At intervals, Suspender had huddled and imbibed with Spurlock. Mim hadn't understood why until now. She hadn't reckoned why he worked for Spurlock when he claimed to hate the death. Now she knew all his work, the contraption he had built with thoughts . . . made a thing that had a shape, a shape as real as a body dangling from a wooden beam.

He asked Mim to cross carefully and continue seeing Beede, to maintain trust. Said to be careful now that she had something extra inside. She savored this job; messing with Beede served the needs of her skin.

One night, she returned to the carnival after the lights were out. Busy on the factory side, she hadn't noticed the late hour. Walking along the boulevard, past slumbering tents and attractions, she surveyed the leftovers from the night's take. Lots of trash, evening must have ended well, fatter than some. Since the flood, rebuilding an audience had been uneven. Mim reckoned everyone had troubles, messes to attend. But things were improving. Bits of junk and crumbles, powdered sugar, and discarded meat cake rinds. Beatrice would eat well tomorrow.

"She has returned," Pelle said from the hotel porch.

In the dimness, he peeled wood from whatever he was carving. His hands were rarely idle; if he wasn't working wood or knitting, he occupied himself with a pocketful of metal pieces. Or spun his ballyhoo coin, always conjuring with his hands.

"How do you do that in the dark?" she asked.

"How do you do what *you* do in the dark?" he asked. "How does anyone do anything?"

Her skin stirred, breeze upon a feather, lifting the afterfeathers of her shell. She exhaled, and the skin settled again.

"Here's your baby," he said. He handed her what he had been carving, small and round. He reached for her other hand and she gave it. He pulled her onto his lap. "You smell like death," he said, but kissed her anyway.

The world gasped beneath her, a wide yawn, and she closed her eyes to deepen the abyss. Relief not to see things. Her body, so tired. He kissed her, and she kissed him, until she couldn't stay awake in the warmth, and everything she had, which wasn't more than meat on bones and tremble inside gut, where the baby kept growing; everything, all of it, cascaded into the open mouth of the world.

Something tapped her cheek. A small bird? A pebble? There were pebbles by the river less gentle than this tap; maybe this was the history of the world. Not metal, but wood on flesh, muted, only a vibration.

From a hundred miles away, he asked, "Are you asleep?"

The tap was not the history of the world, but the carved head, a baby, the head of the person they had created together, to ruin and remake another world.

Small enough to fit in her hand.

The next afternoon in his treehouse, Pelle cleared a work table and arranged parts. Running her hand around the table's perimeter, Mim catalogued: seven desiccated boots, laces removed and organized by length and gauge; a lampshade of cellulose; nine metal ball-chains; a shrunken, brown tangerine; five dull pencils; several vats of glue and plaster. Some boxes. The carved head. And some pointy metal. These objects before her—how long had he hoarded and protected them, how had he known what he would need? *Who gave him permission to dream so fully?*

"You have such good things," she said.

"Finding what's useful. It's something you learn." From a box he produced a fine silken rope, delicious, the color of burnt umber. She touched the rope's sinews three times, traced its path.

"Where did you get this?"

"Knew you'd like that one. It's from my father's house."

"Show me how things work," she said.

He did. She worked on tasks Pelle said his hands were too large to do. Her hands, his. After awhile, she said, "I need to eat."

"Not until you've finished," he said.

She worked quickly on the too-small pieces, made bits ready and lined them up in order, prepared for duty.

III

Goat cheese and paprika mash on toast.

"Shout yer praises! The goats are naturizing!" Lo-Lo said.

Mim helped Lo-Lo fill platters, then sat between Nelda and Cleopatra. Beatrice hunched under the table against Cleopatra, who studied cards, saying nothing. Unusual that Beatrice was inside, but life was different since the flood.

Everyone ate the bounty.

"Mim, you know something I don't," Cleopatra said.

"I don't know what you mean," Mim said.

"She knows how to keep secrets," Lo-Lo said. "A person's allowed to have stories of her own, Eliza-Lou." He often guessed at Cleopatra's true name, watching her face for a reaction. Nelda giggled. Cleopatra spat into her now empty plate and gathered her cards.

Cleopatra and Nelda and Lo-Lo each knew things about Mim. Knowing, not knowing, the compartments blurred and met inside her.

Cleopatra said, "Come, Beatrice. Escape this hole." The beast snuffled behind her grey-blue robe, which pulled a curtain of dirt in its wake.

"I'm off, too," Nelda said. "Wishing Well needs a dredge." She stood and kissed the top of Lo-Lo's head. "Maybe it's a hole, but quite a savory one. *Quel fromage! Merci!*"

Lo-Lo smiled, and spun the moon and the sun. "Now, what's your game, strumplet? I can smell sport on your flesh."

"I'm still hungry," she said.

He got up and assembled another plate. "What's the belly?" he asked.

She ate it all. "More, please."

He looked at her for a while, then gave her more. "Did you hear me?" he asked.

She stared at him, trying to imagine a leaf. Which leaf would this memory bring? This was how she had been able to conjure up that guest. She chewed and thought *leaf, leaf, leaf.* Nothing. Pointless anyway, what would Lo-Lo plot, aside from escape when he tired of the work? Where would he go? This was his home. She would have to wait for nature to see if Lo-Lo held any claims against the carnival.

She washed and dried her plate. "You don't need to protect me anymore." She kissed his cheek.

Quiet beneath the song of the water, he said. "Yes, I do."

IV

Mim decided to weave the father's rope into a basket. Pelle sketched instructions. She sat on the bench beside him, traced with her finger each twist of line, then said, "No. I know what'll work better."

From the table, the father's rope whispered, *help me, help yourself, do what you can to survive, why hesitate? I am snake and delight, soft, strong, waiting . . . I am what you need, what will bind and free and bind you, I am the vessel, I am the method, use me to make what you see in your mind. I will hold the machine-child.*

You always do what comes next, the rope whispered along her cheek, having slithered up her arm, and wound itself around her, the rope learning her body with each breath.

The near-end of rope joined itself and the coil basket fit perfectly under her arm, making a nest for the small person she and Pelle were building. She tucked the last end of rope into the basket handle and offered it to him.

"Sometimes you give me hope," he said.

He dropped a red marble into a glass-encased maze built inside a cracked cooking pot. A series of levers and pulleys and glass tubes. The marble's weight made each next thing happen in this pot-sized world. The two humans listened to its music. He lifted her leg so she straddled the bench, pulled her onto his lap, and she pulled him inside her with his machine-making apparatus, and that sunshine was slower now, late day, gentle, still warm, and she let her head fall back, relaxing her shoulders, dangling her mind. It was unusual, this exhilaration like flying, like the rope wasn't a basket but was, instead, a carriage, a ride, a series of pulleys, and soon all the Impossibles that had ever been untied, throughout all of time, all fibers joined to weave a web of freedom. The wall of wind did not control her. She was held by this enduring rope.

The rope meant life.

As her lover pressed up inside her, the connection was not to him beneath her and the bench beneath him, but to the warm blood of herself and all the life that radiated with fibrous bounds in the air, so she had the simultaneous feeling: falling, yet being cradled.

Loved.

V

The sky pushed down, threatened rain for the first time since the flood. Beede had come to her side of the river this time, flopped his head in her lap. His square mouth spoke of Wistmount, and a cavalcade of other towns. *He must know lots of things,* how to find people. He said he had found his way after his parents had died and hadn't stopped since.

"There's rarely a riddle kept from Beede. A twister girl, she must have secrets inside. You can fly, can't you?" He walked his fingers toward her nipple, played there.

She moved his hand away. "That hurts," she said.

"Plenty of things hurt. Some like hurt."

"Not me." She had noticed a difference in her breasts, how she bore their presence. His head's weight irritated her lap, and her skin rebelled.

She looked down at him, his bota with its secret, leather bag now always against his body. She was only a picture of herself, pasted onto the world. Others could see her, but sometimes she still didn't feel quite solid. She summoned Desiree, dancing in the moving picture, unveiling herself as someone new, and Time stretched back to the actual moment when Desiree was about to undress, after the camera had stopped filming, and Mim could see the beauty emerge, narrower hips than a woman would have. Desiree was insistent, memory captured in a scar. Like the memories captured in Mim's scars from the twister, her twister, and the stained picture of Desiree turned, so Mim could see, could feel her body, the blend of parts—truth, yearning, and emancipation—and despite the world that pressed in above Desiree, and despite the moody sky above Mim, and despite Beede's irritating touch and his square-mouthed head in her lap, and despite all the vivid apprehension of existence: hope. Desiree was hope.

And hope was a baby, inside.

"I might have been a dancer," she said.

"I know some dancers." He rose from her lap and sat beside her.

"But Cleopatra hasn't been able to figure it out," Mim said.

"I'll find you, I will. Need finesse, these situations, don't want to shock the bystanders. Let's say they think you're dead. Let's not cause human expirations out of fate's turn. No hysterics." Said he had seen hearty men faint, after the last war, when kin, presumed dead, walked through the door.

He was stuffed with words, trying to impress. Like always. Though his squawk was louder lately. He knew everything, could do *everything*! But each time she met him, despite how he skewed his chest forward, he looked ever more puny. As Pelle looked ever more strong.

Lo-Lo cooked breakfast of substitute grain and sang, "Witty Mim, full of wonder, seems green but green's a veil." Sometimes when he sang, he would step onto a crate—elevate himself for an audience of one, or sometimes two, counting Beatrice. Today, Mim applauded as usual, though his music leaned minor. He had been suffering insomnia, as they all had. Last night at dinner, Nelda announced her plan to sleep the whole day. Said not to bother her until she rose.

"Make us some coffee?" Lo-Lo asked Cleopatra. "I needs it."

Cleopatra had divined why they couldn't sleep, why now, more than the usual cyclic tossing: The approach of war.

Toward the carnival that fiend crept, riding the clang of current, the sped-up works across the river. When given opportunities to make fire and ruin, Spurlock never said no. Despite personal outbursts of pugilism, the carnies had one thing in common: they all detested war. Conscription was not in their plans. It wasn't the danger; risks were part of life. *Jump on the Electric Trampoline. Climb the Tower of Doom.* But to craft strategies for killing didn't appeal to any of them. There were risks aplenty in this passivity. They couldn't ignore the looming drums. The radio, when it worked, unrolled less music and more stories of build-up, fissures ready to burst. The carnies needed to hear news, to prepare somehow, but too much and their bodies froze from the scratch of radio words, fought relaxing, couldn't settle. To be ready for the Crossing, the physical need to react when called upon—to pack and go—was a sunny walk compared to all this planned death that splashed the world. The radio gave facts, but stole their sleep.

Cleopatra fished out the stained eggshells and poured coffee for whoever asked. It was thick, and opened the shutters inside Mim's skull to let in the day.

"Cookie is haunted by the phantom of conscription, despite our policy against killing work," Nelda said.

"That's not work," Suspender said. "That's cowardice. Insufficient mind on that Spurlock. No long view on him. No, that man is a scared coward. Takes real courage to avoid pugilism. Takes an amount of craft. An amount of art. Invention."

"What Spurlock makes is invention, too," Timmy Zuzu said.

Mim agreed with Zuzu. She had seen some of it, more than other carnies, but didn't want to say.

"No denying," Cleopatra said. "But peer inside a human: you'll see the edges aren't always so clean."

"Sometimes there is mud," Suspender said.

But the radio and newspapers kept up the squawk. Mim found it confusing, the effort it took to fight when just surviving—getting food and maybe some accidental inspiration or song in life—took all their toil and time. Really, the carnies didn't want to fight because they didn't see reason to die before nature made its declaration. Nor to kill anyone else.

During the season of war insomnia, nighttime meant little. Even to the Tobeys. Usually, they slept through loud snores, coughs, and warbling, no matter how the planets aligned, or didn't. Now they fell asleep at lunch, at table, mid-bite. Most of the Tobeys were rough and rude, their deft hands their only savior from the forest. Maybe they had come from the feral forest, like that boy with the samovar shield. Perhaps someone had found each waif, and trained them as Tobeys—some of their work required skill. Who had made those hands, who taught them to work? Some questions Mim would never ask.

Even the Tobeys heeled into the mud and braced against more war. Hated any threat to their bodies.

"Politics say all they want about reasons. Read the newspaper, you'll see. But they're not the ones dying," Nelda said. "That Spurlock's not dying, nor his kin."

Carnies raised their cups and drank and grumbled.

"I doubt any conscription service would bother with us," Suspender said.

"Don't assume," Lo-Lo said. "Yesterday in Wistful Mount I heard men jaw about signing up before they got discovered to be against the effort. Said Politics don't smile on hiders."

"Only the men, right?" Mim asked.

"That I don't know. Yesterday, I heard a guest talking about his girl and how she would suit up like *un homme* over this mess! Crazy," Lo-Lo said. "No matter who you are."

"Clock! Do I smell ready victuals? Is Time among us? Serve up," Suspender said. "Enough embattlement. Don't ruin eat-up time. If they come for us, it'll first be with paper. If they sent paper, we'll get ready for the Crossing. If you lazies will eat-up and get to work."

"Quit the name-calling, you. My work is often invisible," Cleopatra said.

Mim laughed. Her work was often invisible, too.

"War people won't care about invisible," Suspender said. "Seen or unseen, when war papers come, we run."

VI

So much maybe, maybe, maybe. Mim couldn't shut her brain to maybes any more than Lo-Lo or anyone else could sleep. Long after midnight dinner, Mim went down to the lobby and found him pacing the floor. She pulled him onto a setee, curled up beside him, stroked his head, and watched his eyes stay open, even as, in comforting him, she lulled herself calm.

She didn't need any more of his minor-key memories. She only wanted to help him rest. He leaned on her, but did he ever close his eyes? What she had seen inside Lo-Lo, his sad start in trade for coin and melting choco-late—*If those memories were mine, I wouldn't want to close my eyes, either.* Or maybe she would, would cling to anything. Maybe any memory would be better than none.

The nocturne draped its thick coverlet over the hotel, while the two bodies cowered like wary children in the deep sleepless.

During the epoch of war insomnia, the carnies spoke to each other less and less. Speech drained down to the essential. Words they saved for guests. Lo-Lo cooked but never asked what people wanted to eat. They were lucky to have food, he said, and no one complained. They ate to function, spooned up whatever he dumped on their plates. Would carnival guests even notice the missing niceties that usually jeweled their interactions? Cleopatra stopped protecting her guests from intuition's barbs, the future. She simply told what she saw.

One night, Mim sat in her spy-seat behind a screen. An old woman entered. Not often did matrons or crones come to the carnival. When the old woman had cut the deck, Mim didn't even have to do her trick of imagining a leaf, it just appeared, fat, wet, the lobe of an ear of someone who had swum in muck. In the rain, the woman tugs things from a laundry line, pinches her cold fingers on the splintered clothes pegs, soul swollen, yanks fabric from the downpour, and Mim with the woman feels the rain weighing her down . . . her bones swell and pain her. She calls with a tired voice to her grown daughter . . . her *baby* who will never hear her, because she left with that slick man who talked sweetness into the night, lured her across the land to who-knows-where, she got up and out of this dust-palace mudhole just like that, and how? By letting a man between her knees. Leaving her mother with the sour, soaked laundry. Mim feels the twist inside the woman's chest, the heave that follows such raw betrayal. The ungrateful child. And the twist in her chest begins to tear open, and the flood rain gushes inside the cavity where love used to be.

Cleopatra told the woman her daughter would never return. The woman demanded her coin back.

"But it's true," Cleopatra said.

"You're a scourge." The woman left.

"She was crying," Mim said. And this time, Mim had seen why.

Beatrice growled after the crying woman. Even the beast couldn't rest.

SEVENTEEN

LITTLE LON

I

The treehouse shone, innocent and half-pink in the morning light. For a moment, Mim forgot that the carnival's magic was illusion, wasn't actual. Pelle had woken her early to work before breakfast. It took four hands to make the automata whole. She held the body while he wove wire through its cavity, rigged a spine and moveable neck, and finally affixed the carved head.

The shoes of the automata were smaller than Mim's thumb. She tied the laces. She tied one of her hair ropes around its shoulder, in case. The imp was ready. It crawled into Mim's rope basket, tucked itself into a corner, closed its eyes, and waited.

She hadn't rested or slept much the last few days while they worked on possibilities and problems. *Prepare. Test, adjust, and test again. Oil so all parts move smooth. What if this, what if that. Tighten strings, guard the mechanisms from dust.*

After each day's work, they protected their child under a glass bowl.

Pelle removed the bowl, turned the automata over, and with a magnifying glass, examined the felted wool on its knees and elbows. "Dust is unavoidable, but can thwart success." The success of the child.

Small enough to fit in a hand.

"She's Little Lon," Mim said.

"Little Lon," he said.

A flattened leaf.

Young Pelle, at the rough kitchen table, pushes aside his mane and watches the older boy, who is Beede. Young Beede shoves dry bread, cheese, and other foodstuffs into a sack.

"Sad news I know, but your father hung himself in that rafter! Took his own life. Must've lacked your ma too much. Too late for him now. We gotta move, time to move, gotta go, can't stay here," he says, "Ain't gonna take me to the waifs' home, and you neither."

Young Pelle hides behind his hair, curls into a ball, protecting his precious flowered tea bowl, his mother's treasure, which he has wrapped in wool and bundled with a rag, hidden in his vest. (Now Mim knows why he treats his bowl with such care.) Child-body perched upon the chair, he tries not to move. She watches Beede as Pelle watches Beede, and she also sees the swinging body, the vision impossible to erase from whatever Pelle sees in memory, and in life. The body, the body, his father, *and Beede did it* . . . Mim knows along with Pelle that Beede killed his father, shot him in the hayloft and strung him from the rafter; Beede is small but he did it, made and strung up his own contraption, eternal and more haunting than anything Pelle could make, and Pelle thinks that the best and safest thing to do is *try not to move try not to breathe just disappear;* perhaps Beede will take food and go, perhaps the body will not swing there forever, perhaps.

Beede leaves the room, the house. Pelle lets go a breath. Then hears footsteps return.

"You gotta come with, or they'll take you!" Beede grabs Pelle's hand, tight.

Mim hears the train when Pelle does.

"Come on!" Beede hauls Pelle out the door and toward the trail that leads to the tracks. Mim feels spikes in Pelle's gut; he needs to go back, can't ride alongside Death.

Pelle says, "Gotta get my machines," and Mim feels his hand break from Beede's, and there is the train, there it is, louder, louder, and Beede yells and points at a door, a gap in the side of a train car, but Pelle turns and runs back toward home, toward the body. He looks back once, sees Beede disappear into the hungry moving mouth, eaten by the train, gone.

Feet pound back toward home, to the heavy swinging body, still in the rafters, his father. Up Mim climbs with Pelle, up to the loft, and in his midden, despairs at the undone wire-scraped residue of his work, the gashed wood, pieces unmoored, essence gone, more wreckage, more of what Beede killed.

But he digs through the straw nest, and from the ruins, pulls a thick loop of sweet, silky rope, drapes it on his shoulder, and uncovers a small, meticulously-made body. A person.

Small enough to fit in a hand.

The one creation still intact. The one thing Beede has not destroyed.

Pelle, so much smaller than the man he will become, curls up in the straw, curls his shell around his hand and the tiny life that beats inside it.

Mim lit a candle and sang to Little Lon, their mechanical child. "But the briar grows before the rose, and neither grows alone." A song Nelda often sang and Lo-Lo had appropriated to whistle at the stove or when fixing the steam truck. There was sadness in songs, but inevitability drove sound from mouths, like myth rolled from its place at the start of Time, through the Eight Mile Suspended Carnival, through even the death pill factory, stopping briefly to look, linger, and move on, into the future, wherever the future was located. A tune would last forever, as long as people didn't forget to sing, whistle, hum.

She sang to Little Lon, hummed when she forgot words, hummed until she recalled a phrase, knitting sound, which vibrated through her, and hushed the clang inside.

II

Dusk, Mim tucked Little Lon in a corner of the canoe, pushed off and paddled toward the opposite bank. Beede would smell deep and cryptic. His scent had changed. When they met, he smelled of verbena, but recently it was more nutty and bitter. Noticeable inside his wrist, and behind his ear, these places collected his essence; and now the verbena only hinted. The layers, the river, the shore, the canoe, these things collided, crowded into the frame with the memories she had seen, all that brought her to this moment, crossing the river, going to Beede, his square, succulent mouth, hoping she could keep her secrets while giving up her body. Giving, but also keeping.

Water spat from the paddle. She no longer cared when it splashed her, hoped she was upriver from the death pill residue. She would do anything for Pelle because of what was growing inside her, what moved, tentative but real. The thing inside echoed what hid in the basket, the machine-child in its nest, ready to do what it was born to do.

Droplets of cool water splashed her arms, shoulders. The paddle, rough and heavy, the motion of her arms, the animal crowded inside her body.

She reviewed the plan:

1. Wait until Beede falls asleep. Best if he sleeps in the powder room, if not, she would sneak there.

2. Unwrap Little Lon, attach her hands to the lever for the pulley system. Stuff dry club moss into gaps between the lever and Little Lon's hands. Hands the first link in the chain.

When Mim reached the other side, Beede was waiting. He stepped into the river, pulled the canoe to the shore.

"How did you know I would come over?"

"Didn't know. Hoped." He kissed her. All his smells pressed in, but there was something new. She didn't know if it was the bota, or her perception of his smell, or if it was simpler: he hadn't bathed in a while. She followed him toward the powder house.

"Where do you take your bath?" she asked.

"You want to take a bath?"

This wasn't in the plan Pelle had designed, but she could follow a new twist. See where things go. Perhaps she would discover something useful.

They went toward the dormitory, beside which a sizeable freshly painted house loomed. "That's the Good House," he said. "Those chemists and engineers enjoy high-quality lodgings. They use the autos. I would live up there too, but the boss needs me to keep track of the boys." He opened the dormitory door. "Quiet now, don't wake anyone. Take off your shoes."

Inside, barefoot, they snuck down a hall with open doorways on each side, dormitory rooms, two rows of beds to each. Men snored and coughed. Sounds gurgled from underwater, buried beneath flesh and skin. Strong, bitter odors, worse than the wet rope room. This was what she had smelled on Beede, the stench he lived amongst. Why had she never noticed it before? Maybe it had to do with the baby.

The baths were at the end of the hall. He turned on the tub faucet, pressed her against the wall, and kissed her neck.

She needed to wash him. She needed a vat of soap. "Take off your clothes," she said.

"Me? Well, okay, me first." He slipped off his clothes, hung the bota on a nail, and stepped into the filling tub. "Cold!" he said.

She took the soap and dove her hands underwater, into chill like melted ice. She rubbed his chest and back.

"Raise your arms." She tried not to inhale as she lathered and washed.

He giggled. "Get in here!"

"It's too cold."

"Get in!"

To shut him up, she took off her clothes and river scarf. She straddled him. Her knees and shins slid into the murk. The filthy water was so cold it burned, and the hard tub dug into her bones.

He was unready for her.

"What's wrong?" she asked.

"Damnation! Cold water!"

They washed, shivery. Mim didn't want to submerge in his reek, but she needed to occupy herself. Plenty of time until sunrise, plenty of time for the plan.

They dried themselves with greyish linen. She dressed, but Beede whispered, "I need new unders." She waited in the doorway while he entered a roomful of sleeping men, went to a walled-off box in the corner by a window. Slightly more private than the rest of the room. Was that where he slept? She heard a drawer open, then close. On the way back, he tripped on a pair of boots beside a cot, and fell over a man's feet.

"Make it up!" the man yelled from sleep.

Others stirred.

"Shut your hank!" another said.

"Back to sleep, boys, lullabies all around," Beede said.

"I smell something nasty," said the man with the boots, awake now. He stood and pissed in a pot.

"Wilson's perfume," another man said. A few others laughed.

"No, it's nastier," the boot man said.

One of the men was Timmy Zuzu. A rough story hung across Zuzu's face, what he never wore at the carnival. "Dead Louie don't allow visitors," Zuzu said. He looked so sad.

"Go ahead, Zuzu, you turncoat, tell that lifeless bastard," Beede said. "Fuck him." He took an electric lamp from a shelf on the wall, grabbed Mim's hand, and they fled that fetid place.

The warm air calmed her cold-from-the-bath skin. "Who's Dead Louie?"

"An arse and nothing more."

"Will you get in trouble?"

He laughed. "Too late. Fuck Dead Louie and whatever would let him ride its flanks! I'm starting to warm up. Come here." He grabbed her hand and pulled her onward.

"He's always in my meat house. Blamed me for the fire in the eggery. Those chickens were lazy anyway, better off gone. Let me show you something."

They passed the small buildings, moved toward the road.

Beede stopped near a shrub and stomped. The world below sounded hollow. He pulled back a swath of dry grass, revealing the outline of a door, which he opened. "My collection. I don't intend to stay here forever. Hold the light," he said. He handed her the electric lamp and stepped into the ground. She crouched, peered into the pool of light, and heard latches click.

"Wake up, children," he said. He looked up at Mim. "Important artifacts here. There's a market, have no doubt, and I will find it. I've got the plans here! Spurlock would have me skinned. Shine it to the right." He climbed out, unzipped the bota and pulled out a metal tube, slightly wider around than the head of the croquet mallet Lo-Lo used for tenderizing flanks. He opened one end of the tube, removed a cylinder of what looked like hair. Thick felt. He unrolled it, and inside was a piece of paper. "The formula. Touch."

She touched it. Thicker than most paper, more like animal hide. What would Pelle think of this midden?

She knew what to do. "The carnival is leaving, Sunday. Come with us."

"True? Thought that carnival would never budge. Been here a long while. What's the sudden?"

209

"Time to move on, they say. Getting stale. Too many pockets are padlocked."

"Sunday's awful soon," he said.

"Come with us, find somewhere to sell that stuff."

"Find a market."

"Yes, find a market. Wouldn't it be safer?"

"I do sometimes feel my time here is near done. Been cogitating on when, and where. Here is it, maybe."

"Yes. And you can be with me." She touched his lips.

"You're cute. Go with Mim. Okay! I'll pack the odds and ends. Assembled, it's a tight puzzle, been practicing. Oh yes, I've rambled. Your boss won't mind; I can work. I've got some tricks. Sunday?"

"Sunday."

"Don't fret, I'll be there."

After he showed her his things, he replaced the important lump in its pouch, and rolled the plans in their cape of felt, carefully, like wrapping a baby. "Damnation, it's cold," he said.

"Let's go to the powder house," she said.

Just outside the powder house door, he stumbled on a bucket, knocking off its lid, and immediately, the stench choked her.

"Oh hell! Now it's reached air, that stink will only get worse. No capping it now. Hell's arse!" He shoved the lid back on, took the handle and walked toward the river.

She followed. "What're you gonna do with it?"

"Settle the matter! Dump it!" he said.

"But isn't it poison?"

"Your boss is a good storyteller. Water washes it away."

"What *is* it? It smells like death."

"Next best thing," he said. He put the bucket down at the river's edge and pushed up his sleeves. "Stay back. Don't want to spill it on you."

He glubbed the otherworldly stuff into the river. The mess held together, snaky; its joyless sheen resembled the dangling shadow that haunted Pelle . . . the body of the grandfather of the child that now stretched within her womb.

He dropped the bucket, which was strangely clean, and wiped his face. With one hand, he drew a square around his body, same as that shopkeeper in Wistmount had done. He spit. "Going Sunday, then."

He's already gone, she thought, *been gone for years.* Watching Pelle's dead father drift down the river.

"I should go, dinner's soon," she said.

"Stay. Be a good girl and stay. You aren't tired, are you?"

"I need to go."

Beede walked her to the canoe, played with her hair, kissed her, and pulled her dress up. She pulled it down.

"Fine. Leave me all het up, then."

She laughed, pushed off and paddled back. She would tell Pelle about Beede's underground stash, and how the plan had changed.

The two metal kings, so small, smaller than the Chess Game backdrop, small like the chess pieces Pelle had carved from porous wood, one stained with oil, one left bare. But not wood, hers were metal: clash, clash. Everyone had secret places. Mim's was in her head. And in the book she had found with the Impossibles. Not only memories, but also stories, notes, names. Questions. She would write down what Beede had shown her.

But first, tell Pelle.

EIGHTEEN

CHIPPING WITH THE LINE

I

Whom she found knitting on the hotel porch, despite the encroaching chill. His tendency to wait for her there when she crossed the river warmed her insides. Beede made more hoopla of his affection, said big things, but she couldn't trust him. Pelle *showed* her, by works and ways. He made things; he made the whole carnival. She sat beside him. A kitten appeared from anywhere and leapt onto her lap. "Teach me to knit?"

"Easy. Watch." He slowed; the needles poked through holes, twisted yarn, the rhythm a comfort. His hands danced beside each other, touching, kissing as he knitted another row. "Here, do it with me." His hands encircled hers, and they fed the mouths with yarn. Sometimes they dropped stitches and went back to find them. Chains of grey cloud accumulated in their hands. The loops were a kind of knot, but not for untying. Beautiful. In her mind, she could also see them in reverse. See it all unravel.

She told him about the bucket of death, told everything. "He said the water washes it away."

"That water goes somewhere. All those small caskets," he said. "What was it like, down in his hole?"

She didn't understand the question, trying to focus on the knitting.

"Was it clean, for instance?"

"Not really."

"There are ways to work against dirt, but only for so long. He's fortunate to be on top of the hill or it would have flooded. I prefer to stow things higher, despite the climb. But I don't guess he could build a treehouse if he's trying to hide."

"I told him the carnival is leaving. He wants to come."

He put down the needles and wool. "You changed the plan."

"I told him Sunday. We can prepare for the Crossing, as usual, and get him over here," she said. "Who says we have to *go* anywhere?"

He stood. The kitten fled. Pelle stepped off the porch, lifted a big rock and threw it at the night. "You don't change the plan."

"Sometimes a plan needs changing. I know him better than you do. He needed a push."

He came back and pulled her to standing. Stared inside her. "Things need a structure. Things need a scaffold. Predictability. Something to hang everything else on! My plans are scaffolds, don't you see that? They hold everything up."

"I know. They're good scaffolds. They're strong enough to hold up even unexpected things. They *are*."

"There's time for improvisation, and time for chipping with the line!"

"I'm chipping with the line!" she said. "It'll work."

After a long silence, he let her go and said, not to her but to himself, "Dammit. Okay. Need to make adjustments, put the machine together. Need to make that part fit the spot. Make a new spot."

A flicker of his boy face appeared. Beede would be the child now, would need Pelle, pulled along as if to hop on whatever train would carry the carnival *away away away* from this place of dust. To a place of imagination, and fancy, and light, where a baby born could be welcomed, not lost in the woods. A place where Mim could be a mother.

A place without Beede.

Pelle unrolled a plot to pack as if to go, and rope Beede in, so he would unearth his treasures, cross the river, only to find a rearranged carnival.

"And Mother there to greet him," he said.

"Mother?" Mim asked, but he sat down and resumed knitting.

II

Suspender asked Timmy Zuzu to help mend some lacerations in the wine tent on Saturday. Mim was inside, cleaning the tables and jars. The carnival would open soon.

"Across the river, it's a bit irregular," Zuzu said. "Spurlock's leaning too close to those newcomers, those engineers. Before, he's always let the boys off nights. He knows—dang, his family's been knowing forever how dangerous night-work can be. But now these engineers say there's a war coming, increase production. If he doesn't hire more bodies, he'll grind ours into the floor."

"Sure hope Spurlock's no fool," Suspender said.

Mim brought them glasses of wine.

"Sorry I couldn't be friends over there, Mim," Zuzu said.

"I understand."

"You're sweet," Zuzu said.

"When is the war coming?" she asked.

Zuzu laughed. "Hell knows," he said.

"Somebody knows," Suspender said. "It's here already."

Cleaning up after midnight dinner, Lo-Lo whistled a lively song.

"That's tidy," Cleopatra said.

"Called 'Livery Stable Blues.' Warbled out of that broke down radio. Been haunting me. Went to Wistmount for sundries, but really for the record." He did a horse whinny and stomped on the kitchen floor.

Mim laughed. "Silly horsie," she said.

"Never mind horsies, I miss those three goats," he said. "Especially Zlateh. She was a good mother."

"Do you wonder what happened to them?" Mim asked.

Cleopatra turned over a card. "Gone down the river," she said. "That Dunavant deviant from the factory said so. He found one corpse, at least."

"He found three live goats," Mim said. "He killed them."

She unrolled the scene, told them everything, did not spare weight, magnitude, or stench.

"That rat bastard. I would kill him barehanded if I could," Lo-Lo said. "How did you discover this?"

Cleopatra looked at Mim. "You decide. But be careful."

Lo-Lo said, "Mildred Eliza-Lou speaks riddles again. What in Pan's arse do you mean, Mildred?"

"When people remember the past, I sometimes see it," Mim said. "Inside."

"Like this one can?" He pointed at Cleopatra with a greasy plate.

"It's different." Mim explained. A charge went through her; it was power. This power was a fact no one could remove. "Promise you won't tell anyone."

"Does this only occur when you are romantically entwined with a person such as that goat killer?"

"No."

"You can see it all?"

"I can see some things."

"You saw a hell of a lot with those goats."

Cleopatra gathered her cards one by one, returning them to the stack, building a shelf of rock. What a shelf that would be, how strong. And oh, all it would see, all it would know.

Lo-Lo asked Mim if she had seen inside him. She didn't answer.

"Well. Windling. How unusual. How, one might say, unexpected." He got up, and on his way out, hummed an ancient song of bitterness.

"You be careful," Cleopatra told Mim. "Padlock your pockets. It's not the grand world you need to protect yourself from, nothing so large. What you cannot predict is people. You cannot control people." She stood and went toward the stairs, left Mim buffered from her friends by sound and space and all she had to carry inside. The fanciful sun and the moon still enlivened the cylinder on the table . . . were always there, tussling through each day. Mim spun the cylinder slowly, and watched Time get claimed by moon, then sun, then moon again.

III

A babe in the womb knows neither shadow nor light, but knows what its body needs, knows to grapple. Squeezed out into the air, it throws the world into chaos with squalls and gluttony, but still, night, day are irrelevant. The sun and the moon are also natural beings, with types of faces, and needs. Sun needs to light up the world, help froth out the plants, and so forth. Moon needs to shadow and confound our dreams, pull that seawater duvet up to tuck in the sand at night, but the moon is a trickster, covers on, cozy sand, covers off, churning up whatever a miniscule person could stand on.

Those shifts, that rhythmic rise and decay will rouse humans, and their whims.

Later, Lo-Lo lugged the gramophone to the lobby, lit every candle, and filled the hurricane lamps. Carnies crowded around to hear the Original Dixieland Jass Band.

"*Allez, dansons!*" Lo-Lo said.

Mim went to him to dance, but instead he found Nelda and they waltzed across the thin rug to the other side of the room. Upon that rug, flowers used to bloom, but that was long ago. Now it was only whispers of crushed leaves, worn to grey. Full of food and wine, the dancers jumped a tapestry to life, as if the world were not patched up badly and falling apart.

Pelle stagnated in the front doorway.

"Come on!" Mim said, but he would not.

Lo-Lo danced Nelda all the record and several more, shunning Mim. Anton the Younger reached for Cleopatra. Recently, he had declared his love for her. She told Mim she considered him interesting but ultimately irrelevant, a moth. Cleopatra asked, "Anton, are you planning against the cold weather that Tiger predicts? Tiger says it's sure to come soon. But I'm unwilling to bear your fruit. Sorry."

"Tiger's knees are skilled prognosticators," Nelda said.

Anton looked perplexed. "I only need the dance."

Cleopatra stubbed her cigar and took Anton to dance. Willie joined the party, and grabbed Mim. They danced until she was too dizzy. A few of the Tobeys danced with each other, and, eventually, drunk with sound, parked their bulk in stuffed armchairs.

Lo-Lo played "Livery Stable Blues" several times more, then he shouted, "I need beverage!"

Mim followed him to the kitchen. He filled a tall cup with wine.

"Why won't you dance with me?" she asked.

"Don't know what you mean."

"You do."

"Come, there's a party on." He returned to the lobby, but slid to the other side of the room.

She hated the new Lo-Lo-shaped hole. He had become her kin, but now avoided her. His affection awakened part of her insides that needed joy. Her body was colder, not being near him.

She went to Pelle. "Come on, have some fun!" she said.

The boy behind his face peeked out like a sprite. But he said, "I only dance on an empty stomach."

"Come." She pulled him into the warm crowd.

He was awkward, but he took her hand and smiled, and she shimmied, like she had seen the ladies do with their men at the wine tent. Her body's thickness affected her balance.

He pulled her closer. "Save that shaking. You'll go back over tonight, take Little Lon. I'll reset the timer. One more dance, then you get ready."

"Shhh." Touching his lips, she said, "Dance with me."

IV

Every part of Mim's body distilled to two things, and through the sheen of exhaustion, she spoke as she paddled: "Wrap the fuse, sway the man, wrap the fuse, sway the man, wrap the fuse, sway the man," until with push, pull, push, words dissolved into the river. All would be well, all would be well, and she dreamed where the carnival would go, somewhere full of imagination and wonder. Sunshine. No more questions. Time would stretch into a life, and she would have a place, a home, a family. Sway herself and sway the man, sway the man, sway the man. All will be revealed. "We're leaving soon," she said, swaying in the craft with her own efforts, *all will be exhumed,* all Beede had collected would be discovered, along with his foul schemes and goat-lies.

The canoe bumped ashore.

The hour ached toward morning. She picked up the basket, which sheltered the machine-child Little Lon. She had practiced, eyes closed. If she could find the ass-end of the pulley rigging, she could do her job with no extra light.

Randall wasn't at his post; his gun stood alone. He had probably snuck off to pleasure himself, as Beede said Randall did sometimes.

217

"Guarding for pirates, not much work there," Beede had said. "You're the only pirate I know of."

Mim went to the powder house and found the place and affixed Little Lon's hands. Cleopatra had told Mim about baby grips. *Hands so small, but they hold a pinkie like it's their only link to life.* Little Lon was no different. Mim kissed the small head three times for luck. If Little Lon did her job well, she would be unfindable.

"Livery Stable Blues" tinkled in Mim's pirate ears as she swung the empty rope basket to the canoe for her private, watery Crossing.

In the hotel kitchen, Nipsy clattered the dishes.

"Any food left?" Mim asked.

He pointed at a wooden platter of miscellany on the table. "Maybe summat in that mess."

She spread a seedy roll with tobacco butter, which Lo-Lo claimed kept skin smooth and bellies warm. Bake tender leaves at low heat all night until brown, then crumble and sprinkle into a vat of soft butter. Lo-Lo would stir and pack the mess into ramequins and cover with cheesecloth, to rest in the basement for a week, for best flavor and effect. "That was how Mama did, and so do I," Lo-Lo said.

It tasted fine late at night or early morning, when you were tired or too full of wine.

"Goodnight, Nipsy," she said.

"Night." He didn't look up from the dirty water.

She took her comestible to the lobby, carrying it in the rope basket, and curled into a big chair, across from Anton the Younger. His eyes were closed but she could tell he wasn't sleeping.

"Hello," Mim said.

"Your most beautiful friend, Cleopatra, has broken this heart." Anton thumped on his chest. "This heart."

"Has she?" Mim took a bite and licked tobacco butter from her lips. The first bite was always horrible, but the more she ate, the more she needed.

A leaf, nearly translucent, as if most of it had been burned away . . . Anton the Younger is even younger, ten or eleven years old. Runs up a staircase, ornate iron rails, twirling columns like candy-sticks, or spine bones, and Mim stumbles as Anton stumbles on the worn marble steps; both move toward the light above, which comes from an unseen window. Giggles cascade toward them, a flounce of young girl disappears around a corner. Anton and Mim follow, through a cloud of gloomy-sweet smoke, but the girl is gone. Anton throws himself against the uncaring rails, nothing to do but mourn, and Mim feels his yell in her throat, "Ohhh," but no sound comes. She is mute as he is mute as the crackle of a man's voice comes from below.

"*Pouco, ven aqui!*" Anton the Elder stomps toward them, and fear of the father rivets Mim to the wrought iron, and together she and Anton the Younger hide, try to disappear.

In the lobby armchair, Anton the Younger thunked his chest again. "Broken, broken. *Bela cartomante* is good at making broken." He rose and walked toward the hotel staircase.

Later, Mim went upstairs, up and up and up to the top of the world, where the landing emptied directly into the nest of Pelle, right below the attic stairs. Needing to be held, needing sunshine, she put down the rope basket and slowly, silently, crept into his bed.

He stirred. "Your plan makes sense, how a poem makes sense," he said. He went back to sleep.

All night, she watched him breathe.

NINETEEN

NATURE LAUGHS

I

After Saturday night's *fête*, the carnies slept until Suspender sounded his shout-horn. Carnies clanged and banged and prepared for the Crossing under grumble. How could they believe Suspender, even if he said this time wasn't a drill? Mim told Cleopatra and Nelda the plan, and they told Lo-Lo, so he wouldn't sour the food with bitterness. Said it had to do with Beatrice and the goats, and other obvious reasons. Everyone knew Beede was vile. Mim recalled the pot-sized maze in Pelle's treehouse. A marble dropped down could begin the work of something new: the collision of Pelle's plan and the inhabitants of the Eight Mile Suspended Carnival.

With aching hands, Mim disassembled metal parts, oiled, counted, watched in her mind the dropped marble continue on its path, the machine of their actions tumbling forward. She carried the part she had been assigned from Just Knock 'Em Down to the crate outside the construction shop. She worked all day, silent. She watched others. After dinner, Pelle lured her behind a stack of canvas and kissed her. Her skin quivered at this bravado.

"You'll see what I'm building tonight. You'll meet Mother. Now back to work."

She carried the ladder to the entrance, climbed, unlit the Carnival Moon, and began to remove the sign that proclaimed *The Eight Mile Suspended Carnival.*

An automobile and a motor truck charged down the road toward the carnival entrance. From the truck, two men. Spurlock and another man from the auto. They walked to the gate. Spurlock's brown coat dusted the ground. The minion from the auto hovered around Spurlock, moving only when his boss moved.

What was Spurlock doing here? Mim descended the ladder and ran for Suspender, found him at the hotel porch.

"What's the rumpus?" he said.

"Spurlock's here."

The boy behind his face froze for a moment.

"Come." She pulled his arm. They walked back toward the gate, which he unlocked.

"Gentlemen," Suspender said.

"Packing up?" Spurlock asked.

"Conducting a drill. We like to stay limber."

"Alas, we're not here for tricks and games," Spurlock said. "Just hunting an errant worker."

Suspender spun his ballyhoo. "Hunting?"

"Security man. Name of Dunavant."

"This Dunavant, has he a reason to run?" Suspender asked. "Has he misbehaved?"

The minion cringed and nodded. "Mr. Spurlock believes so," he said.

"I haven't seen any of your men over our side. Could be someone hiding in the confusion. You're welcome to reconnoiter. Have time for a beverage?"

"Very kind," Spurlock said. He instructed the motor truck men to look around.

Suspender and Mim led Spurlock and the minion through the grounds. The Tower of Misfortune, the hotel, and Suspender's invisible treehouse were the only points that remained. Everything had come down. The men walked through disarray to the hotel.

"You stay outside, Trowel," Spurlock said to the minion.

Suspender held the door open for Spurlock and Mim. "Please, rest your bones," he said. Spurlock settled into a chair in the lobby; Mim sat across from him.

"Haven't been inside here since I was a child, back when it was a real hotel. Smells the same," he said.

"We're without a maid service—so you might be acquainted with some of this dust," Suspender said.

Spurlock laughed.

From a cabinet, Suspender took a bottle wrapped in gold threads. He handed ridiculously delicate glasses to Spurlock and Mim, and kept one for himself. Uncorked the bottle and filled the glasses with deep amber drink, thick and gleaming. Etched flowers on the crystal distorted the light, made the liquor seem to slither.

As if endorsing the attractions, Suspender used his costume voice. "Braving this mill of illusion, friend? You must itch to find your man."

"You are an apt judge of character." Spurlock raised his glass.

The drink was sweet and bitter, honey troubled by acid, biting inside her mouth as if it contained miniature teeth.

Spurlock turned to Mim. His face was smooth, cleaner than any face she had seen here, apparently unbothered by the spikier details of human circumstance. He smiled and turned back to Suspender. "What lovely counsel surrounds you, sir," he said. His voice snaked, extracted all warmth from her body, from the room, from the world.

"Thank you, Mr. Spurlock," Suspender said.

"Wise. What any businessman would seek." Spurlock turned the fragile glass, and looked through it at Mim. "My grandmother left behind something like this. Charming."

"You're welcome to stay here or join your men in searching. But we best get back to our work." They finished their drinks and went outside. "Be careful with things around here falling. You never know," Suspender said.

"No, you never do know." Spurlock laughed.

"Haven't seen him, sir," the minion said.

"Well, get to work," Spurlock said. He handed Suspender an envelope. "A gift. In case we make a mess. Though, be assured, we endeavor not to. But just in case." Spurlock smiled.

Suspender put the envelope in his coverall pocket. Spurlock and the minion set off in different directions.

Mim said, "Little Lon did her job and Beede . . . Dunavant . . . he's running from them."

Pelle smiled.

Men tidy up, and Nature laughs. Some messes simply cannot help themselves.

Carnies packed and prodded, shoved, filed, categorized, and made meaning from the various parts. Mim was dredging the Wishing Well for coins when, from behind, she heard Beede's voice.

"A party!" he said. He was damp, panting. He grabbed and kissed her. "Some screech threw a boot in the powder house last night, river pulley doused it all. They'll blame me. Time to get outta the death pill business and into amusements!"

"Sounds like a mess," she said.

"Beede survives anything." He kissed her again.

Spurlock would find Beede and take him to the Spurlock Hotel. Let him rot there. It wasn't pleasant but it was fair. Through her body, a full cacophony. Again, that floating mess of death, the glob on the river, Pelle's father killed by Beede. And Beede was then a child! What had he done since? What could he do now? How different would Pelle be if his father hadn't died that way, how much lighter? Would he have done something nobler with his gifts, made buildings, towns, cities? Allowed himself to marry? Found a sympathetic woman with everything his mother had taken, returning him to that gentility Cleopatra sneered at, in guests, but secretly longed for? Cleopatra's chance was stolen by her brief husband's brother. Her chance to suckle and love a life from her own body was gone, more wasted than a roasted goat.

So many orphans.

"We're almost finished," she told Beede. "Help me, would you?" She latched a case full of coins and explained the system of numbered boxes.

Beede helped her pick up the case. He was already carrying three of his own satchels, one square-ish, one like a tube. A third one, lumpish, shifted as if it held a live creature. Mim knew the only thing living in that bag was a pile of bent dreams and unsavory acts. *It's all he has, really.* For a moment, she wished she hadn't lured him over. Was it fair, to trap him? He had killed, but also caressed. Beede was so thorny, but he snaked her in. The authority she had over him when they had sex fooled her shell, and each time, she forgot about his foul aftertaste. Momentarily.

"You shouldn't be here," she said.

"I know, that's the brilliance, no one will suspect it."

"No, Spurlock came here looking for you."

"Raw deerback! Fuck. Well I can't go back now. I'll have to keep my head down." He pulled his collar up and helped Mim carry the case toward the wagons where the other carnies were piling numbered boxes.

And there was the minion, followed by Spurlock. "Hello, Mr. Dunavant," he said.

Beede stopped. One of the henchmen clamped his arms.

Spurlock pointed at Beede, and made that sign with his hands, drawing a square around his body, like the shopkeeper in Wistmount. "What's stowed in the rucksacks?"

"Garments, a few books," Beede said. "You understand, sir, I've decided to pursue a childhood dream. Always wanted to be an entertainer."

"Of course. What boy doesn't want to join the carnival?" Spurlock laughed, and the minion echoed.

Beede laughed, too.

"But Mr. Dunavant, I don't recognize you're a reader. Which books?"

The marble dropped down a hole, for too long made no sound. Finally, with a hollow *plop*, it landed somewhere unknown.

"A volume or two of verse, nothing out of the ordinary. The Book of Holiness. Only what a learned man would carry on his back. We all need inspiration."

Suspender walked up then, as if he had discovered something needed his attention.

Spurlock turned to Suspender. "Turns out this operative has a childhood dream." Then, to Beede. "Which volumes, Mr. Dunavant? I have a warmth for poetry myself." He waved to the minion, who removed Beede's ill-shaped satchel and opened it for Spurlock.

"I see no verse, do you?" Spurlock asked his men.

"It's gotta be in there somewhere." Beede again laughed. "Or maybe I forgot it."

"Forget something as important as inspiration?" Spurlock asked. "Pity. How far does a learned man get when he lacks inspiration, Mr. Dunavant? In your uninspired state, I pause to ask: Do you oppose our commerce? Do you oppose us, in some small way, doing our service for country? Do you, to put it another way, oppose *me?*"

"No, sir," Beede said.

Spurlock turned to Suspender. "Sir, have you hired this man to work in your carnival?"

"No, sir. I didn't know he was here."

Beede glared at Suspender. "I came over here to see my girl," he said.

"Your girl? Is this person yours?" Suspender asked, indicating Mim.

"I don't care who this girl belongs to," Spurlock said. "These *items*, however, are mine." He held up the plans. "Where's the sample? Trowel, look through everything."

By now, the Tobeys had accumulated. "Rumpus?" Anton the Younger asked.

Timmy Zuzu walked up. "Good evening, sir."

"Do I know you?" Spurlock asked.

"I work at the factory. Timothy Zuzu."

"Ah, sure, Timothy Zuzu. And do you also own a person over here? Or will you join the carnival, all whimsy, like our Mr. Dunavant?"

The other men laughed.

"Just doing some extra work," Zuzu said.

"I see. Enterprising of you," Spurlock said. "We'll take Mr. Dunavant to the hotel now."

"Here's the sample," Trowel said.

Beede broke away. Spurlock's men chased and tackled him. One man sat on top, another punched.

"Bring him back here! We'll have time for that later," Spurlock said.

"Just having some fun," the punching man said.

Spurlock whinnied like a horse, and laughed. "Lively, that Dunavant. Shows initiative."

Suspender made an odd sound in his throat.

Spurlock told his men to stop. "We certainly don't want to cause injury. Timothy Zuzu, please join us." Spurlock smiled as if he had given Zuzu an invitation to a fine repast. "You can report the festivities to the factory boys. If you would be so kind. Let them know that theft from Spurlock Munitions has consequences." He turned to Suspender. "We have indeed accomplished. And a good evening to you, sir."

"Evening," Suspender said.

Spurlock and his men took Beede away.

Mim was hollowed out, sick with it all, and so tired she couldn't feel her feet. This day had lasted weeks, months.

Suspender spun his ballyhoo, whistling softly. They watched Spurlock and entourage depart. "Returning, returning, need to make it fit," he said to himself. "Okay citizens, now to recreate. That's it, we'll stay."

"Cannot we wait until the light? There is a thing named sleep," Anton the Younger said.

"We ain't machines! Give us a rest!" another Tobey said.

"No, no, put it all back together now."

Lo-Lo stood close to Suspender, closer than Mim had ever seen him get. "No. Let us sleep." He rubbed his face.

Nelda stood beside Lo-Lo, and said to Suspender, "You drain life from the living. We can't do it! Everyone needs a rest."

Suspender regarded the assembly.

"They're right," Mim said. "We all need sleep. You do, too. It'll be easier in the morning. No harm waiting."

He squinted at Mim, then her growing curve. "Fine. Sleep. Go sleep." He walked toward the gate, and the carnies heaped what they held or carried under tarps.

Lo-Lo hugged Mim. "I'm glad that pile is set to pay for his wrongs. The goats." Then he looked at Mim and stepped away. "Don't read me," he said.

Nelda laughed. "You are a fool," she told Lo-Lo.

"Maybe a fool, but a fool who'll defend his *something inside* against the charm of intruders," he said.

Mim watched Pelle walk to the gate, lock it, and play a phrase on the xylophone.

TWENTY

PREPARATIONS

I

How many layers of dream can a person, sleeping, sustain? How can skin contain the ramifications of dream, the fact of dream, the facets, lit like moving pictures, and the light that only illumines behind slumber-closed lids, flickers of hope, despair, all manner of image and idea, words built toward easy, unexamined meaning . . . words that, when waking, if spoken, crack the mortar between their consonants and vowels, words that have no business abutting each other. In dreams, we never doubt paired objects as logical, as the scaffold of a story, a life. Things in dreams make sense, a cat on someone's head, tables made of other animals, or ice, or sand. Metal melts into water; the dead grandfather of a baby in Mim's womb . . . dead grandfather contained in a bucket, floats off like a shadow to haunt the surface of the river, onward, forever.

Mim woke from dream-haunts before light, then fell back asleep, but the next dreams depicted Beede in the Camera of Illusion's background, giant; his square mouth filled a brilliant blue sky, and mouth moved and words spewed and made even less sense than Willie's poetica. Words tumbled toward Mim faster than she could run. The words grew legs, and she ran and ran, grappled to get away, but Beede's enormous mouth continued to pour forth these legged words, full and deep and laughing, until he himself was Death, and the words, killers.

When she woke it was late, the hotel quiet. After leftovers in the kitchen, she went to Pelle's room. He was still asleep. She sat on the bed, touched his shoulder. He rolled toward her. The man's sadness eclipsed the boy behind his face.

"What's wrong?" she asked.

He exhaled. "I'm sick of walking through porridge."

"Everyone's asleep. We have to get to work, put things back together. If we plan to stay."

"Why stay? Why go? It's all sticky porridge. I can't walk through porridge anymore."

"People won't know what to do. You need to tell them."

"I don't care."

"Yes, you do."

He rolled away from her, faced the wall. Mim touched her middle, summoning the ensconced baby, the marble in the maze, what made everything work. Until it didn't, and just languished, stuck in the tunnel, waiting.

"Get up. People need you. Everyone complains, but where would they be without you, without the carnival? What about me? This is all I have. Get up!" Mim pulled his body over.

He shoved her off. "I don't care! Do whatever you want. Long live the headless octopus. I'm tired."

Mim straddled him and pinned his shoulders. "Get up, now!"

"Get off me! You're pixilated!"

His breath was sweet metal when she kissed him.

He laughed. "Pixilated."

"So what if I am?"

"All this arithmetic, all this work."

"Get up," she said.

He groaned. "Oh, fine-it."

When he got up, when he half-smiled, sunshine crackled through all of her parts.

II

On Tuesday, while the other carnies rebuilt, checked lists, ratcheted bolts, and yelled at each other, Timmy Zuzu returned. Beatrice led him to Lo-Lo,

who called a tea break. In the kitchen, he poured bacon tea into the flowered bowl for Suspender, and coffee into cups for Nelda, Cleopatra, and
Zuzu. Mim held out her cup, but he refused to pour. *So tiresome of him!* She
served herself from the dregs.

Zuzu described what had happened at the jail in Wistmount. "Spurlock
is flinging dice, counting on a win. It's his hotel, why not? Everything was
chippy. Factory boys said the powder house got doused, soaked through
by their own safety measures, no explosion nor fire, but somehow your
river pulley was set off, and shite, did it do the job! Fast. Bucket by bucket.
Powder's drenched—it's paste. They blame Dunavant. Said he neglected the
nightly winding that you advised in the design."

Suspender stirred his tea and took a sip. "They lock Dunavant up?"

Zuzu nodded. "And worse. Spurlock tap danced inside his head while
that garden trowel took notes, transcribed what gibberish Dunavant
disgorged. None of it made sense. They tied him to the clock tower in
Wistmount. Left him there. Humiliation for breakfast, lunch, and dinner.
He ain't going anywhere. Used the pounding rope on him. Then one of the
bodyguards tapped my shoulder. Galloped us back to the factory. Said get
to work."

"How are you here so early?" Nelda asked. "Isn't this your shift?"

"Nobody's paying attention over there, it's complete chopmeat. Night
becomes day. Free season. Anton the Elder left. Said tell the Younger he
would write when he lands somewhere. Dead Louie has too much work;
he's a walking yell machine, what's one or two men gone?" Zuzu leaned
closer to Lo-Lo.

"If we're staying here, we need supplies," Lo-Lo said. "We need food.
None of you want to eat dirt. Well, none except Beatrice."

"Now who's a clown," Cleopatra said. She let Beatrice lick the dregs of
her coffee. "I'm not going."

"Nor me," Nelda said. "Too much mending up to do."

"I'll go," Mim said.

"You've no more business in Wistmount than you have at that death factory. Not safe for your viscera," Cleopatra said.

"I'm going," Mim said.

"Don't look at me," Lo-Lo told her.

"Fool," Nelda said.

"Enough," Suspender said. "She goes with you. I have a list of hardware to get. Zuzu, we sure appreciate the news, and any help with work. Whoever else remains a carny, back to the job."

"I am not riding with that one," Lo-Lo said.

"Shut your ticking, Clock. On you go. And the rest of you—put this carnival back together. Go on now."

Nelda handed Mim a pile of coins. "In case you need a little something."

"Maybe sweets," Mim said.

Carnies got up to leave, but Suspender took Mim's arm and held her back. He put his cheek next to hers. "Find Dunavant," he said. "You heard Zuzu; he's roped up in the public square. Lure him back. I still want him."

"I can't do that."

"You who liberated the Impossibles?" He finished his tea, washed and dried his mother's flowered bowl and returned it to the shelf where it always waited for him.

III

They clanked against each other: Pelle the cutout metal polka dot in his construction shop, the pretty hole. Possibility. Beede the sharp edge on that metal. You could get cut. Their proximity to each other . . . did they forge an unstable coin, ballyhoo to hypnotize a weak-minded guest? A hostile alliance of day and night?

(In the cylinder on the table, always, the moon and the sun, fighting it out.)

Who was waking; who was sleeping?

Mim and Lo-Lo strapped on goggles, and onward toward Wistmount. He sang, "Twist your innocence, constant . . . "

"Please stop singing," she said. "I'm sleepy."

"No. I don't need you to read my thoughts. That's why he wanted you to come, to watch me. He has no faith in people."

"I can't read your thoughts. And wouldn't want to if I could."

He resumed singing.

She put a hand over his mouth. "If I see something, it won't matter whether you're whispering or singing." She removed her hand. "Singing doesn't change anything!"

"My singing changes everything!"

"I wish I couldn't see things. Too many parts. It drains my life. I prefer having friends." She reached for his hand on the steering wheel, but he swatted her away.

"Friends are dandy, but I don't want any person inside my head." He resumed singing, but more quietly.

After awhile, she fell asleep, and woke when the road became less bumpy, past the brick jail, the tall fence.

Lo-Lo said, "Ladies and gentlemen, the Spurlock Hotel. Okay, my throat is parched. Maybe whistling will do."

Mim imagined Beede wearing those dusty red clothes, square mouth babbling. Maybe he was in pain, maybe that body she had been so near all those times now burned. As she conjured the charred skin of his torso, the word *alabaster* drowned in the ashes. Good riddance. But then her closed heart creaked open, just a slice. She was sad for him. He had no one. In this vast world, many had no one, but Beede had rent the fabric between himself and humanity, any humanity he could have touched. Anything kind in him had shriveled, and yet he had touched her gently, and held her roughly. His body seemed to need all of hers, to climb inside the confines of her uncertain skin. Consuming: their meeting, their touch. But he had made the mess himself.

"Lucky we made it here smooth, it's nearly closing time," Lo-Lo said. He parked the steam truck and pulled the pearls. On their way to the store, he stopped whistling only to recite the shopping list, which, as usual, he had memorized alphabetically. He resumed making sounds, left no pause for silence.

They gathered necessities and the extra hardware. Since the flood, they kept discovering things that needed to be replaced. Suspender had a list, fancy items funded, Mim speculated, by the envelope of mess-money from Spurlock. At the hardware store, the clerk loaded their goods into crates.

Mim spent a few of the coins from Nelda on a pocketful of citrus-rind candies from the jar on the counter, and though he asked, she did not share with her driver. "Not until you're my friend again," she said.

"You're a scourge, you. Help me take this bucket of provisions to the cart."

On the right side of her belly, a twinge. "Too heavy," she said. He ignored her but helped her lift it onto the back of the truck.

"You finish securements," he said, "then come find me." He went off to find dumplings for their drive back. She strapped what needed strapping, then hurried toward the clock tower.

A border of knee-high rocks delineated the square, with openings on each side. A cross-shaped path led toward the tower. Against the bottom of the tower: a scene that might be fit for a carnival, a scene for Willie to verse upon, some long-gone Act of Gloom. Something the guests only cared about because they had once cared, because of inertia, an empty ritual to revisit. Beede was tied with a monstrous pounding rope to iron rings at the bottom of the tower. Two shawled women walked past, turned away from him. He still wore his own clothes, shadowed with sweat, and bloody. Torn arm of shirt, torn skin of arm. Head hung down, asleep or half dead. On display like the saddest remnant, *Step right up and See the Discarded Person.* She stopped, unsure what to do.

He coughed. "Don't hurt me," he pleaded.

"It's me," she said. She moved closer. "It's Mim."

"Help." His terrible voice. "Strangling."

The pounding rope was as big as her wrist. She heaved at it, but it wouldn't budge. She heard a baby's cry, and crouched beside him, but kept working on the rope around his neck. A woman hurried by, one arm pulling a small boy, the other holding an infant. Beede let his head lean again.

"Listen. Wake up," she said.

"Away, away," he said through what choked him, "hop a train, give yourself away . . . handiwork of a rat . . . that river pulley. Took squatting at Spurlock Hotel . . . I figured it out . . . fucken clear . . . that no-name man."

"What man?" she asked.

Rope in both hands, seeing the solution before untwisting the gristle of fibers. The rope was stubborn: whoever had tied it was an expert, a brute, devoted to pain. She worked and worked. The rope loosened, fell, and Beede crumpled. She propped him up.

"You're still bleeding." She removed her river scarf and tied it around his arm, helped him stand, and pulled him down the path and into an alley. The song of Lo-Lo, a song of redress, drifted from down the street, grew louder, nearer. She leaned Beede against the wall of a worn building:

the book and map shop, with its musty towers, the friendly woman from Alsace. Oldfields, where Mim had once imagined making a home.

"Can't get you into the truck now. Find your way back to the carnival, if you still want to come with us." She hurried back to the truck.

"Where were you?" Lo-Lo asked.

"Just walking," she said.

They secured themselves in the steam truck. He handed her a dumpling and began to sing.

So many songs, stretching back in time, and forward. So many words, waking up, alive and moving.

IV

Trucks, wagons, the carnival was full. The carnival was different. Canvases wrong, staggered, off-center. The Camera of Illusion was not the only thing that could change, unveil new worlds, predictions, and lies. If someone looked closely, as Mim did, this time things didn't square. Like her skin, which seemed stable from outside but hadn't fit as long as she could remember, that is, since her body had fallen on scratch-land near the Eight Mile Suspended Carnival. *Witness the Tornado Girl's skin, its Surface of Memory!* Her skin stretched over the curled baby, the live marble shrouded inside her depths. The carnival's skin was baggy in places, tight in others, scarred, misplaced. Containers. How full was the world of ill-fitting and uncertain containers.

Lo-Lo honked the horn to part the herd of slow-cattle guests. "I must not be as pretty as Moses," he said. Finally he got through, parked behind the kitchen, and they unloaded the steam truck. Next to the invisible treehouse stood a new container, a wagon-sized machine.

Mim needed to see Cleopatra, but a line of guests waited. She passed the Electric Trampoline. For a while, she helped Tiger at Just Knock 'Em Down. Lots of guests played, but no one knocked them down, which meant no prizes, which meant more money remained with the carnival. They had finally resumed a regular pace. Nelda's Wishing Well was shiny and full. She smiled from her throne. Groups of young men and women, not much older than Mim, ignored the grimier aspects of the carnival, drank wine from the tent—served tonight by Anton—and other stuff from

233

flasks, the warmers of bones. The air was cooler now. Winter approached. Tiger complained that his knees hurt, and Anton the Younger said the ropes were stiff. She couldn't remember winter in her body. Winter would slow the carnival.

She found Pelle on the hotel porch. "Why are you here?" she asked.

"Breathing air, away from the mob." He didn't look at her.

She touched his cheek. "I found Dunavant. He's in bad shape, but he'll come back. I think he will."

He didn't move.

"What's that new machine by the treehouse?"

"Too many memories," he said. "Crowds me out."

Mim wished she could see the crowding memories. Even when she tried to conjure a leaf, it rarely worked; they hadn't found a switch for on and off.

"When I was a boy, I knew that Dunavant. That bag of poison, disguised as a waif."

He took a piece of wood and began to whittle. "He showed up one day at our homestead, all smiles and sunbeams, an orphan in need. My father decided the kid could do some work around the place; maybe he needed a distraction from my mother's being gone. Boy worked hard enough to fool my father, but wouldn't leave me alone, was always at me, wanting to know this or that, like a too-friendly sort, trying to be the good son to my father. As if I wasn't. But that sweet veneer curdled."

"What did he do?" She knew, but needed him to tell.

He stopped whittling. "Shite. I can't say it."

"Maybe I already know," she said.

He stared at her. "Maybe you do. You tell me, then."

She shook her head.

"Shite. Why in arse did I start this?" He twisted off a splinter of stubborn wood, turned the piece, and worked the other side. "One night I heard creaking, someone trying to be quiet, but knocking around. I tracked the ruckus outside, saw my pa go into the barn. Unusual he would go out there after dark, and I didn't understand the whats and whys. Inside the barn, I heard more creaks. I snuck in. Hid near the door. My pa climbed up to the loft where he kept a scrap of money in a metal box under the hay. Dunavant was up there. Pa must've heard him go out there, must've gotten curious. Pa yelled, 'What're you hunting?' and Dunavant laughed and said what I couldn't hear, then the shotgun. Loud, blew a hole through the world. Pa

234

slumped over. Just slumped. I needed to do something but had to be quiet. Dunavant was busy with Pa, tying something. He threw a big rope over a rafter and hoisted Pa's body up. Took him a lot of effort. He didn't see me. He didn't know I saw. I slipped out the door and ran back to the house, hid in bed, didn't know what to do. I was no kind of man."

When he finished telling, neither of them spoke for a while.

"You were a child."

He put down his knife. The wood hid in his hands. Mim wrapped her arms around herself but wasn't warmed.

"How did you find him?" she asked.

"A couple years ago, that explosion at Spurlock's. Newspaper story told about it, back while we were in Springdale. Spurlock fired whoever had been in charge of security. Lucien Dunavant was mentioned, promoted as the new man for the job, and so forth. It's an unusual name."

Mim nodded. She thought of names. Of alabaster.

"Generally it don't feel right, anyone suffering. Doesn't settle right. But who could ignore a wrong like what he did to my pa? All this time, knowing he was across the river, all this time waiting. Waiting like that is enough to kill a man. But it took you to make it happen. To be my method."

"Is that what I am? A method?"

Maybe it was the growing life inside, maybe it was because this place was all she had, but fury upwelled, flung off its veil, stood tall and fully new. Maybe that upwell was the real Mim, or whatever her name was; maybe it was herself beneath any name, maybe it was who she was becoming.

"Answer me!" she said.

"You had no one till you landed here. Don't be so ungrateful. You have a home here long as you'll stay. And I hope you'll stay."

"At least you have memories. I don't know what I had." She looked toward the sky, bright pinpricks in the night's curtain, drops of silver on velvet, memories, and substance: life was everywhere, perfect and undeniable. Like old songs that had traveled so long and would travel farther, singing themselves through Nelda, through Lo-Lo, like Time as it went, and goes, and will go, the stars were *there*, unlike candle flame, which burned until it disappeared. Stars looked down from that wild premise above, looked at everything, and knew. *Knew*. And kept knowing.

"The stars see my memories," she said.

"I suppose so." He touched her hand. "We'll take care of the little one, we'll find some way. Maybe a carnival isn't a proper life for a child, but what is? We'll find some way. That babe won't be alone."

In the pre-dawn, Mim woke to a crash, then a rasping of metal like bones, like a giant gobbling up bones. She pulled on her robe and hurried to the lobby. Others were arriving, all the carnies, and Timmy Zuzu.

Lo-Lo followed Mim toward the din. "Another twister?"

Nelda was so shaken that instead of the usual dungarees, she must have grabbed what was close, her green satin gown. Nipsy babbled about the gate, the ruined gate, now toothless and gaping. Said the xylophone had been pulverized. Said he saw it all from his window on the third floor. The Rules . . . unhinged and busted to shards. A motor truck, collision.

Through a front window, Mim saw Beede.

Arms spread, fists clenched around gate spikes. He howled, called all storm and devastation, everything sinister to assist him. He waved his arms, and rags snowed to the ground: the remains of the banner of The Eight Mile Suspended Carnival, torn like a giant's paper confetti.

Pelle stepped off the porch to watch Beede.

"We have to help," Mim said. She led the carnies and Zuzu through the door and onto the porch. Mim stood beside Lo-Lo, and he let her.

Waving gate spikes like giant claws, Beede spit on the ground five times, then stomped on the spittle, until his body became a coil of anger, a snake. Words with legs spewed from his mouth toward Pelle, some spilling over on the carnies, words armed with pieces of carnival gate, gate unwelded by some giant screw-hand, some colossal gnaw that meant to LOOSEN THE UNIVERSE, crash it down, grind it all to dust.

Pelle went toward Beede, toward the sordid, legged words. Stepped into the cyclone of venom.

"You've shorn your head," Beede said. "Still a fucken little rat, though." Beede jabbed one gate spike into the ground, but kept hold of the other. Around his neck draped the bloody river scarf.

"Surrender that metal," Pelle said.

"I'll keep my spike."

"The devil would," Lo-Lo said.

To the Tobeys, Pelle said, "You lot! Drag his arse to the river. Drag him to the machine I call Mother and strap him down."

236

The Tobeys went for Beede, who roared and swung his spike. Anton blocked Beede's arm and knocked the spike from his hand, then called to Cleopatra, "See me, my lady?" He laughed. "See how easy I do the work of saving?" The Tobeys dragged Beede toward the river.

"What about Rule number Seven?" Cleopatra asked.

Pelle said, "Only applies to the carnival grounds. Hence, to the river."

Tiger picked up the spike. "Someone broke Rule Number Seven for us," he said. "We must defend. Come on, you carnies; boss needs fortification."

Cleopatra picked up Beatrice and linked arms with Tiger. Nelda, Mim, Lo-Lo, Timmy Zuzu, and everyone else followed. The procession like a shadow slid toward the river, where the machine Pelle called Mother waited.

The dead night shadowed these human actions, less from curiosity than inevitability—as, where else would the night go? If a goddess were to turn in bed and regard this affair, the deity might imagine an eccentric and mismatched string of baubles round the neck of a woman, appearing only slightly to move, from the vantage of such heights, toward a prettier line of twinkle, the river, to join and blend and make sense. If a goddess woke, and cared to look. But most would turn away, tumble back into celestial dreams, to fix (or create) more significant problems, problems epic not to one lone man who wished to make beauty by way of contraptions, but to states, to planets, to the intricate matter of galaxies. What goddess could bother to observe this meek vendetta between trinkets on a trivial thread of costume jewelry? An article to be worn by a sad and possibly desperate young woman, eventually chipped, or missing a nugget, set aside for repair when the downtrodden woman could find time to employ her fingers, or the few pennies to pay someone else for fixing? And yet, our woman would keep those precious pieces, stow them safe, and cart them with her from place to place throughout a life, because you never know when you might be invited to *fête*, and find cash for repair, and wear the piece again, thereby restoring sheen and dreams. If not to lure whoever she used to think she needed, couldn't *live* without, then to feel her spine uncurl, to find herself a piddle taller, even if alone, even, *yes, yes, alone,* her embellishment revealing her own self, her aching, long-obscured need of adornment. Her deserved splendor.

237

Beede kicked and flailed; the only way he could go was the river. Pelle ran after, tackled his prey, began to pound. Beede clawed at him and he clawed back. Grapple and punch echoed in the dirt, both men trying to kill and trying to stay alive.

And they bashed and bashed, and the echo of their blows—turbulence tipped on icicle wings—flew to Mim's ears. Everything glazed with ice; everything crackled and spit, then stopped. Things got slow. The limbs of all life had frozen thick and angry, ready to shatter at a breath. While they scrabbled in that nest of fury and burn, Beatrice moaned. Was she remembering her own ordeal at the river? Beede's hand against her back?

Cleopatra started toward the mess, but Nelda seized her arm. "Nothing you can do," she said.

"That fiend abused my Beatrice!"

"I know, dearling." Nelda hugged Cleopatra.

Lo-Lo said, "Nelda's right. The fight is theirs. I don't imagine the goats are the root, but whatever it is belongs equally to each of them."

"Dunavant killed his father," Mim said. "When they were children." Everyone who heard turned toward her. "Shot him dead, then strung him up like a marionette." Mim's eyes smarted with tears.

Lo-Lo spat on the ground.

"Demon. Reap your seeds, you damnable fiend," Cleopatra said.

"Oh, the humanity," Nelda said.

"Poor suckling Suspender," Lo-Lo said. "A haunt like that. Let him do it."

Beede roared, kicked Pelle, then jumped into the river and tried to swim.

Beatrice shrieked and bit Cleopatra, who yelled and dropped her. The animal careened toward the water, a beast-bullet aimed at Beede. Cleopatra followed, screamed the beast's name.

In the river, Beatrice pounced on Beede, attacked and clawed as if starved for food. The train of current took them, carried them along, toward Wistmount, toward the next town, toward whatever lay ahead, toward the broken fist of death, of falsehood, of everything and nothing, and this still-moving gloom turned to murk, like the horrific stuff Beede had poured into the river.

Cleopatra fell on her knees in the flowing murk, wailing. Anton the Younger pulled her out; she pushed him away but didn't go back into the river.

Pelle lay in the dirt. Mim went to him. His bloodied, injured face looked more than ever like the boy inside. She knelt and held him, smelled the molten, red mineral that emanated from his skin, but also, something sweet and green.

After, Mim brought Pelle to rest on a sofa in the lobby and cleaned him up. Carnies, full of the story, animated the hotel, swapped what they thought, what they saw, what they thought they saw. Some stayed outside, their energy too sprawling to leash indoors. Some sat inside to recuperate. Mim found Lo-Lo and ordered a feast.

"Butter, butter the doom-drum," Lo-Lo sang, and dragged his metal spoon through the hotel, across doors, rattling carnies on his way back to his kitchen home to weave fine, savory parts into ecstasy.

Everyone went to eat when it was time.

But Pelle stayed sprawled on the sofa.

"Eat-up time," Mim told him.

"I shall not move from right here," he said.

Someone scraped at the hotel door. Mim went to see who. Beatrice came in, shook mud from her feathers, and dropped something on the rug. "Beatrice is back!" Mim yelled. "Tell Cleopatra!"

Beatrice trotted to Pelle and licked his neck. "Get off me," he said, but laughed.

"What did you bring?" Mim asked Beatrice, and picked up the item. Which was a thumb. She gave it to Pelle. He sat up and studied it.

"His?" he asked.

"Looks like," she said.

Pelle stared at the thumb, his eyes glassy.

Lo-Lo came in and saw Beatrice. "The lost critter! Critter's back." Then he asked, "What's the situation? She okay?" Beatrice nudged Lo-Lo away. "Watch it, you!"

"Go get everyone to eat. We'll be in soon," Mim said.

"Okay," Lo-Lo said. Then he looked at Pelle. "When a thing is done, it's done. Put it behind you now. The ghost can rest. No need to stagnate. You might not see it yet, but up ahead is an island, it's called relief. Old ghosts need their sleep, too."

Pelle nodded. Lo-Lo returned to the kitchen, calling, "Breakfast, eat-up time!"

Mim sat with Pelle, who continued to stare at the thumb. After awhile he lifted his head. There was the boy, the boy behind his face. There was the man the boy had become. There was the baby inside of Mim, growing, no choices or decisions, only growing, always growing.

"What're you gonna do with it?" Mim asked.

He got up and opened the door. "Beatrice," he called. He hurled the thumb onto the porch. He held the door open; she galloped to where it had landed and began to gnaw.

"She earned it." He looked at Mim.

Mim held his hand and led him to the kitchen, where the carnies had begun their morning treat. She washed her hands, then said to Pelle, "Come here." He let her lather his hands, the fondest gift she could conjure. She led him to his place at the table, then retrieved his tea bowl from its shelf and poured tea for him.

She regarded the carnies in their morning tumult, slow, but alive and seething with matter: stories, memories. The impossible ropes hadn't been impossible, that's only how they were named. Mim had worn her name long enough for it to fit. Inside her was the baby, but there was something else, a part that had always been there. Had *always* known what to do. It wasn't memory, but it was real, and part of her. Mim was enough.

She took two lids from the stove and banged them together like cymbals. "Listen up," she said.

"What's the rumpus?" Lo-Lo asked.

"Today, we prepare for the Crossing," Mim said.

A couple carnies laughed. Resumed chat and food.

Mim banged the lids again. "Quiet! It's true. We're finished here. We're leaving. What doesn't fit in wagons the trucks can pull, we leave behind. Jettison what you can recreate. Take the essentials: bolts, wire, rope. Other parts can be found or made elsewhere. Take what you most need. Take what you can use; take what you had when you were born."

Pelle stared at her. Smiled. Drank some tea.

Most carnies groaned out of reflex. But Nelda, Cleopatra, Lo-Lo, and Timmy Zuzu did not. When they had finished their food, they rose. And began preparations.

GRATITUDE

To my parents, ancestors, family, friends, fellow writers, teachers, students, colleagues, red tent sisters and all who've given tangible and intangible sustenance: You carnies know who you are. "Thank you" isn't sufficient coin, but I do thank you, with gusto.

Special thanks to: Virginia Hamilton; Arnold Adoff; Cindy Mapes; Esther Rothman; Don Wallis; Kay Corbin; Eloise Klein Healy; Tara Ison; Lisa Horowitz Brooks; Bernadette Murphy; Chris Benda; Elaine Gale; Vanja Thompson; Jerry Pyle; Laraine Herring; Dee Krieg; Barbara Singleton; Maxine Skuba; Deanna Newsom; Amy Chavez; Chris Tebbetts; Anne Harris; the Maneri family; Diane Baumer; Liz Griffin; Arden Miller; Michael Kelly; Robert Shearman; Mark Beech; Jack Hardy; Susan Suechting and the Hardy family; Luisa Bieri and Sol Rising . . .

To Gayle Brandeis, torrents of love & thanks . . .

To Docent Jim Krusoe for decades of inspiration and encouragement . . .

To generous readers of manuscript drafts: Jahzerah Brooks; Kristin Walrod; Candace Kearns Read; Julia Kress; Shuly Cawood; Tia Acheson . . . and a deluge of love and respect to Melissa Tinker, for always saying *yes* when asked to read, and helping me see and excavate . . .

To Ariel Gore for powering this world with your art, invention, and hexes. If, as you wrote in *We Were Witches,* "Shame is the haunting that's hardest to mop away," thank you for illuminating the mop . . .

To Lynda Barry, unending spirals of gratitude for your existence and methods . . .

To Nick Flynn, for inspiration and guidance toward & through the wilds of Bewilderment . . .

To Seb Doubinsky for help with French phrasing; David Neuhardt for the presentation on the Goes Station munitions factory; Scott Sanders at Antiochiana; Rick Bowes and Jeffrey Ford for suggesting contraptions; Joe Mendelovitz for telling about the Pfeffer boy's father; the Jim Rose Circus Sideshow for twisted inspiration . . . and for their helpful books: Brad Kessler for *Goat Song*; Jeff Brouws and Bruce Caron for *Inside the Live Reptile Tent*; and E. and M. A. Radford for *The Encyclopedia of Superstitions* . . .

For decades, the music of Tom Waits has saturated my consciousness. As I considered an epigraph, "Reeperbahn" sang out. I didn't know why. Then I learned that *Reeperbahn* means ropewalk—*where ropes are made*. With all the hempen fibers that suspend this carnival, could there be better synchronicity? So COLOSSAL thanks to Tom Waits and Kathleen Brennan: Your work is my beacon. And to the Raindogs, especially Kees Lau; and Roger Dorresteijn and especially Connie Ashton for kind help with permissions . . .

To Champion Rod Val Moore: Howls of gratitude through the dented shout-horn for your vision, patience, humor, and radical flexibility...and a thousand thanks to Kate Haake; Gail Wronsky; Karen Kevorkian; Mona Houghton; Chuck Rosenthal; Paul Lieber; Ash Goodwin for lovely design; Gronk Nicandro for utterly perfect art; and to everyone at What Books Press: You make exquisite books!

To Rachel Fulkerson, for publicity support; to Nancy Jane Moore, for wisdom and time; to Kurt Miyazaki & the crew at the Emporium, for sustaining the heartbeat of Yellow Springs . . .

To my Inner Critic, too often by my side—but with a couple mirror tricks, re-routable . . .

To everyone named and unnamed, please know that the gratitude over-flows the vessel . . .

And to Robert Freeman: Hero, book doula, master carnivalian editor-typesetter, etc. Thanks for so often sacrificing your own writing time to help me, and for believing in me.

And to Merida: Thanks for enduring my weirdness, and helping me evolve. I love you.

PHOTOGRAPH BY MERIDA KUDER-WEXLER

Rebecca Kuder's work has appeared in *Los Angeles Review of Books; Hags on Fire; Bayou Magazine; Shadows and Tall Trees; Lunch Ticket; Year's Best Weird Fiction* vols. 3 & 5; *The Rumpus*; and *Crooked Houses*. She received an MFA from Antioch University Los Angeles, and an individual artist excellence award from the Ohio Arts Council. Rebecca lives in Yellow Springs, Ohio, with the writer Robert Freeman Wexler and their child. This is her first novel. www.rebeccakuder.com.

WHAT
BOOKS
PRESS

LOS ANGELES

CPSIA information can be obtained
at www.ICGtesting.com
Printed in the USA
JSHW052139140222
22884JS00003B/18